Joseph Payn

Select Poetry for Children

Joseph Payne

Select Poetry for Children

Reprint of the original, first published in 1874.

1st Edition 2024 | ISBN: 978-3-36884-854-5

Verlag (Publisher): Outlook Verlag GmbH, Zeilweg 44, 60439 Frankfurt, Deutschland
Vertretungsberechtigt (Authorized to represent): E. Roepke, Zeilweg 44, 60439 Frankfurt, Deutschland
Druck (Print): Books on Demand GmbH, In de Tarpen 42, 22848 Norderstedt, Deutschland

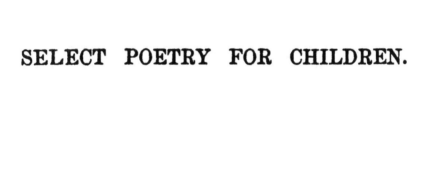

SELECT POETRY FOR CHILDREN.

LONDON : PRINTED BY
SPOTTISWOODE AND CO., NEW-STREET SQUARE
AND PARLIAMENT STREET

THE DEAD SPARROW.

SELECT POETRY

For Children:

WITH

BRIEF EXPLANATORY NOTES.

Arranged for the Use of Schools and Families.

BY

JOSEPH PAYNE,

PROFESSOR OF THE SCIENCE AND ART OF EDUCATION TO THE COLLEGE OF
PRECEPTORS; EDITOR OF "STUDIES IN ENGLISH POETRY,"
"STUDIES IN ENGLISH PROSE," ETC.

EIGHTEENTH EDITION, REVISED AND CONSIDERABLY ENLARGED

Capio Lumen

LONDON:

LOCKWOOD & CO., 7 STATIONERS'-HALL COURT

1874.

PREFACE

sentiments, and especially by touches of pity." St
poetry has a tendency to give to the mind of a cl
that healthful tone which pure air and open sunsh
give to his body.

Should the selection now before the reader
found to approximate even to the idea which
just been presented of what such a book ought
be, the time and labour it has cost will be am
repaid.

Besides the advantages accruing to the taste ɛ
moral character from an early acquaintance w
poetry, which are the greatest and most importa
we must not pass over those which may be deriɩ
from it as a means of exercising and strengthen
the memory, and of cultivating the graces of eloc
tion. The attainment of these benefits will, howev
depend, in some degree, upon the manner in wh
they are sought. The following remarks, sugges
by experience, may, perhaps, be found useful.

When this book is used in schools, it is reco:
mended that the lessons selected from it be learr
simultaneously by small classes. An opportunity
thus afforded for giving that minute attention to 1
meaning and spirit of the poems which is an esse
tial preparation for a just delivery, and for whi
otherwise, probably no time could be found.

would be well for the teacher, in the first place, to
read over to his pupils, with appropriate emphasis
and expression, the passage to be committed to
memory, asking questions on any words or allusions
which may seem likely to occasion difficulty; he
will then direct them to underline with pencil the
words which require peculiar emphasis in the recital,
and to ascertain, or " get up," before they repeat the
lesson, the meaning of such words, phrases, and
allusions as may need explanation. When he hears
the lesson, he may call upon any member of the
class to repeat the whole, or part of it, as may be
convenient, occasionally dropping hints on peculiari-
ties of pronunciation, and putting such questions as
may serve to elicit the author's meaning, and to
illustrate the ingenuity and taste of the composition.
It is advisable, too, that references should be made
from one poem to another where similar expressions
or thoughts occur, or where the same subject is
treated; and that the poems that have been learned
should be occasionally repeated and referred to in
conversation or reading. These directions will
appear unnecessarily minute only to those who do
not know, by experience in teaching, the importance
of attention to details.

Alterations have been made in the originals of
some *of the poems, in* order to adapt them to the

others, than is usually entertained, and believes, n‹ on theory but from experience, that much more ma be made of their minds by acting on this estimat than by treating them as mere babies.

It is gratifying to the Editor to believe, and t some extent to know, that thousands of children t whom schoolbooks generally are an aversion, hav turned to this little book with ever increasin delight, and have found in it "a mirror in whic their best feelings are reflected, and 'whatsoeve things are honest, whatsoever things are just, wha soever things are lovely,' presented to them in th most attractive form."

The present edition has been carefully revised an considerably enlarged by the insertion of sever‹ poems; for permission to use which the publishe‹ are indebted to the generous kindness of Mi‹ Ingelow; Robert Browning, Esq.; Alfred Tennyso‹ Esq.; the Rev. Canon Kingsley; the Right Ho‹ Lord Houghton; William Allingham, Esq.; Edwar‹ Capern, Esq.; and Messrs. Strahan & Co.

4 KILDARE GARDENS, W.
November 1, 1873.

INDEX.

a

SELECT POETRY

CHILDREN.

———◆———

THE VISIBLE CREATION.

THE God of nature and of grace
    In all His works appears;
His goodness through the earth we trace,
    His grandeur in the spheres.[1]

Behold this fair and fertile globe,
    By Him in wisdom planned:
'Twas He who girded, like a robe,
    The ocean round the land.

Lift to the firmament your eye—
    Thither His path pursue;
His glory, boundless as the sky,
    O'erwhelms the wondering view.

The forests in His strength rejoice;
    Hark! on the evening breeze,
As once of old, Jehovah's voice
    Is heard among the trees.[2]

[1] *Spheres*—heavenly bodies.
[2] "And *they heard the voice of the Lord God walking in the garden in the cool of the day.*"—Gen. iii. 8.

B

Here, on the hills, He feeds His herds,
  His flocks in yonder plains;
His praise is warbled by the birds;
  —Oh could we catch their strains,

Mount with the lark, and bear our song
  Up to the gates of light![1]
Or, with the nightingale, prolong
  Our numbers through the night!

His blessings fall in plenteous showers
  Upon the lap of earth,
That teems with foliage, fruits, and flowers,
  And rings with youthful mirth.

If God hath made this world so fair,
  Where sin and death abound;
How beautiful beyond compare[2]
  Will Paradise be found!

Montgomery.

THE VOICE OF SPRING.

I AM coming, I am coming!—
Hark! the little bee is humming;[3]
See, the lark is soaring high
In the blue and sunny sky;

[1] *Gates of light*—the part of the sky from which the light issues in the morning, as if from opening gates. Shakspear writes—

  "Hark! hark! the lark at heaven's gate sings."

[2] *Beyond compare*—beyond comparison.

[3] *Humming*—Observe that many words descriptive of the sounds made by animals are imitations of the sounds themselves; thus the serpent and the goose *hiss*, bees *hum*, flies *buzz*, rooks *caw*, &c.

And the gnats are on the wing,
Wheeling round in airy ring.

See the yellow catkins[1] cover
All the slender willows over;
And on banks of mossy green
Star-like primroses are seen;
And, their[2] clustering leaves below,
White and purple violets blow.

Hark! the new-born lambs are bleating,
And the cawing rooks are meeting
In the elms—a noisy crowd;
All the birds are singing loud;
And the first white butterfly
In the sunshine dances by.

Look around thee—look around!
Flowers in all the fields abound;
Every running stream is bright;
All the orchard trees are white;
And each small and waving shoot
Promises sweet flowers and fruit.

Turn thine eyes to earth and heaven!
God for thee the Spring has given,
Taught the birds their melodies,
Clothed the earth, and cleared the skies,
For thy pleasure or thy food:—
Pour thy soul in gratitude!

Mary Howitt.

[1] *Catkins*—blossoms—a botanical term, denoting the imperfect species of flower peculiar to the willow, hazel, and a few other trees.

[2] *Their, &c.—that is,* below the leaves of the violets mentioned in the next line.

THE FIRST LAMB.

SPORTIVE harbinger[1] of Spring !
Welcome tidings dost thou bring !
Thy short, timid, quivering bleat
Blends, in unison[2] most sweet,
With the newly-wakened song,
Heard the woodland dell along.

While beneath the hawthorn's shade,
Slumbering peacefully thou'rt laid,
Round thee spring the daisies fair ;
Violets scent the balmy air,
And the primrose clusters spread
A soft pillow for thy head :—
Start not !—'tis a harmless guest—
The partridge stealing from her nest ;
Or the bee, whose soothing hum
Tells the crocus-flowers are come !

Lambkin, I will be thy friend,
I my cheerful aid will lend,
Thy weak little feet to guide
To thy tender mother's side.
Soon those tottering feet will bound
O'er the thyme-besprinkled mound ;—
Enlivened by the cheering sun,
Soon the jocund race thou'lt run,
And in the sportive frolic join,
With heart as light and gay as mine.

[1] *Harbinger*—a forerunner—the appearance of n
lambs announces that Spring is coming. See p. 3.
[2] *In unison*—in harmony.

THE PIPER.

Piping down the valleys wild,
　Piping songs of pleasant glee,
On a cloud I saw a child,
　And he, laughing, said to me:—
" Pipe a song about a lamb,"
　So I piped with merry cheer;
" Piper, pipe that song again,"
　So I piped; he wept to hear.
" Drop thy pipe, thy happy pipe,
　Sing thy songs of happy cheer,"
So I sang the same again,
　While he wept with joy to hear.
" Piper, sit thee down and write,
　In a book, that all may read."—
So he vanish'd from my sight.
　And I pluck'd a hollow reed,
And I made a rural pen,
　And I stained the water clear,
And I wrote my happy songs,
　Every child may joy to hear.　*Blake.*

THE SNOW-DROP;

OR, THE RESURRECTION OF THE BODY.

Tell, if thou canst, how yonder flower
　To life and light has burst its way,
Though ten long months beneath the ground
　Its snowy petals [1] torpid lay.[2]

[1] *Petals*—flower-leaves *as* distinguished from the leaves of plants.
[2] *Torpid lay*—lay undeveloped, as if dead, in the bulb.

B 2

Then will I teach thee how a child
 From death's long slumber can awake,
And, to eternal life renewed,
 His robe of heavenly beauty take.

While from the dust, each circling year,
 The snow-drop lifts its humble head,
Say, shall I doubt God's equal power,
 To call me from my lowly bed ?

WISHES AND REALITIES.

A CHILD'S WISHES.

" I WISH I were a little bird,
 To fly so far and high,
And sail along the golden clouds,
 And through the azure sky.
I'd be the first to see the sun
 Up from the ocean spring ;
And ere it[1] touched the glittering spire,
 His ray should gild my wing.

" Above the hills I'd watch him still,
 Far down the crimson west ;
And sing to him my evening song,
 Ere yet I sought my rest.
And many a land I then should see,
 As hill and plain I crossed ;
Nor fear through all the pathless sky
 That I should e'er be lost.

[1] *Ere—before it*—the sun's ray mentioned in the next]

" I'd fly where, round the olive bough,
  The vine its tendrils weaves;
And shelter from the noonbeams seek
  Among the myrtle leaves.
Now if I climb our highest hill,
  How little can I see!
Oh had I but a pair of wings,
  How happy should I be ! "

REPLY.

" Wings cannot soar above the sky,
  As thou *in thought* canst do ;
Nor can the veiling clouds confine
  Thy mental eye's[1] keen view.
Not to the sun dost thou chant forth
  Thy simple evening hymn ;
Thou praisest Him before whose smile
  The noonday sun grows dim.

" But thou mayst learn to trace the sun
  Around the earth and sky,
And see him rising, setting, still,
  Where distant oceans lie.
To other lands the bird may guide
  His pinions through the air ;
Ere yet he rest his wings, thou art
  In thought before him there.

" Though strong and free, his wing may droop,
  Or bands restrain its flight ;
Thought none may stay—more fleet its course
  Than swiftest beams of light ;

---

[1] *Mental eye—the eye* of the mind, which may, figuratively,
be *said to see what it thinks* about.

A lovelier clime than birds can find,
  While summers go and come,
Beyond this earth remains for those
  Whom God doth summon home."

THE CUCKOO.

HAIL, beauteous[1] stranger of the grove,
  Attendant on the Spring!
Now Heaven repairs thy vernal seat,[2]
  And woods thy welcome sing.

Soon as the daisy decks the green,
  Thy certain voice we hear;
Hast thou a star to guide thy path,[3]
  Or mark the rolling year?

Delightful visitant! with thee[4]
  I hail the time of flowers;
And hear the sound of music sweet
  From birds among the bowers.

The schoolboy, wandering in the wood
  To pull the primrose gay,
Starts—the new voice of Spring to hear,
  And imitates thy lay.

---

[1] The Cuckoo is not remarkable for beauty: it is addr
as *beauteous* here, because its coming back is connected
the appearance of the beauties of Spring.

[2] *Now Heaven, &c.*—now Heaven, that is, God, makes
Spring abode, the woods, beautiful again.

[3] *Hast thou a star, &c.*—an allusion either to the pole
which guides the mariner, or to the star which led the
men to the infant Saviour.

[4] *With thee*

Soon as the pea puts on the bloom,
   Thou fliest the vocal vale;[1]
An annual guest in other lands,[2]
   Another Spring to hail.

Sweet bird! thy bower is ever green,
   Thy sky is ever clear;
Thou hast no sorrow in thy song,
   No winter in thy year!

                       Logan.

TO A BUTTERFLY.

I'VE watched you now a short half-hour,
Self-poised upon that yellow flower;
And, little Butterfly! indeed
I know not if you sleep or feed.
How motionless!—not frozen seas
   More motionless!—and then
What joy awaits you, when the breeze
Hath found you out among the trees,
   And calls you forth again!

This plot of orchard ground is ours:
My trees they are, my sister's flowers;
Here rest your wings when they are weary:
Here lodge as in a sanctuary!

[1] The old rhymes respecting the Cuckoo's arrival and departure are—

        "In April
          Come he will.
        In July
          He prepares to fly."

[2] After leaving *England*, the Cuckoo goes to North Africa
and *Asia Minor.*

Come often to us, fear no wrong ;
  Sit near us on the bough,
We'll talk of sunshine and of song,
And summer days, when we were young ;
Sweet childish days, that were as long
  As twenty days are now.

              Wordsworth.

INVITATION TO A ROBIN.

LITTLE bird, with bosom red,
Welcome to my humble shed !
Daily near my table steal,
While I take my scanty meal ;
Doubt not, little though there be,
But I'll cast a crumb to thee ;
Well rewarded if I spy
Pleasure in thy glancing eye,
And see thee when thou'st had thy fill,
Plume [1] thy breast, and wipe thy bill.
Come, my feathered friend, again,
Well thou know'st the broken pane ;
Ask of me thy daily store,
Ever welcome to my door.

              Langhorne

THE BUTTERFLY'S BALL.

Come, take up your hats, and away let us haste,
To the Butterfly's ball and the Grasshopper's feast ;
The trumpeter Gad-fly has summoned the crew,
And the revels are now only waiting for you.

[1] *Plume—to* pick and adjust the feathers.

On the smooth-shaven grass, by the side of a wo
Beneath a broad oak, which for ages has stood,
See the children of earth, and the tenants of air,
For an evening's amusement together repair :

There first came the Beetle, so blind and so black,
Who carried the Emmet, his friend, on his back ;
And there came the Gnat, and the Dragon-fly too,
And all their relations, green, orange, and blue.

And there came the Moth, in his plumage of down,
And the Hornet, in jacket of yellow and brown,
Who with him the Wasp his companion did bring ;
But they promised that evening to lay by their sting.

And the sly little Dormouse crept out of his hole,
And led to the feast his blind brother, the Mole ;
And the Snail, with his horns peeping out from his
    shell,
Came from a great distance—the length of an ell.

A mushroom their table, and on it was laid
A water-dock leaf, which a tablecloth made ;
The viands were various, to each of their taste,
And the Bee brought his honey to crown the repast.

'here, close on his haunches, so solemn and wise,
he Frog from a corner looked up to the skies ;
nd the Squirrel, well pleased such diversion to see,
t cracking his nuts overhead in a tree.

    en out came a Spider, with fingers so fine,
    show his dexterity on the tight line ;
    m one branch *to another* his cobweb he slung,
    as quick as an arrow he darted along.

But just in the middle, oh ! shocking to tell !
From his rope in an instant poor Harlequin fell ;
Yet he touched not the ground, but with talons [1] ou
　　spread,
Hung suspended in air at the end of a thread.

Then the Grasshopper came, with a jerk and
　　spring ;
Very long was his leg, though but short was h
　　wing ;
He took but three leaps, and was soon out of sight,
Then chirped his own praises the rest of the night.

With steps quite majestic the Snail did advance,
And promised the gazers a minuet [2] to dance ;
But they all laughed so loud, that he pulled in h
　　head,
And went in his own little chamber to bed.

Then as evening gave way to the shadows of night,
Their watchman, the Glow-worm, came out with h
　　light ;
Then home let us hasten while yet we can see,
For no watchman is waiting for you and for me.

　　　　　　　　　　　　　　　　　　Rosco

THE BUTTERFLY'S FUNERAL.

Oh ye ! who so lately were blithesome and gay,
At the Butterfly's banquet carousing away ;
Your feasts and your revels of pleasure are fled,
For the chief of the banquet, the Butterfly's dead !

[1] *Talons*—claws.
[2] *Minuet*—an old-fashioned, slow, and stately dance.

No longer the Flies and the Emmets advance,
To join with their friends in the Grasshopper's
    dance,
For see his fine form o'er the favourite bend,
And the Grasshopper mourns for the loss of his
    friend.

And hark to the funeral dirge [1] of the Bee,
And the Beetle, who follows as solemn as he !
And see, where so mournful [2] the green rushes wave,
The Mole is preparing the Butterfly's grave.

The Dormouse attended, but cold and forlorn,
And the Gnat slowly winded his shrill little horn ;
And the Moth, being grieved at the loss of a sister,
Bent over her body, and silently kissed her.

The corpse was embalmed at the set of the sun,
And enclosed in a case which the Silk-worm had
    spun ;
By the help of the Hornet the coffin was laid
On a bier [3] out of myrtle and jessamine made.

In weepers and scarfs [4] came the Butterflies all,
And six of their number supported the pall ;
And the Spider came there in his mourning so
    black,
But the fire of the Glow-worm soon frightened him
    back.

[1] *Dirge*—a mournful song, proper for a funeral service.
[2] *Mournful*—mournfully.
[3] *Bier*—a frame used for supporting and carrying the dead.
[4] *Weepers and scarfs*—articles of dress worn at funerals.

The Grub left his nut-shell to join the sad throng,
And slowly led with him the Book-worm along,
Who wept his poor neighbour's unfortunate doom,
And wrote these few lines, to be placed on his tomb:

EPITAPH.

At this solemn spot, where the green rushes wave,
In sadness we bent o'er the Butterfly's grave;
'Twas here the last tribute to beauty we paid,
As we wept o'er the mound where her ashes are laid.

And here shall the daisy and violet blow.
And the lily discover [1] her bosom of snow;
While under the leaves, in the evenings of spring,
Still mourning his friend, shall the Grasshopper sing.

THE TIGER.

TIGER, tiger, burning bright
In the forest of the night !
What immortal hand or eye
Could frame thy fearful symmetry ?

In what distant deeps or skies
Burnt the ardour of thine eyes?
On what wings dare he aspire—
What the hand dare seize the fire ?

And what shoulder, and what art
Could twist the sinews of thy heart ?
And when thy heart began to beat,
What dread hand formed thy dread feet ?

[1] *Discover, &c.*—display to view her snow-white flower.

What the hammer, what the chain,
In what furnace was thy brain ?—
Did God smile His work to see?
Did He who made the lamb make thee ?
Blake.

THE TRUE STORY OF WEB-SPINNER.[1]

WEB-SPINNER was a miser old,
　　Who came of low degree;[2]
His body was large, his legs were thin,
　　And he kept bad company;
And his visage had the evil look
　　Of a black felon grim;
To all the country he was known,
　　But none spoke well of him.

His house was seven stories high,
　　In a corner of the street,
And it always had a dirty look,
　　When other homes were neat;
Up in his garret dark he lived,
　　And from the windows high,
Looked out in the dusky evening
　　Upon the passers by.

Most people thought he lived alone,
　　Yet many have averred[3]
That dismal cries from out his house
　　Were often loudly heard;

---

[1] *Web-spinner*—the spider.
[2] *Who came, &c.*—who was of mean origin or low rank in ciety.
[3] *Averred*—positively declared.

And that none living left his gate,
    Although a few went in;
For he seized the very beggar old,
    And stripped him to the skin.

And though he prayed for mercy,
    Yet mercy ne'er was shown—
The miser cut his body up,
    And picked him bone from bone.
Thus people said, and all believed
    The dismal story true;
As it was told to me, in truth,
    I tell it so to you.

There was an ancient widow—
    One Madgy de la Moth,
A stranger to the man, or she
    Had ne'er gone there in troth : [1]
But she was poor, and wandered out
    At night-fall [2] in the street,
To beg from rich men's tables
    Dry scraps of broken meat.

So she knocked at old Web-Spinner's door
    With a modest tap, and low,
And down stairs came he speedily
    Like an arrow from a bow.
"Walk in, walk in, mother," said he,
    And shut the door behind—
She thought, for such a gentleman,
    That he was wondrous kind.

---

[1] *Troth*—truth.
[2] *Night-fall*—the beginning of night, evening.

But ere the midnight clock had tolled,
　Like a tiger of the wood,
He had eaten the flesh from off her bones,
　And drunk of her heart's blood !
Now after this foul deed was done,
　A little season's space,
The burly [1] Baron of Bluebottle
　Was riding from the chace.

The sport was dull, the day was hot,
　The sun was sinking down,
When wearily the Baron rode
　Into the dusty town.
Says he, " I'll ask a lodging,
　At the first house I come to ; "
With that,[2] the gate of Web-Spinner
　Came suddenly in view.

Loud was the knock the Baron gave—
　Down came the churl with glee ;
Says Bluebottle, " Good Sir, to-night
　I ask your courtesy ;
I am wearied with a long day's chace—
　My friends are far behind."
" You may need them all," said Web-Spinner,
　" It runneth in my mind."

" A Baron am I," said Bluebottle ;
　" From a foreign land I come ; "
" I thought as much," said Web-Spinner,
　" Fools never stay at home ! "

---

[1] *Burly*—pompous and big.
[2] *With that*—with that time, just at that moment.

Says the Baron, " Churl,[1] what meaneth this?
  I defy you, villain base ! "
And he wished the while, in his inmost heart,
  He was safely from the place.

Web-Spinner ran and locked the door,
  And a loud laugh laughed he,
With that, each one on the other sprang,
  And they wrestled furiously.
The Baron was a man of might,
  A swordsman of renown ;
But the Miser had the stronger arm,
  And kept the Baron down.

Then out he took a little cord,
  From a pocket at his side,
And with many a crafty, cruel knot,
  His hands and feet he tied ;
And bound him down unto the floor,
  And said, in savage jest,
" There is heavy work for you in store;—
  So, Baron, take your rest ! "

Then up and down his house he went,
  Arranging dish and platter,
With a dull and heavy countenance,
  As if nothing were the matter.
At length he seized on Bluebottle,
  That strong and burly man,
And, with many and many a desperate tug,
  To hoist him up began.

And step by step, and step by step,
  He went with heavy tread ;

---

[1] *Churl*—an ill-mannered, miserly person.

But ere he reached the garret door,
  Poor Bluebottle was dead !
Now all this while, a magistrate,
  Who lived in a house hard by,[1]
Had watched Web-Spinner's cruelty
  Through a window privily :

So in he burst, through bolts and bars,
  With a loud and thundering sound,
And vowed to burn the house with fire,
  And level it with the ground ;
But the wicked churl, who all his life
  Had looked for such a day,
Passed through a trap-door in the wall,
  And took himself away.

But where he went, no man could tell :
  'Twas said that under ground
He died a miserable death—
  But his body ne'er was found.
They pulled his house down, stick and stone,
  " For a caitiff[2] vile as he,"
Said they, " within our quiet town
  Shall not a dweller be ! "

                    Mary Howitt.

————◦◦————

THE SPIDER.

THE treacherous Spider, when her nets are spread,
Deep ambushed[3] in her silent den does lie,

[1] *Hard by*—near at hand.
[2] *Caitiff*—villain, base fellow.
[3] *Ambushed*—concealed, with a view to surprise an enemy

And feels, far off, the trembling of her thread,
Whose filmy cord should bind the struggling Fly;
Then, if at last she find him fast beset,
She issues forth, and runs along her loom,[1]
Eager to seize the captive in her net,
And drag the little wretch in triumph home.

Dryden.

THE CONTENTED BLIND BOY.

Oh! say, what is that thing called light,
    Which I must ne'er enjoy?
What are the blessings of the sight?
    Oh! tell a poor Blind Boy!

You talk of wondrous things you *see*;
    You say the sun shines bright;
I feel him warm, but how can he
    Or make it day or night?

My day or night myself I make
    Whene'er I sleep or play;
And could I always keep awake,
    With me 'twere[2] always day.

With heavy sighs I often hear
    You mourn my hapless woe;
But sure with patience I can bear
    A loss I ne'er can know.

Then let not what I cannot have
    My cheer of mind destroy;
While thus I sing, I am a king,
    Although a poor Blind Boy.   *C. Cibber*

[1] *Loom—a weaver's frame*—here, the frame of the spider's web.
[2] *'Twere—it were—it would be.*

WANDERING WILLIE.

WILLIE went out one morning
    The first of the sun to see;
He heard a rivulet laughing,
    " I follow you home," said he.
The river had run for a thousand years,
    Willie had lived for three.

Down by the singing river
    The rushes had made their bed;
" 'Tis me to be king of the castle,"
    Said Will, with a haughty head.
He shouldered a reed as a sentry's gun,
    Pacing with martial tread.

Old Mother Sheep was feeding.—
    " What brings him, that boy, this way ? "
She slowly came after Willie,
    The warrior edged away;
The one that was dumb was in earnest then,
    Neither enjoyed the play.

" This is the giant," said Willie,
    " And I am the valiant knight ;
If only he would not come quite so close,
    I think I should like to fight."
The sheep followed closer, and closer yet,
    Willie grew white with fright.

Over the hedge went Willie,
    And into the ditch fell he;
The ground it was soft, and no limb was scarred,
    Save only *one dimpled* knee.
" *This is the mortal* combat,
    And I am the slain," said he.

For many thousand men,"[1] said he,
" Were slain in that great victory."

" Now tell us what 'twas all about,"
    Young Peterkin, he cries,
And little Wilhelmine looks up
    With wonder-waiting eyes ;
" Now tell us all about the war,
    And what they killed each other for ? "

" It was the English," Kaspar cried,
    " That put the French to rout ;
But what they killed each other for,
    I could not well make out ;
But every body said," quoth[2] he,
" That 'twas a famous victory.

" My father lived at Blenheim then;
    " Yon little stream hard by ;[3]
They burnt his dwelling to the ground,
    And he was forced to fly ;
So with his wife and child he fled,
And knew not where to rest his head.

" With fire and sword the country round
    They wasted far and wide ;
And many a wretched mother, then,
    And new-born infant, died ;
But things like that, you know, must be
At every famous victory.

[1] It is said that 36,000 men were left killed and wo
on the field.
[2] *Quoth*—says or said.
[3] *Yon little stream hard by*—close to yonder little str

"They say it was a shocking sight,
    After the field was won,
For many thousand bodies here
    Lay rotting in the sun;
But things like that, you know, must be
After a famous victory.

" Great praise the Duke of Marlborough won,
    And our good Prince Eugene;"—
" Why 'twas a very wicked thing,"
    Said little Wilhelmine;
" Nay nay, my little girl," quoth he,
" It was a famous victory.

" And every body praised the Duke,
    Who this great fight did win "—
" But what good came of it at last ? "
    Quoth little Peterkin;
" Why, that I cannot tell," said he,
" But 'twas a famous victory."

                Southey.

THE CROCUS;

OR, THE DUTY OF PATIENCE.

Down in my solitude under the snow,
    Where nothing cheering can reach me;
Here, without light to see how to grow,
    I'll trust to nature to teach me.

I will not despair, nor be idle, nor frown,
    Enclosed in so gloomy a dwelling;
My leaves shall run up, and my roots shall run
    down,
    While the bud in my bosom is swelling.

D

And the desert wastes must be
Untracked regions but for thee !

Mary H

———◆◆◆———

TELL ME WHAT THE MILL DOTH S

TELL me what the mill doth say,
Clitter, clatter, night and day ;
When we sleep and when we wake,
Clitter, clatter, it doth make ;
Never idle, never still,
What a worker is the mill !

Hearken what the rill doth say,
As it journeys every day ;
Sweet as skylark on the wing,
Ripple, dipple, it doth sing ;
Never idle, never still,
What a worker is the rill !

Listen to the honey-bee,
As it dances merrily
To the little fairy's drum ;
Humming, drumming, drumming, dru
Never idle, never still,
Humming, drumming, hum it will.

Like the mill, the rill, and bee,
Idleness is not for me.
What says cock-a-doodle-doo ?
" Up, there's work enough for you."
If I work, then, with a will,
It will be but playing still.

E. Ca

CHILDHOOD'S TEARS.

THE tear down childhood's cheek that flows,
Is like the dew-drop on the rose;
When next the summer breeze comes by,
And waves the bush, the flower is dry.

Walter Scott.

—◆◆—

THE DEAD SPARROW.[1]

TELL me not of joy! there's none,
Now my little sparrow's gone:
   He would chirp and play with me;
He would hang his wing awhile—
Till at length he saw me smile
   Oh! how sullen he would be!

He would catch a crumb, and then
Sporting, let it go again;
     He from my lip
     Would moisture sip;
   He would from my trencher feed;
Then would hop, and then would run,
And cry "*phillip*" when he'd done!
   Oh! whose heart can choose but bleed?

Oh! how eager would he fight,
And ne'er hurt, though he did bite!
     No morn did pass,
     But on my glass
   He would sit, and mark and do
What I did; now [2] ruffle all

[1] The author of this piece died in the year 1643, so that it now more than 230 years old.
[2] When the word *now* is repeated, as above, the first *now* signifies, at one time; the second *now*, at another time.

D 2

When at last I was forced from my Sheelah to pai
She said—while the sorrow was big at her heart—
" Oh ! remember your Sheelah, when far, far awa
And be kind, my dear Pat, to our poor dog, Tray

Poor dog ! he was faithful and kind, to be sure,
And he constantly loved me, although I was poor ;
When the sour-looking folks sent me heartless awa
I had always a friend in my poor dog, Tray.

When the road was so dark, and the night was so col
And Pat and his dog were grown weary and old,
How snugly we slept in my old coat of gray,
And he licked me for kindness—my poor dog, Tra

Though my wallet was scant [1] I remembered his ca:
Nor refused my last crust to his pitiful face ;
But he died at my feet on a cold winter's day,
And I played a lament for my poor dog, Tray.

Where now shall I go, poor, forsaken, and blind ?
Can I find one to guide me, so faithful and kind ?
To my sweet native village, so far, far away,
I can never return with my poor dog, Tray.
                                        Campbe

THE BARLEY-MOWERS' SONG.

BARLEY-MOWERS, here we stand,
One, two, three, a steady band ;
True of heart, and strong of limb,
Ready in our harvest trim ;

---

[1] *Though my wallet was scant*—though my bag was i
rnished or nearly empty.

All a-row with spirits blithe,
Now we whet the bended scythe,
lk-a-tink, rink-a-tink, rink-a-tink-a-tink !

Side by side, now bending low, .
Down the swaths [1] of barley go,
Stroke by stroke, as true's [2] the chime
Of the bells, we keep in time ;
Then we whet the ringing scythe,
Standing 'mong the barley lithe,[3]
k-a-tink, rink-a-tink, rink-a-tink-a-tink !

Barley-mowers must be true,
Keeping still the end in view,
One with all, and all with one,
Working on till set of sun,
Bending all with spirits blithe,
Whetting all at once the scythe,
:-a-tink, rink-a-tink, rink-a-tink-a-tink !

Day and night, and night and day,
Time, the mower, will not stay ;
We may hear him in our path
By the falling barley swath ;
While we sing with voices blithe,
We may hear his ringing scythe,
:-a-tink, rink-a-tink, rink-a-tink-a-tink !

Time, the mower, cuts down all,
High and low, and great and small ;
Learn we then for him to grow
Ready, like the field we mow,

ths—*lines of grass or corn cut down by the mower.*
rue's—*as true as.*   [2] *Lithe*—*flexible, waving.*

Like the bending barley lithe,
Ready for the whetted scythe,
Rink-a-tink, rink-a-tink, rink-a-tink-a-tink !
                              Mary Howit

LITTLE MAY.

SEE, she stands, my little May,
   Where the sun and shadow meet;
Shakes her little hands for wings,
   Taps out music with her feet.

Mine she is! this wingèd joy—
   And the thrushes sing and sing,
Loving to keep company
   With so glad, so pure a thing.

Mine! this creature of the dawn,
   With the sweet cool breath of flowers:
That she comes I wonder much
   To a world so cold as ours.

Do I say the world is cold?
   No! she loves me, little May;
From my heart its cloud of care
   With her smiles she draws away;

Strokes my face with dimpled hands;
   With her warm hair, soft and fair,
Crowds my face;—the world looks bright
   Through the sunshine of her hair.

Still she walks in Eden shades,
In her guileless baby white,
With a heart of peace, with eyes
Full of wonder and delight.

Innocent of fruit forbid,
In her thoughts no bitter leaven;
Child, and angel too, she moves
Through a mingled earth and heaven.

I can see her in the light,
As without the gate I stand,
In the shadow, in the cold—
See the angel, sword in hand.

I must strive with weed and thorn,
I must suffer, watch, and wait,
I must lay this body down,
Ere I can repass the gate.

Gracious spirits that love man
Whisper through her rosy sleep,
And she smiles; if they should come
Whisp'ring me, I could but weep.

Dumb things love my little May;
Could they shrink from eyes like these?
Full of faith that knows no fear,
Eyes that hold no mysteries.

On the gravel Mop will rush,
Gambol, keep her tiny pace,
Heedful to *her baby talk*,
Slowly turn the wisest face;

Watch her hand for crumbled cake,
  Wait her will, and begging stand,
Have long patience till she please,
  Take it softly from her hand;

Willing on her baby knee
  Lay his head without a fear;
Shut his lazy eyes and sleep
  While she curls his shaggy ear.

At her round pink finger-tips
  Tenderly the dove will peck;
Nestle, white as innocence,
  With his head against her neck;

Coo his gentle soul to her,
  Knowing that her heart is meek;
And the kitten makes his paw
  Velvet soft, and pats her cheek.

Jane Mores

THE PET LAMB.

THE dew was falling fast, the stars began to blink;
I heard a voice; it said, " Drink, pretty creatu
    drink ! "
And looking o'er the hedge, before me I espied
A snow-white mountain lamb, with a maiden at
    side.

No other sheep were near, the lamb was all alone,
And by a slender cord was tethered [1] to a stone;
With one knee on the grass did the little maid
    kneel,
While to that mountain lamb she gave its eveni
    meal.

[1] *Tethered*—fastened.

'Twas little Barbara Lewthwaite, a child of beauty
   rare!
I watched them with delight, they were a lovely pair;
And now with empty can the maiden turned away;
But ere ten yards were gone, her footsteps did she
   stay.

Towards the lamb she looked, and from that shady
   place
I unobserved could see the workings of her face;
If nature to her tongue could measured numbers
   bring,[1]
Thus, thought I, to her lamb that little maid might
   sing :—

" What ails thee, young one? what? why pull so at
   thy cord?
Is it not well with thee, well both for bed and board?
Thy plot of grass is soft, and green as grass can be ;
Rest, little young one, rest; what is't that aileth thee?

" What is it thou wouldst seek? What is wanting
   to thy heart?
Thy limbs are they not strong?—and beautiful thou
   art;
This grass is tender grass; these flowers they have
   no peers ;[2]
And that green corn, all day, is rustling in thy ears!

" If the sun be shining hot, do but stretch thy woollen
   chain;
The beech is standing by, its covert thou canst gain;

[1] *If nature, &c.*—if she could utter her feelings in verse.
[2] *Peers—equals.*

E

For rain and mountain storms ! the like thou need'st
    not fear—
The rain and storm are things which scarcely can
    come here.

" Rest, little young one, rest ! hast thou forgot the day
When my father found thee first in places far away?
Many flocks were on the hills, but thou wert owned
    by none ;
And thy mother from thy side for evermore was gone.

" He took thee in his arms, and in pity brought thee
    home :
A blessed day for thee ! then whither wouldst thou
    roam ?
A faithful nurse thou hast; the dam that did thee
    yean [1]
Upon the mountain tops, no kinder could have been.

" Thou know'st that twice a day I have brought thee
    in this can
Fresh water from the brook, as clear as ever ran :
And twice, too, in the day, when the ground is wet
    with dew,
I bring thee draughts of milk ; warm milk it is, and
    new.

" It will not, will not rest !—Poor creature, can it be
That 'tis thy mother's heart that is working so in thee?
Things that I know not of, belike to thee are dear,
And dreams of things which thou canst neither see
    nor hear.

---

[1] *That did thee yean*—that gave birth to thee.

s ! the mountain tops, that look so green and fair !
heard of fearful winds and darkness that come
there ;
little brooks that seem all pastime and all play,
n they are angry, roar like lions for their prey.

:e thou need'st not fear the raven in the sky ;
t and day thou'rt safe—our cottage is hard by.
  bleat so after me ? why pull so at thy chain ?
—and at break of day I will come to thee
again ? "   *Wordsworth.*

THE WEDDING AMONG THE FLOWERS.[1]

grand convocation which Flora enacted,
:e the business of all her domain was transacted,
s hinted, there yet remained one regulation
:rfect her glorious administration.
)me, strength and masculine beauty were given,
stical air, and an eye meeting heaven ;
en virtues to many, to others perfume,
ugh each variation of sweetness and bloom :
: therefore suggested, with Flora's compliance,
ite every charm in some splendid alliance.
:oyal assent to the motion was gained.
: passed at three sittings, and duly ordained.

: now most amusing to traverse the shade,
hear the remarks that were privately made :

his elegant little poem, which was originally published
  year 1808, in a separate form, is reprinted here by the
  permission of the accomplished authoress—now Mrs.
  t, *of Nottingham.*

Such whispers, inquiries, and investigations!
Such balancing merits and marshalling stations!
The nobles protested they never would yield
To debase their high sap with the weeds of the field;
For, indeed there was nothing so vulgar and rude,
As to let every ill-bred young wild-flower intrude;
Their daughters should never dishonour their houses,
By taking such rabble as these for their spouses!

At length, my Lord SUNFLOWER, whom public opinion
Confessed as the pride of the blooming dominion,
Avowed an affection he'd often betrayed
For sweet Lady LILY, the queen of the shade;
And said, should her friends nor the public with-
    stand,
He would dare to solicit her elegant hand.

A whisper, like that which on fine summer eves
Young zephyrs address to the frolicsome leaves,
Immediately ran through the whole congregation,
Expressive of pleasure and high approbation.
No line was degraded, no family pride
Insulted, by either the bridegroom or bride;
For in him all was majesty, beauty, and splendour,
In her all was elegant, simple, and tender.

Now nothing remained but to win her consent,
And Miss IRIS, her friend, as the messenger went,
The arts of entreaty and argument trying,
Till at length she returned, and announced her com-
    plying.
Complete satisfaction the tidings conveyed,
And whispers and dimples the pleasure displayed.
Will COCKSCOMB, indeed, and a few POWDERED BEAUX
Who *were* *not* *little* vain of their figure and clothes,

ooked down with chagrin which they could not
    disguise,
hat *they* were not fixed on to carry the prize.

t length the young nobleman ventured to name
ie following spring, and supported his claim
y duly consulting a reverend Seer,
ANDELION, who augured the wedding that year,
oved to give his opinion by breath of perfume,
nd nodding assent with his silvery plume.
or licence, his lordship in person applied
o the high CROWN IMPERIAL, whose court he
    descried
y the GOLDEN ROD, ensign of state, by his side.
eturning from thence in the course of his journey,
e ordered the deeds of JONQUIL, the attorney;
nd anxious a speedy conclusion to bring,
t LOVE-CHAIN and GOLD-DUST to work on the ring.

ow April came garnished with smiles, and the day
as fixed for the first of luxuriant May.
long the green garden, in shade or in sun,
ll was business and bustle, and frolic and fun;
or, as Flora had granted a full dispensation
o all the gay tribes in her blooming creation,
y which at the festival all might appear,
ho else were on duty but parts of the year;
iere was now such a concourse of beauty and
    grace,
s had not, since Eden, appeared in one place;
id cards were dispersed, with consent of the fair,
o every great family through the parterre.[1]

[1] *Parterre*—a flower-garden.
B 2

There was one city lady, indeed, whom the bride
Did not wish to attend, which was Miss LONDO
    PRIDE ;
And his lordship declared he would rather not mee
So doubtful a person as young BITTER-SWEET.
Sir MICHAELMAS DAISY was asked to appear,
But was gone out of town for best part of the year :
And though he was sent for, NARCISSUS declined
Out of pique, and preferred to keep sulking behind
For, having beheld his fine form in the water,
He thought himself equal to any flower's daughter,
And would not consent to increase a parade,
The hero of which he himself should have made.
Dr. CAMOMILE was to have been of the party,
But was summoned to town to old Alderman Heart
Old ALOE, a worthy respectable don,
Could not go in the clothes that just then he had o
And his tailor was such a slow fellow, he guessed
That it might be a century before he was dressed.[1]
Excuses were sent, too, from very near all
The ladies residing at Great Green-house Hall,
Who had been so confined, were so chilly and spar
It might cost them their lives to be out in the air.
The SENSITIVE PLANT hoped her friend would excus
    her ;
It thrilled every nerve in her frame to refuse her,
But she did not believe she had courage to view
The solemn transaction she'd summoned her to.
Widow WAIL had a ticket, but would not attend,
For fear her low spirits should sadden her friend ;

---

[1] *In allusion to the* vulgar error, that the aloe requires
hundred years to arrive at maturity.

d, too wild to regard either lady or lord,
NEY-SUCKLE, as usual, was gadding abroad.
twithstanding all which, preparations were made
the very first style for the splendid parade.
e CLOTH-PLANT, a clothier of settled repute,
dertook to provide every beau with a suit,
mmed with BACHELORS'-BUTTONS; but these, I
   presume,
re rejected, as out of the proper costume.
ss SATIN-FLOWER, fancy-dress-maker from town,
d silks of all colours and patterns sent down;
· which LADIES'-RIBBON could hardly prepare
r trimmings, so fast as bespoke by the fair.
o noted perfumers from Shrubbery Lane,
ssrs. MUSK-ROSE and LAVENDER, essenced the
   train,
d ere the last twilight of April expired,
whole blooming band was completely attired.

length the bright morning, with glittering eye,
ped o'er the green earth from the rose-coloured
   sky;
d soon as the lark flitted out of her nest,
bridal assembly was ready and dressed.
long the most lovely, far lovelier shone
bride, with an elegance purely her own:
r tall slender figure green tissue arrayed,
th diamonds strung loose on the shining brocade:
ap of white velvet, in graceful costume,
orned her fair forehead—a silvery plume
ped with gold, from the centre half-negligent
   hung,
th *strings of white* pearl scattered loosely among:

The last (such as fairies are fancied to wear,)
Aurora[1] herself had disposed in her hair.
To meet her and welcome the high-omened day,
The bridegroom stepped forth in majestic array—
A rough velvet suit, mingled russet and green,
Around his fine figure, broad flowing was seen;
His front, warm and manly, a diadem graced,
Of regal appearance, resplendent as chaste;
The centre was puckered in velvet of brown,
With golden vandykes, which encircled the crown.
Since nature's first morning, ne'er glittered a pair,
The one so commanding, the other so fair!
Many ladies of fashion had offered to wait
As bridemaids, the honour was reckoned so great;
These famed for their beauty, for fragrancy those,
ANEMONE splendid, or sweet-smelling ROSE;
But gentle and free from a tincture of pride,
A sweet country cousin was called by the bride,
Who long in a valley had sheltered unknown,
Or was traced to the shade by her sweetness alone;
She timid appeared in the meekest array,
With pearls of clear dew on an evergreen spray.

Now moved the procession from dressing-room
    bowers,
A brilliant display of illustrious flowers:
Young HEART'S-EASE in purple and gold ran before,
To welcome them in at the great temple door;
Where old Bishop MONK'S-HOOD had taken his stand,
To weave and to sanction the conjugal band:
The trumpeter SUCKLING, with musical air,
Preceded as herald;—then came the young pair,

[1] *Aurora*—the goddess of the morning—the dawn.

'ith little Miss LILY, as bridemaid behind,
lone her fair head on her bosom reclined.
he old Duke of PEONY, richly arrayed
ı coquelicot,[1] headed the long cavalcade;
uchess Dowager ROSE leading up at his side,
'ith her daughters, some blooming, some fair as
    the bride;
y Lady CARNATION, excessively dashing,
ouged highly, and new in the Rotterdam fashion,[2]
iscoursing of rank and of pedigree, came
'ith a beau of distinction, Van TULIP by name;
ield-officer POPPY, in trim militaire;
n unfortunate youth, HYACINTHUS the fair;
'ith Major CONVOLVULUS, fresh from parade,
nd his son, though a Minor, in purple cockade;
 pair from the country, affecting no show,
RETTY BETSY the belle, and SWEET-WILLIAM the
    beau,
ıcceeded; and next, in the simplest attire,
iss JESSAMINE pale, and her lover SWEET-BRIAR;
URICULA came, in puce velvet and white,
'ith her spouse POLYANTHUS, a rich city knight;
essrs. STOCKS from 'Change Alley,[3] in crimson
    array;
he twin-brother LARKSPURS, two fops of the day;

[1] *Coquelicot*—the red poppy—here used to describe the
lour of the dress.
[2] *Rotterdam*—The carnation and tulip are especially culti-
ted in Holland—hence the reference to Rotterdam, a town
that country, and to *Van* tulip, Van being a Dutch title of
nk.
[3] *'Change Alley*—for Exchange Alley, a passage near where
e old Royal Exchange stood, much frequented by dealers
Stock, as money is sometimes called.

With light-hearted COLUMBINE, playing the fool,
And footing away, like a frolic from school;
Then a distant relation, 'twas said, of the bride,
WATER-LILY, a nymph from the rivulet's side,
And last, hand-in-hand, at the end of the train,
VIOLETTA and DAISY, from Hazel-nut lane.
MEZEREON had fully designed to be there,
But was only half dressed, and obliged to forbear;
And the EVENING PRIMROSE was pale with chagrin
That her cap did not come till the day had closed i
So each remained pouting behind in the shade,
As winding along moved the brilliant parade.

At length the fair temple appeared to their view,
All blushing with beauty and spangled with dew :
Tall hollyhock pillars encircled it round,
With tendrils of pea and sweet eglantine[2] bound ;
The roof was a trellis[3] of myrtle and vine,
Which knots and festoons of nasturtium combine:
Surmounting each pillar, the cornice displayed
The midsummer star-wort, relieving the shade;
And, wreathed into loops of the tenderest green,
Antirrhinum waved loose to the zephyrs between.
The passion-flower fond to the portico clung,
And guelder-rose glittered the foliage among ;
A mossy mosaic[4] the pavement displayed,
With tufts of hepatica richly inlaid ;

---

[1] The flowers of the mezereon appear on the naked ste
before the leaves are unfolded.

[2] *Eglantine*—the sweet-briar.

[3] *Trellis*—a lattice, or frame of cross-barred work of wo
&c.

[4] *Mosaic*—an imitation of a painting, made with pebbl
marbles, shells, or, as in the passage above, of moss of dif
lours.

ιd high in the centre an altar was reared,
hich wreathen with net-work of flowers appeared :
here sunbeams, by dews in the trellis condensed,
om herbs aromatic sweet odours dispensed :
love were suspended the merry blue-bells,
ly rites to enliven with musical swells.

ιd now the train enters, the altar burns bright,
esh fragrance escapes from the centrical light;
fore the green shrine, the young couple await
ch form ceremonious ordained by the state ;
ιd mystical vows understood but by flowers,
hich elude observation of senses like ours.
vas only perceived that the Bishop profound
ιar dews from his urn sprinkled thrice on the
   ground;
ιd Zephyr, or some such invisible thing,
rice fluttered the air with his butterfly wing.
length the rites closed in a grand benediction,
ιd merriment burst without any restriction.
w blushed in the banquet along the parterre,
ch dainty that nature or art could prepare :—
MASK ROSE on the lawn had a table-cloth spread,
e FLESH PLANT provided the dish at the head,
ιd CORNBOTTLE furnished the table with bread.
usewife BUTTERCUP sent a supply from her churn;
e SNOWDROP iced dews in a white Crocus urn ;
ιd CANDY TUFT, skilled in the art of preserving,
splendid dessert had the honour of serving.
ιE BURGUNDY, vintner, the goblet supplied
th neat[1] foreign wines, and made[2] cowslip beside ;

Neat—pure.   [2] *Made—that is, home made,*

Campanula cups, filled with gentle spring rain,
Were served to the ladies who wished for it plain;
And all was so elegant, splendid, and rare,
That I could not name half the fine things that were
    there.
When finished, SNAP-DRAGONS produced a good joke,
And ROCKETS went up to amuse the young folk.
In return for past favours, a band of young bees
Hummed a midsummer tune through the neigh-
    bouring trees;
And linnet and lark, as by accident, met
And surprised the young pair with a charming duet.
And now mirth and revelry were at their height,
The little ones crept to the shade in affright;
The ladies had danced in the heat of the sun,
Till their dresses were limp and their spirits outdone;
And Flora, who witnessed the scene with concern,
Beckoned forward to Vesper[1] to empty her urn.
At once, as by magic, the merriment died,
Not a whisper was heard, not a gambol was tried!
Returned to their stations in border or bed,
Each shut up his eye, or hung graceful her head;
And those who had left foreign mountains and vales,
Rode home in snug parties, on zephyrs and gales;
So that ere the first star wandered out with a beam,
They were all sound asleep, and beginning to dream!
          Ann Taylor.

JOHN BARLEYCORN.

THERE went three kings into the east,
  Three kings both great and high,

[1] *Vesper*—the evening star—evening itself.

And they have sworn a solemn oath,
   John Barleycorn shall die.

They took a plough and ploughed him down,
   Put clods upon his head;
And they have sworn a solemn oath,
   John Barleycorn was dead.

But the cheerful spring came kindly on,
   And showers began to fall;
John Barleycorn got up again,
   And sore surprised them all.

The sultry suns of summer came,
   And he grew thick and strong;
His head well armed with pointed spears,
   That no one should him wrong.

The sober autumn entered mild,
   And he grew wan and pale;
His bending joints and drooping head
   Showed he began to fail.

His colour sickened more and more,
   He faded into age;
And then his enemies began
   To show their deadly rage.

They took a weapon long and sharp,
   And cut him by the knee;
Then tied him fast upon a cart,
   Like a rogue for forgery.

They laid him down upon his back,
   And cudgelled him full sore;
They hung him up before the storm,
   And turned him o'er and o'er.

F

They filled up then a darksome pit
  With water to the brim;
And heaved in poor John Barleycorn,
  To let him sink or swim.

They laid him out upon the floor,
  To work him further woe;
And still, as signs of life appeared,
  They tossed him to and fro.

They wasted o'er a scorching flame
  The marrow of his bones;
But the miller used him worst of all,
  For he crushed him between two stones.

And they have taken his very heart's blood
  And drunk it round and round;—
And so farewell, John Barleycorn!
  Thy fate thou now hast found.

Burn

THE LADY-BIRD IN THE HOUSE.

OH! lady-bird, lady-bird, why do you roam
So far from your children, so far from your home?
Why do you, who can revel all day in the air,
And the sweets of the grove and the garden can shar
In the fold of a leaf who can find a green bower,
And a palace enjoy in the tube of a flower,—
Ah! why, simple lady-bird, why do you venture
The dwellings of men so familiar [1] to enter?
Too soon you may find that your trust is misplace(
When by some cruel child you are wantonly chase(

[1] *Familiar*—for familiarly.

d your bright scarlet coat, so bespotted with bla
orn by his barbarous hands from your back :
! then you'll regret you were tempted to rove
ɔm the tall climbing hop, or the hazel's thick grov
ɪd will fondly remember each arbour and tree,
here lately you wandered contented and free :—
en fly, simple lady-bird !—fly away home,
  more from your nest and your children to roam.
                               Charlotte Smith.

THE LADY-BIRD IN THE FIELDS.

DY-BIRD ! lady-bird ! fly away home ;
The field-mouse has gone to her nest ;
e daisies have shut up their sleepy red eyes,
And the bees and the birds are at rest.

'y-bird ! lady-bird ! fly away home,
 he glow-worm is lighting his lamp ;
  dew's falling fast, and your fine speckled wings
 ill be wet with the close-clinging damp.

 -bird ! lady-bird ! fly away home,
 ɘ fairy-bells tinkle afar ;
  haste, or they'll catch you, and harness you fast
 :h a cobweb to Oberon's [1] car.

TO A BEE.

 ʋert out betimes, thou busy, busy bee !
 ɪn abroad I took my early way,

[1] *Oberon*—the king of the fairies.

Before the cow from her resting-place
Had risen up, and left her trace
  On the meadow with dew so grey,
I saw thee, thou busy, busy bee!

Thou wert alive, thou busy, busy bee!
  When the crowd in their sleep were dead;
Thou wert abroad in the freshest hour,
When the sweetest odour comes from the flower;
  Man will not learn to leave his bed,
And be wise and copy thee, thou busy, busy bee

Thou wert working late, thou busy, busy bee!
  After the fall of the cistus flower; [1]
When the evening primrose was ready to burst;
I heard thee last, as I saw thee first;
  In the silence of the evening hour,
I heard thee, thou busy, busy bee!

Thou art a miser, thou busy, busy bee!
  Late and early at employ;
Still on thy golden stores intent,
Thy summer in heaping and hoarding is spent
  What thy winter will never enjoy;
Wise lesson this for me, thou busy, busy bee!

Little dost thou think, thou busy, busy bee!
  What is the end of thy toil!
When the latest flowers of the ivy are gone,
And all thy work for the year is done,
  Thy master comes for the spoil;—
Woe then for thee, thou busy, busy bee!

South

[1] *The gum cistus flower lives but one day.*

THE FROST.

ae Frost looked forth, one still clear night,
nd whispered, "Now I shall be out of sight;
, through the valley and over the height,
   In silence I'll take my way:
will not go on like that blustering train,
he wind and the snow, the hail and the rain,
ho make so much bustle and noise in vain,
   But I'll be as busy as they."

hen he flew to the mountain and powdered its crest;
e lit on the trees, and their boughs he dressed
ı diamond beads—and over the breast
   Of the quivering lake he spread
coat of mail, that it need not fear
he downward point of many a spear
hat he hung on its margin, far and near,
   Where a rock could rear its head.

e went to the windows of those who slept,
nd over each pane, like a fairy, crept;
Therever he breathed, wherever he stept,
   By the light of the moon were seen
lost beautiful things:—there were flowers and trees;
here were bevies of birds and swarms of bees;
here were cities with temples and towers, and these
   All pictured in silver sheen![1]

ut he did one thing that was hardly fair;
le peeped in the cupboard, and finding there
'hat all had forgotten for him to prepare—
   "Now just to set them a thinking,

[1] *Sheen*—brightness, splendour.

F 2

I'll bite this basket of fruit," said he,
" This costly pitcher I'll burst in three,
And the glass of water they've left for me
        Shall ' *tchick !* ' to tell them I'm drinking."
                                    Miss Gould.

THE LION.

Lion, thou art girt with might !
King by uncontested right;
Strength, and majesty, and pride,
Are in thee personified !
Slavish doubt, or timid fear,
Never came thy spirit near ;
What it is to fly, or bow
To a mightier than thou,
Never has been known to thee,
Creature, terrible and free !

Power the mightiest gave the Lion,
Sinews like to bands of iron ;
Gave him force which never failed ;
Gave a heart that never quailed.[1]
Triple-mailèd [2] coat of steel,
Plates of brass from head to heel.
Less defensive were [3] in wearing,
Than the Lion's heart of daring ;
Nor could towers of strength impart
Trust like that which keeps his heart.

---

[1] *Quailed*—sank into dejection.
[2] *Mailèd*—covered with armour. This word must be here
pronounced in two syllables, for the sake of the verse.
[3] *Were*—would be.

When he sends his roaring forth,
Silence falls upon the earth ;
For the creatures, great and small,
Know his terror-breathing call ;
And, as if by death pursued,
Leave to him a solitude.

Lion, thou art made to dwell
In hot lands, intractable,
And thyself, the sun, the sand,
Are a tyrannous triple band ; [1]—
Lion-king and desert throne,
All the region is your own !

Mary Howitt.

THE BEGGAR MAN.

AROUND the fire, one wintry night,
  The farmer's rosy children sat ;
The faggot lent its blazing light ;
  And jokes went round and careless chat.

When, hark ! a gentle hand they hear,
  Low tapping at the bolted door ;
And, thus to gain their willing ear,
  A feeble voice was heard to implore :—

" Cold blows the blast across the moor ;
  The sleet drives hissing in the wind ;
Yon toilsome mountain lies before ;
  A dreary, treeless waste behind.

[1] *Tyrannous triple band*—a threefold band of tyrants—a
nd *of three tyrants.*

" My eyes are weak and dim with age ;
　No road, no path, can I descry ;
And these poor rags ill stand the rage
　Of such a keen, inclement sky.

" So faint I am, these tottering feet
　No more my feeble frame can bear ;
My sinking heart forgets to beat,
　And drifting snows my tomb prepare.

" Open your hospitable door,
　And shield me from the biting blast ;
Cold, cold it blows across the moor,
　The weary moor that I have past ! "

With hasty steps the farmer ran,
　And close beside the fire they place
The poor half-frozen beggar man,
　With shaking limbs and pallid face.

The little children flocking came,
　And warmed his stiffening hands in thei
And busily the good old dame
　A comfortable mess prepares.

Their kindness cheered his drooping soul ;
　And slowly down his wrinkled cheek
The big round tear was seen to roll,
　And told the thanks he could not speak.

The children, too, began to sigh,
　And all their merry chat was o'er ;
And yet they felt, they knew not why,
　More glad than they had done before.

　　　　　　　　　　　　　Miss ⅃

THE LAMB.

LITTLE lamb, who made thee?
Dost thou know who made thee?
Gave thee life, and bid thee feed
By the stream and o'er the mead;
Gave thee clothing of delight,
Softest clothing, woolly, bright;
Gave thee such a tender voice,
Making all the vales rejoice:
    Little lamb, who made thee;
    Dost thou know who made thee?

Little lamb, I'll tell thee;
Little lamb, I'll tell thee.
 He is called by thy name,
For He calls Himself a Lamb.
He is meek, and He is mild;
He became a little child:
I, a child, and thou, a lamb,
We are called by His name.
    Little lamb, God bless thee;
    Little lamb, God bless thee.

Blake.

THE KITTENS AND THE VIPER.

CLOSE by the threshold of a door nailed fast
Three kittens sat; each kitten looked aghast;
I, passing swift and inattentive by,
At the three kittens cast a careless eye;
Little concerned *to know* what they did there;
Not deeming kittens worth a poet's care.

But presently a loud and furious hiss
Caused me to stop and to exclaim, " What's this ? "
When lo ! with head erect and fiery eye,
A dusky viper on the ground I spy.
Forth from his head his forked tongue he throws,
Darting it full against a kitten's nose !
Who, never having seen in field or house
The like, sat still and silent as a mouse ;
Only projecting, with attention due,
Her whiskered face, she asked him, " Who are you '
On to the hall went I, with pace not slow
But swift as lightning, for a long Dutch hoe ;
With which, well armed, I hastened to the spot
To find the viper ;—but I found him not ;
And turning up the leaves and shrubs around,
Found only—that he was not to be found.
But still the kittens, sitting as before,
Were watching close the bottom of the door.
" I hope," said I, " the villain I would kill
Has slipped between the door and the door-sill ;
And if I make despatch, and follow hard
No doubt but I shall find him in the yard."
(For long ere now it should have been rehearsed,
'Twas in the garden that I found him first.)
Ev'n there I found him ; there the full-grown cat
His head, with velvet paw, did gently pat ;
As curious as the kittens erst[1] had been
To learn what this phenomenon[2] might mean.
Filled with heroic ardour at the sight,
And fearing every moment he would bite,.

---

[1] *Erst*—before, formerly. [2] *Phenomenon*—an appearan
a *remarkable* appearance ; the plural is *phenomena.*

And rob our household of the only cat
That was of age to combat with a rat,
With outstretched hoe I slew him at the door,
And taught him NEVER TO COME THERE NO MORE!

Cowper.

THE BIRD CAUGHT AT SEA.

PRETTY little feathered fellow,
　Why so far from home dost [1] rove?
What misfortune brought thee hither
　From the green, embowering grove?

Let thy throbbing heart be still;
　Here secure from danger rest thee;
No one here shall use thee ill,
　Here no cruel boy molest thee.

Barley-corns and crumbs of bread,
　Crystal [2] water, too, shall cheer thee;
On soft sails recline thy head,
　Sleep, and fear no danger near thee:

And when kindly winds shall speed us
　To the land we wish to see,
Then, sweet captive, thou shalt leave us,—
　Then amidst the groves be free.

A. Hill.

THE THRUSH.

How void of care yon merry thrush,
　That sings melodious in the bush,

---

[1] *Dost*—dost thou?

[2] *Crystal*—a transparent mineral; *crystal water*—water as clear as crystal.

That has no stores of wealth to keep,
No lands to plough, no corn to reap!

He never frets for worthless things,
But lives in peace, and sweetly sings;
Enjoys the present with his mate,
Unmindful of to-morrow's fate.

Of true felicity possessed,
He glides through life supremely blest;
And for his daily meal relies
On Him whose love the world supplies.

Rejoiced he finds his morning fare,
His dinner lies—he knows not where;
Still to the unfailing hand he chants
His grateful song, and never wants.

Williams

THE ANT AND THE CRICKET.

A silly young cricket, accustomed to sing
Through the warm sunny months of the summer and
　　spring,
Began to complain, when he found that at home
His cupboard was empty, and winter was come.
　　　　Not a crumb to be found
　　　　On the snow-covered ground;
　　　　Not a flower could he see,
　　　　Not a leaf on a tree;—
" Oh ! what will become," said the cricket, " of me ? "

At last, by starvation and famine made bold,
All dripping with wet, and all trembling with cold,

Away he set off to a miserly ant,
To see if, to keep him alive, he would grant
    A shelter from rain,
    And a mouthful of grain.
    He wished only to borrow,
    And repay it to-morrow;
If not, he must die of starvation and sorrow.

Said the ant to the cricket, " I'm your servant and
    friend ;
But we ants never borrow, we ants never lend.
But tell me, dear sir, did you lay nothing by
When the weather was warm ? " Said the cricket,
    " Not I !
    My heart was so light
    That I sang day and night,
    For all nature looked gay."
    " You sang, sir, you say ?
Go, then," said the ant, " and dance winter away."
Thus ending, he hastily opened the wicket,
And out of the door turned the poor little cricket.

Though this is a fable, the moral is good :—
If you live without work, you will go without food.

THE LULLABY.

SLEEP, my child, my darling child, my lovely child,
    sleep :
    The sun sleepeth upon the green fields ;
    The moon sleepeth upon the blue waves ;
    The *morning sleepeth* upon a bed of roses ;
              G

The evening sleepeth on the tops of the dark hills;
The winds sleep in the hollow of the rocks ;
The stars sleep upon a pillow of clouds :—
Sleep, my child, my darling child, my lovely child,
    sleep.

The mist sleepeth in the bosom of the valley,
And the broad lake under the shadow of the trees.
The flowers sleep while the night dew falls,
And the wild bird sleeps upon the mountain :—
Sleep in quiet, sleep in joy, my darling,
May thy sleep never be the sleep of sorrow !
Sleep, my child, my darling child, my lovely child,
    sleep.

THE MILLER OF THE DEE.

THERE dwelt a miller hale and bold
    Beside the river Dee ;
He worked and sang from morn till night,
    No lark more blithe than he ;
And this the burden of his song
    For ever used to be,—
" I envy nobody ; no, not I,
    And nobody envies me ! "

" Thou'rt wrong, my friend ! " said old King Hal,
    " Thou'rt wrong as wrong can be ;
For could my heart be light as thine,
    I'd gladly change with thee.
And tell me now what makes thee sing
    With voice so loud and free,
While I am sad, though I'm a king,
    Beside the river Dee ? "

The miller smiled and doff'd his cap :
" I earn my bread," quoth.he ;
' I love my wife, I love my friend,
　I love my children three ;
I owe no penny I cannot pay ;
　I thank the river Dee,
That turns the mill, that grinds the corn,
　To feed my babes and me."

Good friend," said Hal, and sigh'd the while,
" Farewell ! and happy be ;
But say no more, if thou'dst be true,
　That no one envies thee.
Thy mealy cap is worth my crown,
　Thy mill my kingdom's fee !
Such men as thou are England's boast,
　O miller of the Dee ! "　　　　　*Mackay.*

A SNAKE IN THE GRASS:

A TALE FOUNDED ON FACTS.

She had a secret of her own,
That little girl of whom we speak,
O'er which she oft would muse alone,
Till the blush came across her cheek ;
A rosy cloud that glowed awhile,
Then melted in a sunny smile.

There was so much to charm the eye,
So much to move delightful thought,
Awake at night she loved to lie,
Darkness to her that image brought ;
She *murmured of it* in her dreams,
Like the low sound of gurgling streams.

What secret thus the soul possessed
Of one so young and innocent?
Oh! nothing but a robin's nest,
O'er which in ecstasy she bent;—
That treasure she herself had found,
With five brown eggs, upon the ground.

When first it flashed upon her sight,
Bolt flew the dam above her head;
She stooped, and almost shrieked with fright;
But spying soon that little bed,
With feathers, moss, and horse-hairs twined,
Rapture and wonder filled her mind.

Breathless and beautiful she stood,
Her ringlets o'er her bosom fell,
With hands uplift, in attitude
As though a pulse might break the spell,
While through the shade, her pale, fine face
Shone like a star amidst the place.

She stood so silent, stayed so long,
The parent birds forgot their fear;
Cock-robin trolled his small sweet song,
In notes like dew-drops, trembling, clear;
From spray to spray the shyer hen
Dropped softly on her nest again.

There Lucy marked her slender bill
On this side, and on that her tail
Peered o'er the edge—while, fixed and still,
Two bright black eyes her own assail,
Which in eye-language seemed to say,
"*Peep, pretty* maiden, then away!"

Away, away, at length she crept,
So pleased, she knew not how she trode,
Yet light on tottering tip-toe stept,
As if birds' eggs strewed all the road :
With folded arms and lips comprest,
To keep her joy within her breast.

Morn, noon, and eve, from day to day,
By stealth she visited that spot :
Alike her lessons and her play,
Were slightly conned, or half forgot;
And when the callow young were hatched,
With infant fondness Lucy watched :—

Watched the kind parents dealing food
To clamorous suppliants all agape;
Watched the small, naked, unformed brood
Improve in size, in plume, and shape,
Till feathers clad the fluttering things,
And the whole group seemed bills and wings.

Inconsciously within her breast,
There many a brooding fancy lay,
She planned to bear the tiny nest
And chirping choristers away,
In stately cage to tune their throats,
And learn untaught their mother-notes.

One morn, when fairly fledged for flight,
The Lucy, on her visit, found
What seemed a necklace, glittering bright,
Twined round the nest, twined round and round,
With emeralds, pearls, and sapphires set,
as my lady's coronet.

She stretched her hand to seize the prize,
When up a serpent popped its head,
But glid like wild-fire from her eyes,
Hissing and rustling as it fled;
She uttered one short, thrilling scream,
Then stood, as startled from a dream.

Her brother Tom, who long had known
That something drew her feet that way,
Curious to catch her there alone,
Had followed her that fine May-day;
Lucy, bewildered by her trance,
Came to herself at his first glance.

Then in her eyes sprang welcome tears,
They fell as showers in April fall;
He kissed her, coaxed her, soothed her fears,
Till she in frankness told him all:
Tom was a bold adventurous boy,
And heard the dreadful tale with joy.

For he had learnt—in some far land,
How children catch the sleeping snake;
Eager himself to try his hand,
He cut a hazel from the brake,
And like a hero set to work,
To make a stout, long-handled fork.

Brother and sister then withdrew,
Leaving the nestlings safely there;
Between their heads the mother flew,
Prompt to resume her nursery care;
But Tom, whose breast for glory burned,
In less than half an hour returned.

With him came Ned, as cool and sly
As Tom was resolute and stout;
So, fair and softly, they drew nigh,
Cowering [1] and keeping sharp look-out
Till they had reached the copse, to see
But not alarm the enemy.

Guess with what transport they descried
How, as before, the serpent lay
Coiled round the nest, in slumbering pride;
The urchins chuckled o'er their prey,
And Tom's right hand was lifted soon,
Like Greenland whaler's with harpoon.[2]

Across its neck the fork he brought,
And pinned it fast upon the ground;
The reptile woke, and quick as thought,
Curled round the stick, curled round and round,
While head and tail Ned's nimble hands
Tied at each end with packthread bands.

'carce was the enemy secured,
Vhen Lucy timidly drew near,
ut, by their shouting well assured,
ved the green reptile without fear;
ie lads, stark wild with victory, flung
eir caps aloft—they danced, they sung.

t Lucy with an anxious look
ned to her own dear nest, when lo!
legs and wings the young ones took,
ping and tumbling to and fro;

Cowering—sinking by bending the knees.
Harpoon—a dart to strike whales with.

The parents chattering from above,
With all the earnestness of love.

Alighting now among their train,
They pecked them on new feats to try,
But many a lesson seemed in vain
Before the giddy things would fly.
Lucy both laughed and cried to see
How ill they played at liberty.

I need not tell the snake's sad doom,
You may be sure he lived not long;
Corked in a bottle, for a tomb,
Preserved in spirits and in song,
His skin in Tom's museum shines,
You read his story in these lines.

Montgomei

THE MOUSE'S PETITION:

FOUND IN THE TRAP, WHERE HE HAD BEEN CONFIN ALL NIGHT.

Oh, hear a pensive prisoner's prayer,
   For liberty that sighs;
And never let thy heart be shut
   Against the wretch's cries!

For here forlorn and sad I sit
   Within this wiry grate;
And tremble at the approaching morn,
   Which brings impending fate.

If e'er thy breast with freedom glowed,
   And spurned a tyrant's chain,
Let not thy strong, oppressive force
   A free-born mouse detain.

Oh ! do not stain with guiltless blood
   Thy hospitable hearth ;
Nor triumph that thy wiles [1] betrayed
   A prize so little worth !

The scattered gleanings of a feast
   My frugal meals supply :
But, if thine unrelenting heart
   That slender boon deny,—

The cheerful light, the vital air,
   Are blessings widely given ;
Let nature's commoners [2] enjoy
   The common gifts of heaven.

Barbauld.

LOVING AND LIKING.

ADDRESSED TO A CHILD.

Say not you *love* a roasted fowl,
But you may love a screaming owl,
And, if you can, the unwieldy toad
That crawls from his secure abode,
Within the grassy garden wall,
When evening dews begin to fall.
Oh! mark the beauty of his eye,
What wonders in that circle lie !
So clear, so bright, our fathers said
He wears a jewel in his head !
And when, upon some showery day,
Into a path or public way,

[1] *Wiles—snares.*   [2] *Nature's commoners—those who have a common right to nature's gifts.*

A frog leaps out from bordering grass
Startling the timid as they pass,
Do you observe him, and endeavour
To take the intruder into favour;
Learning from him to find a reason
For a light heart in a dull season.
And you may love the strawberry flower,
And love the strawberry in its bower:
But when the fruit, so often praised
For beauty, to your lip is raised,
Say not you *love* the delicate treat,
But *like* it, enjoy it, and thankfully eat.

Miss Wordsworth.

THE SWALLOW.

Swallow! that on rapid wing
Sweep'st along in sportive ring,
Now here, now there, now low, now high,
Chasing keen the painted fly;—
Could I skim away with thee
Over land and over sea,
What streams would flow, what cities rise,
What landscapes dance before mine eyes!
First from England's southern shore
'Cross the Channel we would soar,
And our venturous course advance
To the plains of sprightly France;
Sport among the feathered choir
On the verdant banks of Loire;
Skim Garonne's majestic tide,
Where Bordeaux adorns his side;

Cross the towering Pyrenees,
'Mid myrtle groves and orange trees ;
Enter then the wild domain
Where wolves prowl round the flocks of Spain,
Where silkworms spin, and olives grow,
And mules plod surely on and slow.
Steering thus for many a day
Far to south our course away,
From Gibraltar's rocky steep,
Dashing o'er the foaming deep,
On sultry Afric's fruitful shore
We'd rest at length, our journey o'er,
Till vernal gales should gently play,
To waft us on our homeward way.

Miss Aikin.

HOME THOUGHTS FROM ABROAD.

OH, to be in England
Now that April's there,
And whoever wakes in England
Sees, some morning, unaware,
That the lowest boughs and the brushwood sheaf
Round the elm-tree bole are in tiny leaf,
While the chaffinch sings on the orchard bough
In England—now !

And after April, when May follows,
And the white-throat builds, and all the swallows—
Hark ! where my blossomed pear-tree in the hedge
Leans to the field, and scatters on the clover
Blossoms and dew-drops—at the bent spray's edge—
That's the *wise thrush ;* he sings each song twice over,

Lest you should think he never could re-capture
The first fine careless rapture !
And though the fields look rough with hoary dew,
All will be gay when noontide wakes anew
The buttercups, the little children's dower,
—Far brighter than this gaudy melon-flower !

R. Browning.

OLD CHRISTMAS.

Now he who knows old Christmas,
  He knows a carle[1] of worth;
For he is as good a fellow,
  As any upon the earth !

He comes warm cloaked and coated,
  And buttoned up to the chin;
And soon as he comes a-nigh the door
  'Twill open and let him in.

We know that he will not fail us,
  So we sweep the hearth up clean;
We set him the old arm-chair,
  And a cushion whereon to lean.

And with sprigs of holly and ivy
  We make the house look gay;
Just out of an old regard to him,—
  For it was his ancient way.

He comes with a cordial voice,
  That does one good to hear;
He shakes one heartily by the hand,
  As he hath done many a year.

---

[1] *Carle*—a robust, strong, hearty fellow.

And after the little children
　He asks in a cheerful tone,
Jack, Kate, and little Annie,—
　He remembers them every one !

What a fine old fellow he is !
　With his faculties all as clear,
And his heart as warm and light,
　As a man in his fortieth year !

What a fine old fellow, in troth,[1]
　Not one of your griping elves,[2]
Who, with plenty of money to spare,
　Think only about themselves.

Not he ! for he loveth the children,
　And holiday begs for all ;
And comes with his pockets full of gifts,
　For the great ones and the small !

And he tells us witty old stories ;
　And singeth with might and main ;
And we talk of the old man's visit
　Till the day that he comes again !
                              Mary Howitt.

———◦◦◦———

TO A HEDGE SPARROW.

LITTLE flutterer ! swiftly flying,
　Here is none to harm thee near ;
Kite, nor hawk, nor schoolboy prying ;—
　Little flutterer ! cease to fear.

---

[1] *Troth*—truth.
[2] *Elves*—plural of *elf*, which properly means a fairy or
spirit ; sometimes, as *here,* an unnatural kind of being, one
different *from men in general.*

H

One who would protect thee ever
　From the schoolboy, kite, and hawk,
Musing, now obtrudes, but never
　Dreamt of plunder in his walk.

He no weasel, stealing slily,
　Would permit thy eggs to take ;
Nor the polecat, nor the wily
　Adder, nor the speckled snake.

May no cuckoo, wandering near thee,
　Lay her egg within thy nest;
Nor thy young ones, born to cheer thee,
　Be destroyed by such a guest ! [1]

Little flutterer ! swiftly flying,
　Here is none to harm thee near;
Kite, nor hawk, nor schoolboy prying ;—
　Little flutterer ! cease to fear.

———◆———

THE MOSS-ROSE.

FROM THE GERMAN OF KRUMMACHER.

THE Angel of the flowers, one day,
Beneath a rose-tree sleeping lay ;
That spirit to whose charge 'tis given
To bathe young buds in dews of heaven ;—
Awaking from his light repose,
The Angel whispered to the rose :

---

[1] The cuckoo usually deposits her egg in the nest of the hedge-sparrow, who hatches it, and tends the young one as *her own*—a *service* which the little cuckoo repays by speedily *turning* out all the other nestlings.

" O fondest object of my care,
  Still fairest found, where all are fair;
  For the sweet shade thou givest to me,
  Ask what thou wilt, 'tis granted thee!"
" Then," said the rose, with deepened glow,
" On me another grace bestow:"
  The spirit paused in silent thought,—
  What grace was there that flower had not?
  'Twas but a moment—o'er the rose
  A veil of moss the Angel throws,
  And, robed in nature's simplest weed,
  Could there a flower that rose exceed?

ANSWER TO A CHILD'S QUESTION.

Do you ask what the birds say? The sparrow, the
    dove,
The linnet, and thrush say, " I love and I love!"
In the winter they're silent—the wind is so strong;
What it says I don't know, but it sings a loud song.
But green leaves, and blossoms, and sunny warm
    weather,
And singing, and loving—all come back together.
But the lark is so brimful of gladness and love,
The green fields below him, the blue sky above,
That he sings, and he sings; and for ever sings he—
" I love my Love, and my Love loves me."

Coleridge.

SUMMER EVENING AT THE FARM.

Down *the deep* and miry lane,
Creaking comes the empty wain;

And driver on the shaft-horse sits,
Whistling now and then by fits;
And oft, with his accustomed call,
Urging on the sluggish Ball.
The barn is still, the master's gone,
The thresher puts his jacket on,
While Dick upon the ladder tall,
Nails the dead kite to the wall.

Here comes shepherd Jack at last,—
He has penned the sheep-cote fast;
For 'twas but two nights before,
A lamb was eaten on the moor;
His empty wallet *Rover* carries,
Nor for Jack, when near home, tarries;
With lolling tongue he runs to try
If the horse-trough be not dry.

The milk is settled in the pans,
And supper messes in the cans;
In the hovel carts are wheeled,
And both the colts are driven a-field;
The snare for Mister Fox is set,
The leaven laid, the thatching wet,
And Bess has slunk away to talk
With Roger, in the holly-walk.

Kirke White

MORNING OR EVENING HYMN.

GREAT God! how endless is Thy love!
   Thy gifts are every morning new,
And morning mercies from above
   Gently distil, like early dew.

Thou spread'st the curtains of the night,
  Great guardian of my sleeping hours!
Thy sovereign word restores the light,
  And quickens all my drowsy powers.

I yield my powers to Thy command,
  To thee I consecrate my days;
Perpetual blessings from Thy hand
  Demand perpetual songs of praise.
                              Watts.

THE NIGHTINGALE AND GLOW-WORM.

A NIGHTINGALE, that all day long
Had cheered the village with his song,
Nor yet at eve his note suspended,
Nor yet when eventide was ended,
Began to feel,—as well he might,—
The keen demands of appetite;
When, looking eagerly around,
He spied, far off, upon the ground,
A something shining in the dark,
And knew the glow-worm by his spark;
So, stooping down from hawthorn top,
He thought to put him in his crop.
The worm, aware of his intent,
Harangued him thus, quite eloquent—
" Did you admire my lamp," quoth he,
" As much as I your minstrelsy,
  You would abhor to do me wrong,
  As much as I to spoil your song;
  For 'twas the *self*-same power divine
  Taught you to sing, and me to shine;
             H 2

That you with music, I with light,
Might beautify and cheer the night."
The songster heard his short oration,
And, warbling out his approbation,
Released him as my story tells,
And found a supper somewhere else.

Cowper.

MORAL.[1]

From this short fable, youth may learn
Their real interest to discern ;
That brother should not strive with brother,
And worry and oppress each other ;
But, joined in unity and peace,
Their mutual happiness increase :
Well pleased another's faults to hide,
And in his virtues feel a pride.

WE ARE SEVEN;

OR, A CHILD'S NOTION OF DEATH.

A SIMPLE child, dear brother Jim,
  That lightly draws its breath,
And feels its life in every limb,
  What should it know of death ?

I met a little cottage girl,
  She was eight years old, she said;
Her hair was thick with many a curl
  That clustered round her head.

[1] The moral here given is by an unknown hand.

She had a rustic, woodland air,
　　And she was wildly clad :
Her eyes were fair, and very fair,
　　—Her beauty made me glad.

" Sisters and brothers, little maid,
　　How many may you be ? "
" How many ?　Seven in all," she said,
　　And, wondering, looked at me.

" And where are they ?　I pray you tell."
　　She answered, " Seven are we ;
And two of us at Conway[1] dwell,
　　And two are gone to sea.

" Two of us in the church-yard lie,
　　My sister and my brother ;
And in the church-yard cottage, I
　　Dwell near them with my mother."

" You say that two at Conway dwell,
　　And two are gone to sea ;
Yet you are seven !—I pray you tell,
　　Sweet maid, how this may be."

Then did the little maid reply,
　　" Seven boys and girls are we ;
Two of us in the church-yard lie,
　　Beneath the church-yard tree."

" You run about, my little maid,
　　Your limbs they are alive ;
If two are in the church-yard laid,
　　Then you are only five."

[1] *Conway—or more properly* Conwy, *a town in North Wales, situated near the* mouth of the *river* Conwy.

" Their graves are green, they may be seen,"
   The little maid replied,
" Twelve steps or more from mother's door,
   And they are side by side.

" My stockings there I often knit,
   My kerchief there I hem;
And there upon the ground I sit—
   I sit and sing to them.

" And, often after sunset, Sir,
   When it is light and fair,
I take my little porringer,
   And eat my supper there.

" The first that died was little Jane;
   In bed she moaning lay,
Till God released her from her pain,
   And then she went away.

" So in the church-yard she was laid;
   And all the summer dry,
Together round her grave we played,
   My brother John and I.

" And when the ground was white with snow,
   And I could run and slide,
My brother John was forced to go,
   And he lies by her side."

" How many are you then," said I,
   " If they two are in heaven ? "
The little maiden did reply,
   " O master! we are seven."

" But they are dead; those two are dead;
   Their spirits are in heaven ! "
'Twas throwing words away; for still
The little maid would have her will,
   And said, " Nay, we are seven."
              Wordsworth.

THE MILKMAID.

A MILKMAID, who poised a full pail on her head,
Thus mused on her prospects in life, it is said:
" Let me see—I should think that this milk will
     procure
One hundred good eggs, or fourscore, to be sure.

" Well then—stop a bit—it must not be forgotten,
Some of these may be broken, and some may be
     rotten ;
But if twenty for accident should be detached,
't will leave me just sixty sound eggs to be hatched.

Well, sixty sound eggs—no, sound chickens, I
     mean :
'these some may die—we'll suppose seventeen,
venteen ! not so many—say ten at the most,
nich will leave fifty chickens to boil or to roast.

ut then, there's their barley, how much will they
     need ?
y they take but one grain at a time when they
     feed—
iat's a mere trifle; now then, let us see,
     fair market price how much money there'll be.

" Six shillings a pair—five—four—three-and-six.
To prevent all mistakes, that low price I will fix :
Now what will that make ? fifty chickens, I said—
Fifty times three-and-sixpence — *I'll ask brother
    Ned.*

"O ! but stop—three-and-sixpence a *pair* I must
    sell 'em ;
Well, a pair is a couple—now then let us tell 'em ;
A couple in fifty will go—(my poor brain !)
Why just a score times, and five pair will remain.

" Twenty-five pair of fowls—now how tiresome it is
That I can't reckon up such money as this !
Well there's no use in trying, so let's give a guess—
I'll say twenty pounds, *and it can't be no less.*

" Twenty pounds, I am certain, will buy me a cow,
Thirty geese and two turkeys—eight pigs and a
    sow ;
Now if these turn out well, at the end of the year,
I shall fill both my pockets with guineas, 'tis clear."

Forgetting her burden, when this she had said,
The maid superciliously [1] tossed up her head ;
When, alas ! for her prospects—her milk-pail de-
    scended,
And so all her schemes for the future were ended.

This moral, I think, may be safely attached,—
" Reckon not on your chickens before they are
    hatched."

Jeffreys Taylor.

---

[1] *Superciliously*—consequentially, contemptuously.

THE GOLDFINCH STARVED IN HIS CAGE.

TIME was when I was free as air,
The thistle's downy seed my fare,
 My drink the morning dew ;
I perched at will on every spray,
My form genteel, my plumage gay,
 My strains for ever new.

But gaudy plumage, sprightly strain,
And form genteel, were all in vain,
 And of a transient date ;[1]
For, caught, and caged, and starved to death,
In dying sighs my little breath
 Soon passed the wiry grate.

Thanks, gentle swain, for all my woes,
And thanks for this effectual close
 And cure of every ill !
More cruelty could none express ;
And I, if you had shown me less,
 Had been your prisoner still.

Cowper.

THE WIND IN A FROLIC.

THE wind one morning sprang up from sleep,
Saying, "Now for a frolic ! now for a leap !
Now for a mad-cap galloping chace !
I'll make a commotion in every place ! "

---

 [1] *Of a transient date*—of short duration.

So it swept with a bustle right through a great town,
Cracking the signs and scattering down
Shutters; and whisking, with merciless squalls,
Old women's bonnets and gingerbread stalls.
There never was heard a much lustier shout,
As the apples and oranges trundled about;
And the urchins that stand with their thievish eyes
For ever on watch, ran off each with a prize.

Then away to the field it went, blustering and
    humming,
And the cattle all wondered whatever was coming;
It plucked by the tails the grave matronly cows,
And tossed the colts' manes all about their brows;
Till, offended at such an unusual salute,
They all turned their backs, and stood sulky and
    mute.

So on it went capering and playing its pranks.
Whistling with reeds on the broad river's banks,
Puffing the birds as they sat on the spray,
Or the traveller grave on the king's highway.
It was not too nice to hustle the bags
Of the beggar, and flutter his dirty rags;
'Twas so bold, that it feared not to play its joke
With the doctor's wig or the gentleman's cloak.
Through the forest it roared, and cried, gaily, " Now,
You sturdy old oaks, I'll make you bow ! "
And it made them bow without more ado,
Or it cracked their great branches through and
    through.

Then it rushed like a monster on cottage and farm,
Striking their dwellers with sudden alarm;

And they ran out like bees in a midsummer swarm;
There were dames with their kerchiefs tied over
    their caps,
To see if their poultry were free from mishaps;
The turkeys they gobbled, the geese screamed aloud,
And the hens crept to roost in a terrified crowd;
There was rearing of ladders, and logs laying on,
Where the thatch from the roof threatened soon to
    be gone.

But the wind had swept on, and had met in a lane
With a schoolboy, who panted and struggled in vain;
For it tossed him and twirled him, then passed, and
    he stood
With his hat in a pool and his shoes in the mud.

Then away went the wind in its holiday glee,
And now it was far on the billowy sea,
And the lordly ships felt its staggering blow,
And the little boats darted to and fro.
But lo! it was night, and it sank to rest
On the sea-bird's rock in the gleaming west,
Laughing to think, in its fearful fun,
How little of mischief it had done.

William Howitt.

THE COMPLAINTS OF THE POOR.

" AND wherefore do the poor complain ? "
    The rich man asked of me ;—
" Come walk *abroad* with me," I said,
    "And I will answer thee."

'Twas evening, and the frozen streets
   Were cheerless to behold;
And we were wrapped and coated well,
   And yet we were a-cold.

We met an old, bare-headed man;
   His locks were few and white;
I asked him what he did abroad
   In that cold winter's night.

'Twas bitter keen, indeed, he said,
   But at home no fire had he,
And therefore he had come abroad
   To ask for charity.

We met a young bare-footed child,
   And she begged loud and bold;
I asked her what she did abroad
   When the wind it blew so cold.

She said her father was at home,
   And he lay sick in bed;
And therefore was it she was sent
   Abroad to beg for bread.

We saw a woman sitting down
   Upon a stone to rest;
She had a baby at her back
   And another at her breast.

I asked her why she loitered there,
   When the night-wind was so chill;
She turned her head, and bade the child,
   That screamed behind, be still.

She told us that her husband served,
  A soldier, far away ;
And therefore to her parish she
  Was begging back her way.

I turned me to the rich man then,
  For silently stood he ;—
" You asked me why the poor complain,
  And these have answered thee !"
Southey

CHILDHOOD'S SPORTS.

'NEATH yonder elm, that stands upon the moor,
When the clock spoke the hour of labour o'er,
What clamorous throngs, what happy groups were
    seen,
In various postures scattering o'er the green !
Some shoot the marble, others join the chace
Of self-made stag, or run the emulous race ;
While others, seated on the dappled [1] grass,
With doleful tales the light-winged minutes pass.
Well I remember how, with gesture starched,
A band of soldiers, oft with pride we marched ;
For banners, to a tall ash we did bind
Our kerchiefs, flapping to the whistling wind ;
And for our warlike arms we sought the mead,
And guns and spears we made of brittle reed :
Then, in uncouth array, our feats to crown,
We stormed some ruined pig-stye for a town.
Kirke White.

[1] *Dappled—of different colours, streaked.*

THE HARE AND THE TORTOISE.

A FORWARD hare, of swiftness vain,
The genius of the neighbouring plain,
Would oft deride the drudging crowd ;—
For geniuses are ever proud.
He'd boast his flight 'twere vain to follow,
For dog and horse he'd beat them hollow ;—
Nay, if he put forth all his strength,
Outstrip his brethren *half a length.*
A tortoise heard his vain oration,
And vented thus his indignation :
" O puss ! it bodes thee dire disgrace
When I defy thee to the race.
Come, 'tis a match ; nay, no denial,
I lay my shell upon the trial."
'Twas ' done ' and ' done,' ' all fair,' ' a bet,' [1]
Judges prepared, and distance set.
The scampering hare outstripped the wind ;
The creeping tortoise lagged behind,
And scarce had passed a single pole
When puss had almost reached the goal. [2]
" Friend tortoise," quoth the jeering hare,
" Your burden's more than you can bear ;
To help your speed it were as well
That I should ease you of your shell ;
Jog on a little faster, prithee : [3]
I'll take a nap and then be with thee."
The tortoise heard his taunting jeer,
But still resolved to persevere ;

---

[1] *Done, &c.*—terms used on the race-course.
[2] *Goal*—the point to which racers run.
[3] *Prithee*—I pray thee.

On to the goal securely crept,
While puss, unknowing, soundly slept.
The bets were won, the hare awoke,
When thus the victor tortoise spoke:
" Puss, though I own thy quicker parts,
Things are not always done by starts:
You may deride my awkward pace;
But *slow* and *steady* wins the race ! "

Lloyd.

A CHARADE.

ʀOUNCED as one letter, and written with three,
  letters there are and two only in me;
double, I'm single, I'm black, blue, and grey,
  read from both ends, and the same either way.
  restless and wandering, steady and fixed,
  you know not one hour what I may be the
  next;
It and I kindle, beseech and defy,
  watery and moist, I am fiery and dry.
  scornful and scowling, compassionate, meek,
  light, I am dark, I am strong, I am weak.
piercing and clear, I am heavy and dull,
ressive and languid, contracted and full.
a globe and a mirror, a window, a door,
index, an organ, and fifty things more.
long to all animals under the sun,
  to those which were long understood to have
  none.
some I am said to exist in the mind,
I am found *in potatoes*, and needles, and wind.
e jackets I own, of glass, water, and horn,

And I wore them all three on the day I was born.
I am covered quite snug, have a lid and a fringe,
Yet I move every way on invisible hinge.
A pupil I have, a most whimsical wight,
Who is little by day, and grows big in the night,
Whom I cherish with care as a part of myself;
For in truth I depend on this delicate elf,
Who collects all my food, and with wonderful knack
Throws it into a net, which I keep at my back;
And though heels over head it arrives, in a trice
It is sent up to table all proper and nice.
I am spoken of sometimes as if I were glass,
But then it is false, and the trick will not pass.
A blow makes me run, though I have not a limb;
Though I neither have fins, nor a bladder, I swim.
Like many more couples, my partner and I
At times will look cross at each other, and shy;
Yet still though we differ in what we're about,
One will do all the work when the other is out.
I am least apt to cry, as they always remark,
When trimmed with good lashes, or kept in the dark;
Should I fret and be heated, they put me to bed,
And leave me to cool upon water and bread.
But if hardened I grow they make use of the knife,
Lest an obstinate humour endanger my life;
Or you may, though the treatment appears to be rough,
Run a spit through my side, and with safety enough.
Like boys who are fond of their fruit and their play,
I am seen with my ball and my apple all day.
My belt is a rainbow, I reel and I dance;
I am said to retire, though I never advance.
I am read by physicians, as one of their books,
And am used by the ladies to fasten their hooks.

My language is plain, though it cannot be heard,
And I speak without ever pronouncing a word.
Some call me a diamond, some say I am jet ;
Others talk of my water, or how I am set.
I'm a borough in England, in Scotland a stream,
And an isle of the sea in the Irishman's dream.
The earth without me would no loveliness wear,
And sun, moon, and stars at my wish disappear ;
Yet so frail is my tenure, so brittle my joy,
That a speck gives me pain, and a drop can destroy.

MARION LEE.

NOT a care hath Marion Lee,
Dwelling by the sounding sea !
Her young life's a flowery way :—
Without toil from day to day.
Without bodings for the morrow—
Marion was not made for sorrow !
Like the summer-billows wild,
Leaps the happy-hearted child ;
Sees her father's fishing-boat
O'er the waters gaily float ;
Hears her brother's fishing-song
On the light gale borne along ;
Half a league she hears the lay,
Ere they turn into the bay,
And with *glee*, o'er cliff and main,
Sings an answer back again,

Which by man and boy is heard,
Like the carol of a bird.
Look, she sitteth laughing there,
Wreathing sea-weed in her hair;
Saw ye e'er a thing so fair?

Mary E

HARVEST HOME.

HARK! from woodlands far away,
Sounds the merry roundelay;[1]
Now, across the russet plain,
Slowly moves the loaded wain;
Greet the reapers as they come—
Happy, happy harvest home!

Never fear the wintry blast,
Summer suns will shine at last;
See the golden grain appear,
See the produce of the year.
Greet the reapers as they come—
Happy, happy harvest home!

Children join the jocund ring,
Young and old come forth and sing
Stripling blithe, and maiden gay,
Hail the rural holiday.
Greet the reapers as they come—
Happy, happy harvest home!

[1] *Roundelay*—a song in which the passages or
repeated.

Peace and plenty be our lot,
All the pangs of war forgot;
Strength to toil, and ample store,
Bless Old England evermore.
Greet the reapers as they come—
Happy, happy harvest home !

THE ORPHANS.

My chaise the village inn did gain,
  Just as the setting sun's last ray
Tipped with refulgent gold the vane
  Of the old church across the way.

Across the way I silent sped,
  The time till supper to beguile
In moralizing o'er the dead
  That mouldered round the ancient pile.

There many an humble green grave showed
  Where want, and pain, and toil did rest;
And many a flattering stone I viewed
  O'er those who once had wealth possest.

A shaded beech its shadow brown
  Threw o'er a grave where sorrow slept,
On which, though scarce with grass o'ergrown,
  Two ragged children sat and wept.

A piece of bread between them lay,
  Which neither seemed inclined to take,
And yet they *looked* so much a prey
  To want, it made my heart to ache.

"Then since no parent we have here,
　　We'll go and search for God around,
Lady, pray, can you tell us where
　　That God, our Father, may be found?

"He lives in Heaven, mother said,
　　And Goody says that mother's there!
So, if she knows we want his aid,
　　I think perhaps she'll send him here."

I clasped the prattlers to my breast,
　　And cried, "Come both and live with m
I'll clothe you, feed you, give you rest,
　　And will a second mother be.

"And God shall be your Father still;
　　'Twas He in mercy sent me here,
To teach you to obey His will,
　　Your steps to guide, your hearts to cheer

———◦◦◦———

THE WINTER'S DAY.

WHEN raging storms deform the air
　　And clouds of snow descend,
And o'er the landscape, once so fair,
　　Stern winter's shadows blend;

When biting frost rides on the wind
　　Bleak from the north and east,
And wealth is at his ease reclined,
　　Prepared to laugh and feast;

When the poor traveller treads the plain,
　All dubious of his way,
And crawls with still increasing pain,
　And dreads the parting day;

When poverty, in scant attire,
　Shrinks from the biting blast,
Or hovers o'er the pigmy fire,
　And fears it will not last;

When the fond mother clasps her child
　Still closer to her breast,
And the poor infant, frost-beguiled,[1]
　Scarce feels that it is pressed;—

Then let your bounteous hand extend
　Its blessings to the poor,
Nor spurn the wretched, as they bend
　All suppliant at your door.

———◦◇◦———

THE TRAVELLER'S RETURN.

Sweet to the morning traveller
　The song amid the sky,
Where, twinkling in the dewy light,
　The skylark soars on high.

And cheering to the traveller
　The gales that round him play,
When faint and heavily he drags
　Along his noontide way.

[1] *Frost-beguiled*—benumbed, and rendered insensible by the frost.

K

And when beneath the unclouded sun
  Full wearily toils he,
The flowing water makes to him
  A soothing melody.

And when the evening light decays,
  And all is calm around,
There is sweet music to his ear
  In the distant sheep-bell's sound.

But oh! of all delightful sounds
  Of evening or of morn,
The sweetest is the voice of love
  That welcomes his return.

Southe

THE MISER AND THE MOUSE.

FROM THE GREEK ANTHOLOGY.

A MISER, traversing his house,
Espied, unusual there, a mouse,
And thus his uninvited guest,
Briskly inquisitive, addressed:
" Tell me, my dear, to what cause is it
I owe this unexpected visit ? "
The mouse her host obliquely [1] eyed,
And, smiling, pleasantly replied :
" Fear not, good fellow, for your hoard !
I come to *lodge*, and not to *board !* "

Cowp

---

[1] *Obliquely*—with a sort of arch, sidelong glance

EPITAPH ON A HERO.

HERE lies one who never drew
Blood himself, yet many slew;
Gave the gun its aim, and figure
Made in field, yet ne'er pulled trigger.
Armed men have gladly made
Him their guide, and him obeyed;
At his signified desire,
Would advance, present, and fire.
Stout he was, and large of limb,
Scores have fled at sight of him;
And to all this fame he rose
By only following his nose.
Neptune was he called, not he
Who controls the boisterous sea,
But of happier command,
Neptune of the furrowed land;
And your wonder vain to shorten,
Pointer [1] to *Sir John Throckmorton.* [2]

Cowper.

——◆◆——

THE PET PLANT.

̷ORIST a sweet little blossom espied,
̷ch bloomed, like its ancestors, by the road-side;
̷olours were simple, its charms they were few,
̷ the flower looked fair on the spot where it
grew;—

̷ointer—a dog that by its peculiar gestures points out
̷ame to the sportsman.
̷ friend of *Cowper,* who lived at Weston, near Olney,
̷inghamshire.

The florist beheld it, and cried, " I'll enchant
The botanical world with this sweet little plant—
Its leaves shall be sheltered and carefully nursed,
It shall charm all the world, though I met with it first
        Under a hedge."

He carried it home to his hot-house with care,
And he said, " Though the rarest exotics [1] are there,
My little pet plant, when I've nourished its stem,
In tint and in fragrance shall emulate them,
Though none shall suspect from the road-side it came;
Rhodum Sidum I'll call it—a beautiful name—
When botanists look through their glasses and view
Its beauties, they'll never suspect that it grew
        Under a hedge."

The little pet plant, when it shook off the dirt
Of its own native ditch, began to grow pert,
And tossed its small head; for perceiving that none
But exotics were round it, it thought itself one :
As a field-flower, all would have said it was fair,
And praised it, though gaudier blossoms were there;
But when it assumes hot-house airs we see through
The forced tint of its leaves, and suspect that it grew
        Under a hedge.

In the bye-ways of life, oh ! how many there are,
Who being born under some fortunate star,
Assisted by talent or beauty, grow rich,
And bloom in a hot-house instead of a ditch !
And while they disdain not their own simple stem,
The honours they grasp may gain honour for them;
But when, like the pet plant, such people grow pert,
We soon trace them to their original dirt
        Under a hedge.

[1] *Exotics*—foreign plants.

THE BABE IN HEAVEN TO ITS MOTHER.

O WEEP not, mother dear,
  Since I can weep no more,
For God has wiped away the tear
  That dimmed my eyes before.

In yonder house of clay
  I could not speak to thee;
I could not that sweet voice obey
  Which breathed such love to me.

But now on angel's wing,
  I trace my heavenly flight,
And now an angel's song I sing,
  And soar in fields of light.

I learn His name to bless,
  Who came an infant here;
Who sojourned in this wilderness,
  Because our souls were dear.

Weep not that I am blest,
  That, through redeeming grace,
Mine is a better rest
  Than even thy kind embrace.

Thou couldst not save from woe,
  Or quell my foes within;
Too soon I might have strayed below,
  And sought the path of sin.

But safe for ever here,
  I tread on holy ground;
And still I *watch thee,* mother dear,
  And, viewless, hover round.

x 2

And when thy spirit flies
To this bright world of love,
Then will I gladly close thine eyes,
And welcome thee above.

———◦◦◦———

EPITAPH ON AN INFANT.

ERE sin could blight or sorrow fade,
Death came, with friendly care,
The opening bud to heaven conveyed,
And bade it blossom there.

Coler

———◦◦◦———

THE THREE SONS.

I HAVE a son, a little son, a boy just five years o
With eyes of thoughtful earnestness, and min
gentle mould ;
They tell me that unusual grace in all his ⟩
appears,
That my child is grave and wise of head, beyon(
childish years.
I cannot say how this may be; I know his fa(
fair,
And yet his chiefest comeliness is his sweet
serious air ;
I know his heart is kind and fond, I know he lo
me,
And loveth too his mother dear, with gra
fervency.

But that which others most admire is the thought
    that fills his mind,
The food for grave inquiring speech he everywhere
    doth find.
Strange questions doth he ask of me, when we
    together walk,
He scarcely thinks as children think, or talks as
    children talk ;
Nor cares he much for childish play, doats not on
    bat or ball,
But looks on manhood's ways and works, and aptly
    mimics all.
His little head is busy still, and oftentimes per-
    plexed
With thoughts about this world of care, and thoughts
    about the next.
He kneels at his dear mother's knee; she teacheth
    him to pray,
And strange, and sweet, and solemn are the words
    which he will say.
Oh ! should my gentle child be spared to manhood's
    years like me,
A holier and a wiser man I trust that he will be ;
And when I look into his eyes, and stroke his
    thoughtful brow,
I dare not think what I should feel, were I to lose
    him now.

I have a son, a second son, a simple child of three ;
I'll not declare how bright and fair his little features
    be ;
How silver sweet those tones of his when he prattles
    on *my knee.*

I do not think his light blue eyes are, like his
    brother's, keen,
Nor his brow so full of childish thought as his hath
    ever been;
But his little heart's a fountain pure of mind and
    tender feeling,
And his very look's a gleam of light, rich depths of
    love revealing.
When he walks with me, the country folks, who pass
    him in the street,
Will shout for joy, and bless my boy; he looks so
    mild and sweet.
A playfellow he is to all, and yet, with cheerful
    tone,
Will sing his song of love, when left to play alone.
His presence is like sunshine, sent to gladden
    home and hearth,
To comfort us in all our griefs, and sweeten all our
    mirth.
Should he grow up to riper years, God grant his
    heart may prove
As meet a home for heavenly grace, as now for
    earthly love;
And if beside his grave the tears our aching eyes
    may dim,
God comfort us for all the love that we shall lose in
    him.

I have a son, a third sweet son; his age I cannot
    tell,
For they reckon not by months and years, where he
    is gone to dwell;

To us for fourteen anxious months his infant smiles
　　were given,
And then he bade farewell to earth, and went to live
　　in heaven.
I cannot tell what form is his, what looks he weareth
　　now,
Nor guess how bright a glory crowns his shining
　　seraph brow :
The thoughts that fill his sinless soul, the bliss which
　　he doth feel,
Are numbered with the secret things, which God
　　will not reveal.
But I know, for God doth tell me this, that now he
　　is at rest,
Where other blessed infants be, on their Saviour's
　　loving breast ;
I know his spirit feels no more the weary load of
　　flesh,
But his sleep is blest with endless dreams of joy for
　　ever fresh.
I know that we shall meet our babe, his mother dear
　　and I,
When God himself shall wipe away all tears from
　　every eye.
Whate'er befalls his brethren twain, his bliss can
　　never cease ;
Their lot may here be grief and care, but his is
　　certain peace.
It may be that the tempter's wiles their souls from
　　bliss may sever,
But if our own poor faith fail not, *he* must be ours
　　for ever.

When we think of what our darling is, and what we
    still may be,
When we muse on that world's perfect bliss, and this
    world's misery,
When we groan beneath this load of sin, and feel
    this grief and pain,
Oh ! we'd rather lose our other two, than have him
    here again.

Moultrie.

A SUMMER EVENING.

How fine has the day been, how bright was the sun,
How lovely and joyful the course that he run,
Though he rose in a mist when his race he begun,
    And there followed some droppings of rain !
But now the fair traveller's come to the west,
His rays are all gold, and his beauties are best ;
He paints the sky gay as he sinks to his rest,
    And foretells a bright rising again.

Just such is the Christian : his course he begins
Like the sun in a mist, while he mourns for his sins,
And melts into tears; then he breaks out and shines,
    And travels his heavenly way :
But when he comes nearer to finish his race,
Like a fine setting sun he looks richer in grace,
And gives a sure hope, at the end of his days,
    Of rising in brighter array.

Watts.

THE HUMMING-BIRD.

THE humming-bird ! the humming-bird !
  So fairy-like and bright ;
It lives among the sunny flowers,
  A creature of delight !

In the radiant islands of the East,
  Where fragrant spices grow,
A thousand, thousand humming-birds
  Go glancing to and fro.

Like living fires they flit about,
  Scarce larger than a bee,
Among the broad palmetto leaves,
  And through the fan-palm tree.

And in those wild and verdant woods,
  · Where stately moras tower,
Where hangs from branching tree to tree
  The scarlet passion-flower ;

Where on the mighty river banks,
  La Plate and Amazon,
The cayman,[1] like an old tree trunk,
  Lies basking in the sun ;

There builds her nest the humming-bird,
  Within the ancient wood—
Her nest of silky cotton down,
  And rears her tiny brood.

---

[1] *Cayman*—the American alligator.

She hangs it to a slender twig,
　　Where waves it light and free,
　As the campanero [1] tolls his song,
　　And rocks the mighty tree.

All crimson is her shining breast,
　　Like to the red, red rose;
Her wing is the changeful green and blue
　　That the neck of the peacock shows.

Thou, happy, happy humming-bird,
　　No winter round thee lours;
Thou never saw'st a leafless tree,
　　Nor land without sweet flowers.

A reign of summer joyfulness
　　To thee for life is given;
Thy food, the honey from the flower,
　　Thy drink, the dew from heaven!

　　　　　　　　　　　　Mary Howitt.

———◆◇◆———

LINES FROM THE PERSIAN OF HAFIZ.

On parent's knees, a naked new-born babe,
Weeping, thou sat'st, while all around thee smiled;
So live, that sinking in thy last sad sleep,
Calm, *thou* mayst smile, while all around thee weep.

　　　　　　　　　　　　Sir W. Jones.

---

[1] *Campanero*—a West Indian bird whose note may be heard nearly three miles off like the toll of a distant convent

LUCY GRAY.

No mate, no comrade, Lucy knew;
  She dwelt on a wide moor;
The sweetest thing that ever grew
  Beside a cottage door!

You yet may spy the fawn at play,
  The hare upon the green;
But the sweet face of Lucy Gray
  Will never more be seen.

" To-night will be a stormy night;
  You to the town must go;
And take a lantern, child, to light
  Your mother through the snow."

" That, father, I will gladly do;
  'Tis scarcely afternoon—
The minster [1] clock has just struck two,
  And yonder is the moon."

At this the father raised his hook,
  And snapped a faggot band;
He plied his work, and Lucy took
  The lantern in her hand.

Not blither is the mountain roe;
  With many a wanton stroke
Her feet disperse the powdery snow,
  That rises up like smoke.

[1] *Minster*—cathedral church.

L

The storm came on before its time ;
   She wandered up and down,
And many a hill did Lucy climb,
   But never reached the town.

The wretched parents all that night
   Went shouting far and wide;
But there was neither sound nor sight
   To serve them for a guide.

At day-break on a hill they stood
   That overlooked the moor ;
And thence they saw the bridge of wood,
   A furlong from the door.

They wept, and turning homeward, cried,
   " In heaven we all shall meet,"—
When in the snow the mother spied
   The print of Lucy's feet !

Half breathless, from the steep hill's edge
   They tracked the footmarks small;
And through the broken hawthorn hedge,
   And by the long stone wall ;

And then an open field they crossed—
   The marks were still the same ;
They tracked them on, nor ever lost,
   And to the bridge they came.

They followed from the snowy bank
   Those footmarks, one by one,
Into the middle of the plank—
   And further there were none !

You yet may spy the fawn at play,
  The hare upon the green ;
But the sweet face of Lucy Gray
  Will never more be seen.
Wordsworth.

THE ROSE OF MAY.

AH ! there's the lily, marble pale,
The bonnie broom, the cistus frail ;
The rich sweet pea, the iris blue,
The larkspur with its peacock hue ;
All these are fair, yet hold I will
That the Rose of May is fairer still.

'Tis grand 'neath palace walls to grow,
To blaze where lords and ladies go ;
To hang o'er marble founts, and shine
In modern gardens, trim and fine ;
But the Rose of May is only seen
Where the great of other days have been.

The house is mouldering stone by stone,
The garden-walks are overgrown ;
The flowers are low, the weeds are high,
The fountain-stream is choked and dry,
The dial-stone with moss is green,
Where'er the Rose of May is seen.

The Rose of May its pride display'd
Along the old stone balustrade ;
And ancient ladies, quaintly dight,
In its pink *blossoms* took delight ;

And on the steps would make a stand
To scent its fragrance—fan in hand.

Long have been dead those ladies gay ;
Their very heirs have passed away ;
And their old portraits, prim and tall,
Are mould'ring in the mould'ring hall ;
The terrace and the balustrade
Lie broken, weedy and decayed.

But blithe and tall the Rose of May
Shoots upward through the ruin grey ;
With scented flower, and leaf pale green,
Such rose as it hath ever been,
Left, like a noble deed, to grace
The memory of an ancient race.

Mary Howi

MORNING INVITATION TO A CHILD.

THE house is a prison, the schoolroom's a cell ;
Leave study and books for the upland and dell ;
Lay aside the dull poring, quit home and quit car
Sally forth ! sally forth ! let us breathe the fre
    air !
The sky dons [1] its holiday mantle of blue ;
The sun sips his morning refreshment of dew,
Shakes, joyously laughing, his tresses of light,
And here and there turns his eye piercing ai
    bright ;
Then jocund mounts up on his glorious car,
With smiles to the morn—for he means to go far—

---

[1] *Dons*—puts on.

While the clouds that had newly paid court at his
    levee,[1]
Spread sails to the breeze, and glide off in a bevy.[2]
Lofty trees, tufted hedge-rows, and sparkling between,
Dewy meadows enamelled [3] in gold and in green,
With king-cups and daisies, that all the year please,
Sprays, petals,[4] and leaflets that nod in the breeze,
With carpets, and garlands, and wreaths, deck the
    way,
And tempt the blithe spirit still onward to stray,
Itself its own home ;—far away ! far away !
The butterflies flutter in pairs round the bower,
The humble-bee sings in each bell of each flower ;
The bee hums o'er heather[5] and breeze-wooing
    hill,[6]
And forgets in the sunshine his toil and his skill ;
The birds carol gladly !—the lark mounts on high !
The swallows on wing make their tune to the eye,
And, as birds of good omen, that summer loves well,
Ever wheeling, weave ever some magical spell.
The hunt is abroad :—hark ! the horn sounds its
    note,
And seems to invite us to regions remote.
The horse in the meadows is stirred by the sound,
And, neighing impatient, o'erleaps the low mound ;

---

[1] *Levee*—a crowd of inferiors waiting on or visiting some
great personage.
[2] *Bevy*—properly a flock of birds—a company.
[3] *Enamelled*—inlaid with various colours.
[4] *Petals*—flower leaves.
[5] *Heather*—heath.
[6] *Breeze-wooing hill*—a hill which, as it were, courts or
invites the wind to stay near it—high and exposed.

Then proud in his speed o'er the champaign [1] h
    bounds
To the whoop of the huntsmen, and tongue of th
    hounds;
Then stay not within, for on such a blest day
We can never quit home, while with Nature w
    stray, far away! far away!   *J. H. Greei*

————◦◇◦————

SOLILOQUY OF A WATER-WAGTAIL.

"HEAR your sovereign's proclamation,
    All good subjects, young and old!
I'm the Lord of the Creation,
    I—a water-wagtail bold!
    All around, and all you see,
    All the world was made for ME!

"Yonder sun, so proudly shining,
    Rises—when I leave my nest;
And, behind the hills declining,
    Sets—when I retire to rest.
    Morn and evening, thus you see,
    Day and night, were made for ME!

"Vernal gales to love invite me;
    Summer sheds for me her beams;
Autumn's genial scenes delight me;
    Winter paves with ice my streams;
    All the year is mine you see;
    Seasons change like moons for ME;

[1] *Champaign*—open, flat country.

" On the heads of giant mountains,
  Or beneath the shady trees;
  By the banks of warbling fountains
  I enjoy myself at ease:
  Hills and valleys, thus you see,
  Groves and rivers, made for ME!

" Boundless are my vast dominions;
  I can hop, or swim, or fly;
  When I please, my towering pinions
  Trace my empire through the sky:
  Air and elements, you see,
  Heaven and earth, were made for ME!

" Birds and insects, beasts and fishes,
  All their humble distance keep;
  Man, subservient to my wishes,
  Sows the harvest which I reap:
  Mighty man himself, you see,
  All that breathe, were made for ME?

" 'Twas for my accommodation
  Nature rose when I was born;
  Should I die—the whole creation
  Back to nothing would return:
  Sun, moon, stars, the world, you see,
  Sprung—exist—will fall with ME."

Here the pretty prattler, ending,
Spread his wings to soar away;
But a cruel hawk, descending,
Pounced him up—a helpless prey.
Couldst thou not, poor wagtail, see
That the hawk was made for THEE?

Montgomery.

THE FIRST GRIEF.

" Oh ! call my brother back to me ;
    I cannot play alone ;
  The summer comes with flower and bee—
    Where is my brother gone ?

" The butterfly is glancing bright
    Across the sunbeam's track ;
  I care not now to chase its flight—
    Oh ! call my brother back.

" The flowers run wild—the flowers we sowed
    Around our garden-tree ;
  Our vine is drooping with its load—
    Oh ! call him back to me."

" He would not hear my voice, fair child !
    He may not come to thee ;
  The face that once like spring-time smiled
    On earth no more thou'lt see !

" A rose's brief, bright life of joy,
    Such unto him was given ;
  Go—thou must play alone, my boy—
    Thy brother is in heaven ! "

" And has he left the birds and flowers,
    And must I call in vain ;
  And through the long, long summer hours,
    Will he not come again ?

" And by the brook, and in the glade,
    Are all our wanderings o'er ?
  Oh ! while my brother with me played,
    *W*ould I had loved him more !' "

Mrs. Heman

OUR ENGLISH HOME.

OH ! who would leave our happy land,
   Where peace and plenty dwell,
To roam upon a foreign strand,
   Whose wonders travellers tell ?

The orange sheds its sweet perfume
   Beneath Hispania's [1] skies ;
But we've the apple's ruddy bloom,
   The orchard's rich supplies !

The cocoa and the date-tree spread
   Their boughs in India's clime ;
The yellow mango hangs o'erhead,
   And stately grows the lime ;

But we've the cherry's tempting bough,
   The currant's coral gem ;
What English child will not allow
   That these may vie with them ?

Italy boasts its citron groves,
   And walks of lemon trees ;
Ceylon, its spicy nuts and cloves,
   That scent the summer breeze ;

But we've the peach, and nectarine red,
   The ripe and blooming plum,
The strawberry, in its leafy bed,
   When holidays are come.

[1] *Hispania*—Spain.

The purple vine its harvest yields,
   France, in thy fertile plain;
But we've the yellow waving fields
   Of golden British grain.

Heaven on our favoured land hath smiled;
   From want and war we're free;
The noble's heir, the peasant's child,
   Alike have liberty.

Grateful we'll praise the mighty hand
   That sheds such blessings here,
Protecting still our native land
   From ills that others fear.

Still let us love this spot of earth—
   The best where'er we roam—
And duly estimate the worth
   Of our dear English home.
                 Mrs. C. B. Wilso

CHILDREN LISTENING TO A LARK.

See, the lark prunes his active wings,
Rises to heaven, and soars, and sings!
His morning hymns, his mid-day lays,
Are one continued song of praise;
He speaks his Maker all he can,
And shames the silent tongue of man.
When the declining orb of light
Reminds him of approaching night,

His warbling vespers [1] swell his breast,
And, as he sings, he sinks to rest.
Shall birds instructive lessons teach,
And we be deaf to what they preach ?
No, ye dear nestlings of my heart,
Go, act the wiser songster's part ;
Spurn your warm couch at early dawn,
And with your God begin the morn ;
To Him your grateful tribute pay
Through every period of the day ;
To Him your evening songs direct ;
His eye shall watch, His arm protect ;
Though darkness reigns, He's with you still ;
Then sleep, my babes, and fear no ill.

Cotton.

THE BIRD'S NEST.

It wins my admiration
To view the structure of that little work,
A bird's nest.   Mark it well within, without !
No tool had he that wrought, no knife to cut,
No nail to fix, no bodkin to insert,
No glue to join : his little beak was all—
And yet how neatly finished ! what nice hand,
With every implement and means of art,
And twenty years' apprenticeship to boot,[1]
Could make me such another ?   Vainly, then,

---

[1] *Vespers*—properly, the evening service of the Roman Catholic church ; here, evening songs.
[2] *To boot*—in addition.

We boast of excellence, whose noblest skill
Instinctive genius foils.

Hurdi.

———◆◆———

THE TOAD'S JOURNAL. [1]

In a land for antiquities greatly renowned,
A traveller had dug wide and deep under ground
A temple for ages entombed to disclose—
When lo ! he disturbed in its secret repose
A toad, from whose journal it plainly appears
It had lodged in that mansion some thousands
  years.
The roll, which this reptile's long history records,
A treat to the sage antiquarian affords :
The sense by obscure hieroglyphics concealed,
Deep learning, at length, with long labour revealed
The first thousand years as a specimen take ;—
The dates are omitted for brevity's sake.
—— "Crawled forth from some rubbish, an
  winked with one eye ;
Half opened the other, but could not tell why ;
Stretched out my left leg, as it felt rather queer,
Then drew all together and slept for a year.
Awakened, felt chilly—crept under a stone ;
Was vastly contented with living alone.
One toe became wedged in the stone like a peg,
Could not get it away—had the cramp in my leg ;

---

[1] It is said that Belzoni, the traveller in Egypt, discover
a living toad in a temple which had been for ages buried
the sand. This circumstance gave rise to the poem, the fir
twelve lines of which were not written by the ingenious a
thor of the rest, but prefixed by some unknown hand.

Began half to wish for a neighbour at hand
To loosen the stone, which was fast in the sand;
Pulled harder—then dozed, as I found 'twas no
    use;—
Awoke the next summer, and lo! it was loose.
Crawled forth from the stone when completely awake;
Crept into a corner and grinned at a snake.
Retreated, and found that I needed repose;
Curled up my damp limbs and prepared for a doze:
Fell sounder to sleep than was usual before,
And did not awake for a century or more;
But had a sweet dream, as I rather believe:—
Methought it was light, and a fine summer's eve;
And I in some garden deliciously fed
In the pleasant moist shade of a strawberry bed.
There fine speckled creatures claimed kindred with
    me,
And others that hopped, most enchanting to see.
Here long I regaled with emotion extreme;—
Awoke—disconcerted to find it a dream;
Grew pensive—discovered that life is a load;
Began to get weary of being a toad;
Was fretful at first, and then shed a few tears."—
Here ends the account of the first thousand years.

MORAL.

It seems that life is all a void,
On selfish thoughts alone employed:
That length of days is not a good,
Unless their use be understood;
While if good deeds *one* year engage,
That may be longer than an age:

M

But if a year in trifles go,
Perhaps you'd spend a thousand so.
Time cannot stay to make us wise—
We must improve it as it flies.

Jane Tayl(

INVITATION TO BIRDS.

Ye gentle warblers! hither fly,
　　And shun the noontide heat ;
My shrubs a cooling shade supply,
　　My groves a safe retreat.

Here freely hop from spray to spray,
　　And weave the mossy nest ;
Here rove and sing the live-long day,
　　At night here sweetly rest.

Amid this cool transparent rill,
　　That trickles down the glade,
Here bathe your plumes, here drink your
　　And revel in the shade.

No school-boy rude, to mischief prone,
　　Here shows his ruddy face ;
Or twangs his bow, or hurls a stone
　　In this sequestered place.

Hither the vocal thrush repairs ;
　　Secure the linnet sings ;
The goldfinch dreads no slimy snares
　　To clog her painted wings.

Sweet nightingale ! oh, quit thy haunt,
   Yon distant woods among,
And round my friendly grotto chant
   Thy sadly-pleasing song.

Let not the harmless redbreast fear,
   Domestic bird, to come
And seek a safe asylum here,
   With one that loves his home.

My trees for you, ye artless tribe,
   Shall store of fruit preserve ;
Oh ! let me thus your friendship bribe—
   Come feed without reserve.

For you these cherries I protect,
   To you these plums belong ;
Sweet is the fruit that you have pecked,
   But sweeter far your song.

Graves.

BETH-GELERT;[1]

OR, THE GRAVE OF THE GREYHOUND.

THE spearman heard the bugle sound,
   And gaily smiled the morn,
And many a brach,[2] and many a hound,
   Attend Llewellyn's horn.

[1] The name of a village in North Wales. The circumstances narrated in this poem occurred in the reign of King John of England, when Llewellyn the Great was the independent Prince of North Wales.

[2] *Brach—a female hound.*

And still he blew a louder blast,
   And gave a louder cheer ;
" Come, Gelert, why art thou the last
   Llewellyn's horn to hear ?

" Where does my faithful Gelert roam ?
   The flower of all his race ;
So true, so brave ; a lamb at home,
   A lion in the chace."

'Twas only at Llewellyn's board
   The faithful Gelert fed ;
He watched, he served, he cheered his lor
   And sentineled[1] his bed.

In sooth he was a peerless hound,
   The gift of royal John :[2]
But now no Gelert could be found,
   And all the chace rode on.

And now, as over rocks and dells
   The huntsmen's cheerings rise,
All Snowdon's craggy chaos[3] yells
   With many mingled cries.

That day Llewellyn little loved
   The chace of hart or hare,
And scant and small the booty proved,
   For Gelert was not there.

Unpleased, Llewellyn homeward hied ;
   When near the portal seat,[4]

---

[1] *Sentineled*—watched as a sentinel.
[2] *Royal John*—King John of England.
[3] *Craggy chaos*—confused mass of craggy rocks
formed the mountain.
[4] *Portal seat*—seat at the door of his castle.

His truant Gelert he espied,
  Bounding his lord to greet.

But when he gained his castle door
  Aghast the chieftain stood;
The hound was smeared with drops of gore,
  His lips and fangs [1] ran blood!

Llewellyn gazed with wild surprise,
  Unused such looks to meet;
His favourite checked his joyful guise,[2]
  And crouched and licked his feet.

Onward in haste Llewellyn past,
  And on went Gelert too;
And still where'er his eyes he cast
  Fresh blood-drops shocked his view!

O'erturned his infant's bed he found,
  The blood-stained covert[3] rent;
And all around the walls and ground
  With recent blood besprent.[4]

He called his child; no voice replied—
  He searched with terror wild;
Blood! blood he found on every side,
  But nowhere found his child!

"Hell-hound! by thee my child's devoured!"
  The frantic father cried;
And to the hilt his vengeful sword
  He plunged in Gelert's side.

[1] *Fangs*—long tusks or teeth.
[2] *Guise*—manner, appearance.
[3] *Covert*—for coverlet, the outermost of the bed-clothes.
[4] *Besprent*—sprinkled.

His suppliant look, as prone[1] he fell,
   No pity could impart,
Yet mournfully his dying yell
   Sank in Llewellyn's heart.

Aroused by Gelert's dying yell,
   Some slumberer wakened nigh—
What words the parent's joy can tell
   To hear his infant's cry ?

Concealed amidst a mingled heap
   His hurried search had missed,
All glowing from his rosy sleep,
   His cherub boy he kissed.

Nor wound had he nor harm, nor dread,
   But, the same couch beneath,
Lay a great wolf,[2] all torn and dead,—
   Tremendous still in death.

Ah ! what was then Llewellyn's pain?—
   For now the truth was clear;
The gallant hound the wolf had slain
   And saved Llewellyn's heir.

Vain, vain was all Llewellyn's woe;
   " Best of thy kind, adieu !
The frantic deed which laid thee low,
   This heart shall ever rue ! "[3]

And now a gallant tomb they raise,
   With costly sculpture decked;

[1] *Prone*—headlong.
[2] *Wolf*—wolves were at this time numerous and formidal
'n *North Wales.*
[3] *Rue*—regret, lament.

And marbles, storied[1] with his praise,
　Poor Gelert's bones protect.

Here never could the spearman pass,
　Or forester, unmoved;
Here oft the tear-besprinkled grass
　Llewellyn's sorrow proved.

And here he hung his horn and spear,
　And oft, as evening fell,
In fancy's piercing sounds would hear
　Poor Gelert's dying yell!

W. Spenser.

TO A WASP.

WINGED wanderer of the sky,
From your wonted path on high,
With your fearful dragon tail,
Crested head, and coat of mail,
Why do you my peace molest?
Why do you disturb my rest?
While the sunny meads are seen
Decked with purest white and green;
And the gardens and the bowers,
And the forests and the flowers,
Don their robes of various dye,
Blending fitly to the eye;—
Did *I* chase you in your flight?
Did *I* put you in a fright?

---

[1] *Storied*—engraved, or written over.

Did *I* spoil your treasures hid ?
Well you know I never did.
Foolish trifler, pray beware !
Tempt my anger—if you dare.
Trust not in your strength of wing,
Trust not in your length of sting ;
You are lost if here you stay ;
Haste then, trifler, haste away !

Bruce.

THE WINTER FIRE.

A FIRE's a good companionable friend,
A comfortable friend, who meets your face
With welcome glad, and makes the poorest shed
As pleasant as a palace !   Are you cold ?
He warms you—weary ? he refreshes you—
Hungry ? he doth prepare your food for you.
Are you in darkness ? he gives light to you—
In a strange land ? he wears a face that is
Familiar from your childhood.   Are you poor ?—
What matters it to him ?   He knows no difference
Between an emperor and the poorest beggar !
Where is the friend, that bears the name of man,
Will do as much for you ?

Mary Howitt.

THE MOTHER TRIED.

" OH ! blessed is my baby boy ! "
Thus spoke a mother to her child,
And kissed him with excess of joy—
He looked into her face and smiled.

But as the mother breathed his name,
  The fervent prayer was scarcely said,
Convulsions shook his infant frame—
  The mother's only hope was dead !

Yet still her faith in Him she kept,
  On Him who turned to grief her joy ;
And still she whispered, as she wept,
  " Oh ! blessed *is* my baby boy ! "
S. C. Hall.

A CHILD'S WISH.

OH! how I wish that I had lived
  In the ages that are gone !
Like a brother of the Wandering Jew,
  And yet kept living on ;

For then in its early glory,
  I could have proudly paced
The City of the Wilderness,[1]
  Old Tadmor of the waste ;

And have seen the Queen of Sheba,[2]
  With her camels riding on,
With spices rich, and precious stones,
  To great King Solomon ;

And have talked with grey Phœnicians
  Of dark and solemn seas,
And heard the wild and dismal tales
  Of their far voyages.

[1] *Tadmor* or *Palmyra*—a city built by Solomon ; see 2nd Chronicles, viii. 4.
[2] *Queen of Sheba*—see 2nd Chronicles, vi. 1.

I could have solved all mysteries
　Of Egypt old and vast,
And read each hieroglyphic scroll,
　From the first word to the last.

I should have known what cities
　In the desert wastes were hid;
And have walked, as in my father's house,
　Through each great pyramid.

I might have sat on Homer's knees,
　A little prattling boy,
And listened to the story strange
　Of the ten years' siege of Troy.

I might have walked with Plato
　In the groves of Academe;[1]
And have talked with him of sylvan Pan,
　And the Naiads of each stream.

What joy to have climbed th' Acropolis,[2]
　With its stately Parthenon;
And in after days to the seven-hilled Rome
　With eager steps to have gone!

To have stood by warlike Romulus,
　In council and in fray,
And with his horde of robbers dwelt,
　In reed-roofed huts of clay!

Think of ambitious Cæsar,
　And Pompey great and brave;—

[1] *Academe*—a garden in one of the suburbs of Athens,
out in walks shaded by trees, and adorned with statues
fountains. It was a favourite resort of learned men.

[2] *Acropolis*—a rocky eminence about 150 feet high, ar
id at the foot of which Athens was built, and on ʋ
mit stood the Parthenon or Temple of Minerva.

To have seen their legions in the field,
  Their galleys on the wave!

I should have seen Rome's glory dimmed,
  When round her leaguered [1] wall
Came down the Vandal and the Goth,
  The Scythian and the Gaul;

And the dwarfish Huns by myriads,
  From the unknown northern shores;
As if the very earth gave up
  The brown men of the moors.

I should have seen old Wodin [2]
  And his seven sons go forth,
From the green banks of the Caspian Sea
  To the dim wilds of the North;

To the dark and piny forests,
  Where he made his drear abode,
And taught his wild and fearful faith,
  And thus became their god.

And the terrible Vikingr,[3]
  Dwellers on the stormy sea,
The Norsemen [4] and their Runic [5] lore
  Had all been known to me.

[1] *Leaguered*—besieged.

[2] *Wodin*—one of the deified heroes of Saxon Mythology: we have his name in Wednesday, that is Wodin's-day.

[3] *Vikingr*—men of the creeks or bays; pirates so called, famous in our early history.

[4] *Norsemen*—northern-men, from the north of Europe.

[5] *Runic*—mysterious, a name given to certain alphabetic characters cut in *stones found* in Norway, Sweden, and some other *countries.*

Think only of the dismal tales,
   And the mysteries I should know,
If my long life had but begun,
   Three thousand years ago !

Mary E

LAPLAND.

" WITH blue cold nose and wrinkled bro'
Traveller, whence comest thou ? "
" From Lapland's woods and hills of fros
By the rapid reindeer crost ;
Where tapering glows the gloomy fir
And the stunted [1] juniper ;
Where the wild hare and the crow
Whiten in surrounding snow ;
Where the shivering huntsmen tear
His fur coat from the grim white bear :
Where the wolf and arctic fox
Prowl along the lonely rocks ;
And tardy suns to deserts drear
Give days and nights of half-a-year ;
—From icy oceans, where the whale
Tosses in foam his lashing tail ;
Where the snorting sea-horse shows
His ivory teeth in grinning rows ;
Where, tumbling in their seal-skin boa
Fearless the hungry fishers float,
And from teeming [2] seas supply
The food their niggard plains deny.

Miss

[1] *Stunted*—hindered from growth, dwarf.
[2] *Teeming*—full, abundant.

ANIMALS AND THEIR COUNTRIES.

O'ER Afric's sand the tawny lion stalks;[1]
On Phasis'[1] banks the graceful pheasant walks;
The lonely eagle builds on Kilda's[2] shore:
Germania's forests feed the tusky boar:
From Alp to Alp the sprightly ibex bounds;
With peaceful lowings Britain's isle resounds;
The Lapland peasant o'er the frozen mere[3]
Is drawn in sledges by the swift reindeer;
The river-horse and scaly crocodile
Infest the reedy banks of fruitful Nile;
The dipsas[4] hisses over Mauritania's plain,[5]
And seals and spouting whales sport in the northern
    main.[6]

Barbauld.

———◦◊◦———

THE NEGRO BOY.[7]

WHEN avarice enslaves the mind,
   And selfish views alone bear sway,
Man turns a savage to his kind,
   And blood and rapine mark his way.
   Alas! for this poor, simple toy,
   I sold a happy negro boy.

[1] *Phasis*—a river in Persia. [2] *Kilda*—an island of Scotland; the most western of the Hebrides. [3] *Mere*—a large lake. [4] *Dipsas*—a venomous serpent, whose bite produces intolerable thirst. [5] *Mauritania*—the ancient name of northwestern Africa, now Fez and Morocco. [6] *Main*—main-*sea*—ocean.

[7] An African prince, who once visited England, was asked what he had given for his watch; he answered, "What I will *never give again*—a fine boy."

N

His father's hope, his mother's pride,
  Though black, yet comely to their view,
I tore him helpless from their side,
  And gave him to a ruffian crew;
    To fiends that Afric's coast annoy,
    I sold the trembling negro boy.

From country, friends, and parents torn,
  His tender limbs in chains confined,
I saw him o'er the billows borne,
  And marked his agony of mind;
    But still to gain the simple toy,
    I gave the weeping negro boy.

Beneath a tyrant's harsh command,
  He wears away his youthful prime,
Far distant from his native land,
  A stranger in a foreign clime.
    Sad thoughts his days and nights emplo:
    A poor, dejected negro boy.

His wretched parents long shall mourn,
  Shall long explore the distant main,
Eager to see the youth return,—
  But all their hopes and sighs are vain;
    They never shall the sight enjoy
    Of their lamented negro boy.

                Sam

THE BIRD IN A CAGE.

OH! who would keep a little bird confined
When cowslip-bells are nodding in the wind,

When every hedge as with "good-morrow" rings,
And, heard from wood to wood, the blackbird sings?
Oh! who would keep a little bird confined
In his cold wiry prison?—Let him fly,
And hear him sing, "How sweet is liberty!"

W. L. Bowles.

THE STREAMLET.

I SAW a little streamlet flow
  Along a peaceful vale;
A thread of silver, soft and slow,
  It wandered down the dale;
Just to do good it seemed to move,
Directed by the hand of Love.

The valley smiled in living green;
  A tree, which near it gave
From noon-tide heat a friendly screen,
  Drank from its limpid [1] wave.
The swallow brushed it with her wing,
And followed its meandering.[2]

But not alone to plant and bird
  That little stream was known;
Its gentle murmur far was heard—
  A friend's familiar tone!
It glided by the cotter's [3] door,
It blessed the labour of the poor.

And would that I could thus be found,
  While travelling life's brief way,

[1] *Limpid*—clear.   [2] *Meandering*—winding course.
[3] *Cotter*—cottager.

An humble friend to all around,
　Where'er my footsteps stray ;
Like that pure stream, with tranquil b
Like it, still blessing, and still blest.

M. A.

THE DAISY.

WHAT hand but His who arched the sk
　And pours the day-spring's [1] living 1
Wondrous alike in all He tries,
　Could raise the daisy's purple bud,
Mould its green cup, its wiry stem,
　Its fringed border nicely spin,
And cut the gold-embossed gem,
　That, set in silver, gleams within,
And fling it, unrestrained and free
　O'er hill and dale, and desert sod :
That man, where'er he walks, may see
　At every step the stamp of God ?

Mas

PRINCIPLE PUT TO THE TEST.

A YOUNGSTER at school, more sedate than th
Had once his integrity put to the test :—
His comrades had plotted an orchard to rok
And asked him to go and assist in the job.

He was very much shocked, and answered,
What, rob our poor neighbour ! I pray you

[1] *Day-spring*—rise of day—dawn.　[2] Living floo

Besides the man's poor, his orchard's his bread ;
Then think of his children, for they must be fed."

" You speak very fine, and you look very grave,
But apples we want, and apples we'll have ;
If you will go with us, we'll give you a share,
If not, you shall have neither apple nor pear."

They spoke, and Tom pondered, "I see they will
    go ;
Poor man ! what a pity to injure him so ;
Poor man ! I would save him his fruit if I could,
But staying behind will do him no good.

" If this matter depended alone upon me,
His apples might hang till they dropped from the
    tree ;
But since they *will* take them, I think I'll go too ;
He will lose none by me, though I get a few."

His scruples thus silenced, Tom felt more at ease,
And went with his comrades the apples to seize ;
He blamed and protested, but joined in the plan ;
He shared in the plunder, but pitied the man.

Conscience slumbered awhile, but soon woke in his
    breast,
And in language severe the delinquent addressed :
" With such empty and selfish pretences away !
By your *actions* you're judged, be your speech what
    it may." [1]

                          Cowper.

[1] *The last verse is* added by another hand.

N 2

THE GLADNESS OF NATURE.

Is this a time to be cloudy and sad,
  When all is smiling above and around;
When even the deep blue heavens look glad,
  And gladness breathes from the blossoming
  ground?

There are notes of joy from the blackbird and wren,
  And the gossip of swallows through all the sky;
The ground-squirrel gaily chirps by his den,
  And the wilding bee hums merrily by.

The clouds are at play in the azure space,
  And their shadows sport in the deep green vale;
And here they stretch to the frolic chace,
  And there they roll in the easy gale.

There's a dance of leaves in that aspen bower,
  There's a titter of winds in that beechen tree,
There's a smile on the fruit, and a smile on the
  flower,
  And a laugh from the brook that runs to the sea.

And look at the broad-faced sun, how he smiles
  On the dewy earth that smiles in his ray,
On the leaping waters and gay young isles,—
  Ay, look, and he'll smile all thy gloom away.
                     W. C. Bryant

———•◦•———

EVENING HYMN.

God, that madest earth and heaven,
  Darkness and light!
Who the day for toil hast given,
  For rest the night;

May Thine angel guards defend us,
  Slumber sweet Thy mercy send us,
Holy dreams and hopes attend us,
  This livelong night!

Heber.

THE FIRST SWALLOW.

THE gorse is yellow on the heath;
The banks with speed-well flowers are gay;
The oaks are budding, and beneath,
The hawthorn soon will bear the wreath,
  The silver wreath of May.

The welcome guest of settled spring,
The swallow, too, is come at last;
Just at sun-set, when thrushes sing,
I saw her dash with rapid wing,
  And hailed her as she past.

Come, summer visitant, attach
To my reed roof your nest of clay,
And let my ear your music catch,
Low twittering underneath the thatch,
  At the grey dawn of day.

Charlotte Smith.

THE FAKENHAM GHOST.

THE lawns were dry in Euston park:
  (Here truth [1] inspires my tale,)
The lonely footpath, still and dark,
  Led over hill and dale.

[1] *This ballad is founded on fact.*

Benighted was an ancient dame,
   And fearful haste she made
To gain the vale of Fakenham,[1]
   And hail its willow shade.

Her footsteps knew no idle stops,
   But followed faster still;
And echoed to the darksome copse
   That whispered on the hill,

Where clamorous rooks, yet scarcely hus
   Bespoke a peopled shade;
And many a wing the foliage brushed,
   And hovering circuits made.

The dappled [2] herd of grazing deer,
   That sought the shades by day,
Now started from their paths with fear,
   And gave the stranger way.

Darker it grew, and darker fears
   Came o'er her troubled mind;
When now, a short, quick step she hears
   Come patting close behind.

She turned, it stopped; nought could sh
   Upon the gloomy plain;
But as she strove the sprite to flee,
   She heard the same again.

Now terror seized her quaking frame,
   For, where the path was bare,
The trotting ghost kept on the same—
   She muttered many a prayer.

[1] *Fakenham*—a village in Suffolk.
[2] *Dappled*—variegated—spotted.

Yet once again, amidst her fright,
   She tried what sight could do ;
When, through the cheating glooms of night,
   A MONSTER ! stood in view.

Regardless of whate'er she felt,
   It followed down the plain ;
She owned her sins, and down she knelt,
   And said her prayers again.

Then on she sped, and hope grew strong,
   The white park-gate in view ;
Which pushing hard, so long it swung,
   That ghost and all passed through !

Loud fell the gate against the post,
   Her heart-strings like to crack ;
For much she feared the grisly [1] ghost
   Would leap upon her back.

Still on—pit—pat—the goblin went,
   As it had done before :
Her strength and resolution spent,
   She fainted at the door.

Out came her husband, much surprised,
   Out came her daughter dear ;
Good-natured souls ! all unadvised
   Of what they had to fear.

The candle's gleam pierced through the night,
   Some short space o'er the green ;
And there the little trotting sprite
   Distinctly might be seen.

---

[1] *Grisly*—dreadful—hideous.

An ass's foal had lost its dam
  Within the spacious park ;
And, simple as a playful lamb,
  Had followed in the dark.

No goblin he ; no imp of sin ;
  No crimes had ever known ;—
They took the shaggy stranger in,
  And reared him as their own.[1]

His little hoofs would rattle round
  Upon the cottage floor ;
The matron learned to love the sound
  That frightened her before.

A favourite the ghost became
  And 'twas his fate to thrive ;
And long he lived, and spread his fame,
  And kept the joke alive ;

For many a laugh went through the vale
  And some conviction too—
Each thought some other goblin tale
  Perhaps was just as true.

Bloom,

———◦◦◦———

THE FAITHFUL FRIEND.

The greenhouse is my summer seat ;
My shrubs, displaced from that retreat,
    Enjoyed the open air ;
Two goldfinches, whose sprightly song
Had been their mutual solace long,
    Lived happy prisoners there.

[1] *It does* not distinctly appear that they had any rig
lo this.

They sang as blithe as finches sing
That flutter loose on golden wing,
    And frolic where they list; [1]
Strangers to liberty, 'tis true,
But that delight they never knew,
    And therefore never missed.

But nature works in every breast,
With force not easily supprest;
    And Dick felt some desires,
Which, after many an effort vain,
Instructed him at length to gain
    A pass between the wires.

The open windows seemed to invite
The freeman to a farewell flight;
    But Tom was still confined;
And Dick, although his way was clear,
Was much too generous and sincere
    To leave his friend behind.

So settling on his cage, by play,
And chirp, and kiss, he seemed to say,
    "You must not live alone,"—
Nor would he quit that chosen stand,
Till I with slow and cautious hand
    Returned him to his own.

O ye, who never taste the joys
Of friendship, satisfied with noise,
    Fandango,[2] ball, and rout!
Blush, when I tell you how a bird
A prison with a friend preferred,
    To liberty without.   Cowper.

    [1] *List*—wish, please.
    [2] *Fandango*—a Spanish dance.

SONG OF THE BEES.

WE watch for the light of the morn to break,
　And colour the eastern sky
With its blended hues of saffron and lake;
Then say to each other, " Awake! awake!
For our winter's honey is all to make,
　And our bread for a long supply."

And off we hie to the hill and dell,
　To the field, to the meadow and bower;
We love in the columbine's horn to dwell,
To dip in the lily with snow-white bell,
To search for the balm in its fragrant cell,
　The mint and the rosemary flower.

We seek the bloom of the eglantine,[1]
　Of the painted thistle and brier;
And follow the steps of the wandering vine,
Whether it trail on the earth supine,[2]
Or round the aspiring tree-top twine,
　And aim at a state still higher.

While each, on the good of her sister bent,
　Is busy, and cares for all,
We hope for an evening of heart's content
In the winter of life, without lament
That summer is gone, or its hours misspent,
　And the harvest is past recall.

　　　　　　　　　　　　　　　Miss Gou

---

[1] *Eglantine*—properly the sweet-brier; here the hon
suckle is probably intended.
[2] *Supine*—lying along on the ground.

THE SNAIL.

FROM THE LATIN OF VINCENT BOURNE.

To grass, or leaf, or fruit, or wall,
The snail sticks close, nor fears to fall,
As if he grew there, house and all
        Together.

Within that house secure he hides,
When danger imminent betides
Of storm, or other harm besides
        Of weather.

Give but his horns the slightest touch,
His self-collecting power is such,
He shrinks into his house with much
        Displeasure.

Where'er he dwells he dwells alone,
Except himself, has chattels [1] none,
Well satisfied to be his own
        Whole treasure.

Thus, hermit-like, his life he leads,
Nor partner of his banquet needs,
And if he meets one, only feeds
        The faster.

Who seeks him must be worse than blind,
(He and his house are so combined)
If finding it, he fails to find
        Its master.

        Cowper.

[1] *Chattels*—movable property.

O

THE ROMANCE OF THE SWAN'S NEST.

LITTLE Ellie sits alone
'Mid the beeches of a meadow,
By a stream-side on the grass;
And the trees are showering down
Doubles of their leaves in shadow
On the shining hair and face.

She has thrown her bonnet by;
And her feet she has been dipping
In the shallow waters' flow—
Now she holds them nakedly
In her hands, all sleek and dripping,
While she rocketh to and fro.

Little Ellie sits alone,
And the smile she softly useth
Fills the silence like a speech:
While she thinks what shall be done,
And the sweetest pleasure chooseth
For her future, within reach.

Little Ellie in her smile
Chooseth—" I will have a lover
Riding on a steed of steeds!
He shall love me without guile;
And to *him* I will discover
That swan's nest among the reeds.

" And the steed it shall be red-roan,
And the lover shall be noble,
With an eye that takes the breath;

And the lute he plays upon
Shall strike ladies into trouble,
As his sword strikes men to death.

" And the steed it shall be shod
All in silver, housed in azure,
And the mane shall swim the wind,
And the hoofs along the sod
Shall flash onward and keep measure,
Till the shepherds look behind.

" He will kiss me on the mouth
Then, and lead me as a lover
Through the crowds that praise his deeds;
And, when soul tied by one troth,
Unto *him* I will discover
That swan's nest among the reeds."

Little Ellie, with her smile
Not yet ended, rose up gaily,—
Tied the bonnet, donn'd the shoe,
And went homeward round a mile,
Just to see, as she did daily,
What more eggs were with the two.

Pushing through the elm-tree copse,
Winding by the stream, light-hearted,
Where the osier pathway leads—
Past the boughs she stoops and stops:
So! the wild swan had deserted,
And a rat had gnaw'd the reeds.

Ellie went home sad and slow.
If she found the lover ever,
With his red-roan steed of steeds,

Sooth I know not! but I know
She could never show him—never—
That swan's nest among the reeds.

                                 E. B. Browning.

THE CHILDREN IN THE WOOD.[1]

Now ponder well, you parents dear,
　These words which I shall write;
A doleful story you shall hear,
　In time brought forth to light:

A gentleman of good account
　In Norfolk dwelt of late,
Who did in honour far surmount [2]
　Most men of his estate.

Sore sick he was, and like to die,
　No help his life could save;
His wife by him as sick did lie,
　And both possessed one grave.

No love between these two was lost,
　Each was to other kind;
In love they lived, in love they died,
　And left two babes behind:—

The one a fine and pretty boy,
　Not passing three years old;

---

[1] This very popular ballad is here reprinted from Percy's
Reliques, with such slight alterations, both in the orthography
and the style, as were necessary to fit it for this Selection.
The original copy is thought to be more than two hundred
years old.

[2] *Surmount*—exceed.

The other a girl, more young than he,
   And framed in beauty's mould.

The father left his little son,
   As plainly doth appear,
When he to perfect age [1] should come,
   Three hundred pounds a year.

And to his little daughter Jane
   Five hundred pounds in gold,
To be paid down on marriage day ;
   Which might not be controlled.

But if the children chanced to die,
   Ere they to age should come,
Their uncle should possess their wealth—
   For so the will did run.

" Now, brother," said the dying man,
   "Look to my children dear ;
Be good unto my boy and girl,
   No friends else have they here ;

" To God and you I recommend
   My children dear this day ;
But little while, be sure, we have
   Within this world to stay.

" You must be father and mother both
   And uncle all in one ;
God knows what will become of them,
   When I am dead and gone."

----

[1] *Perfect age*—the age of 21.

With that out spoke their mother dea
"O brother kind," quoth [1] she,
"You are the man must bring our bab
To wealth or misery.

"And if you keep them carefully,
Then God will you reward;
But if you otherwise should deal,
God will your deeds regard." [2]

With lips as cold as any stone
They kissed their children small:
"God bless you both, my children dea
And then their tears did fall.

These words did then their brother sp
To this sick couple there:
"The keeping of your little ones,
Sweet sister, do not fear;

"God never prosper me nor mine,
Nor aught else that I have,
If I do wrong your children dear,
When you are in the grave."

The parents being dead and gone,
The children home he takes,
And brings them straight unto his hor
Where much of them he makes.

He had not kept these pretty babes
A twelvemonth and a day,

[1] *Quoth*—says or said.
[2] R......l ....ard and punish

When, for their wealth, he did devise
To make them both away.[1]

He bargained with two ruffians strong,
Which were of furious mood,
That they should take these children young,
And slay them in a wood.

He told his wife an artful tale—
He would the children send
To be brought up in fair London,
With one that was his friend.

Away then went these pretty babes,
Rejoicing at that tide,[2]
Rejoicing with a merry mind,
They should on cock-horse ride.

They prate and prattle pleasantly,
As they rode on their way,
To those that should their murderers be,
And work their lives' decay ;

So that the pretty speech they had
Made murder's heart relent,
And they that undertook the deed
Full sore did now repent.

Yet one of them, more hard of heart,
Did vow to do his charge,[3]
Because the wretch that hired him
Had paid him very large.[4]

[1] *To make them both away*—to make away with them—to ill them.　　　　　　[2] *Tide*—time.
[3] *His charge*—that which he had been charged with.
[4] *Large*—for largely.

The other won't agree thereto :
　So here they fall to strife ;
With one another they did fight
　About the children's life :

And he that was of mildest mood
　Did slay the other there,
Within an unfrequented wood—
　The babes did quake for fear !

He took the children by the hand,
　Tears standing in their eye,
And bade them straightway follow him
　And look [1] they did not cry.

And two long miles he led them on,
　While they for bread complain ;
" Stay here," quoth he ; " I'll bring you
　When I come back again."

These pretty babes, with hand in hand
　Went wandering up and down,
But never more could see the man
　Approaching from the town.

Their pretty lips with blackberries
　Were all besmeared and dyed,
And when they saw the darksome nigl
　They sat them down and cried.

Thus wandered these poor innocents,
　Till death did end their grief ;
In one another's arms they died,
　For want of due relief.

　　　　　　　[1] *Look*—take care.

No burial this pretty pair
  Of any man receives,
Till Robin Redbreast painfully [1]
  Did cover them with leaves.

And now the heavy wrath of God
  Upon their uncle fell;
Yea, fearful fiends did haunt his house,
  His conscience felt a hell.

His barns were fired, his goods consumed,
  His lands were barren made;
His cattle died within the field,
  And nothing with him staid.

And in a voyage to Portugal
  Two of his sons did die;
And, to conclude, himself was brought
  To want and misery.

He pawned and mortgaged [2] all his land,
  Ere seven years came about,
And now at length his wicked act
  Did by this means come out:

The fellow that did take in hand
  These children dear to kill,
Was for a robbery judged to die,
  (Such was God's blessed will!)

[1] *Painfully*—with pains or trouble—carefully. Some copies read "piously."

[2] *Mortgaged all his land*—gave up his land as security for the repayment of the money that he had borrowed.

Who did confess the very truth,
　　As here hath been displayed;
Their uncle having died in gaol,
　　Where he for debt was laid.

You that executors [1] be made,
　　And overseers eke,[2]
Of children that be fatherless,
　　And their undoing [3] seek,

Take your example by this thing,
　　And yield to each his right,
Lest God with such-like misery
　　Your wicked deeds requite.

————◦◦◦————

THE THRUSH'S MEDITATION.

AIRY budding ash-tree,
　　You have made a throne,
And the sweetest thrush in all the world
　　Is sitting there alone;
Drawn in links of tender brown
　　Against a keen blue sky,
He sings up and he sings down—
　　Who can pass him by?

Through the thin leaves thrilling
　　Goes each glittering note,
Till hearts of happy trees are drawn
　　Into this one bird-throat;

---

[1] *Executor*—one who carries into effect the will
deceased person.
[2] *Eke*—also.　　　　　　　　[3] Undoing—destruction

And all the growing blooms of morn
(His music is so strong)
Are reached and blended and up-borne
And uttered into song.

Now he asks a question!
The answer who can guess?
While sparrows chirp a pettish "no,"
And doves keep murmuring "yes:"
" O will the months be kind and clear,
Unvexed by needless rain,
And will the summer last this year
Till spring time comes again?"

Now he states a dogma—
His view of day and night,
Proclaiming volubly and loud
No other bird is right;
But, half-way through his creed, he checks
At some sweet chance of sound,
And, catching it, no longer recks
If heaven or earth go round.

Now he labours gravely;
Each moment pays itself;
No singer ever worked so hard
For art or fame or pelf;
And now he knows the pretty phrase
And scatters it like rain,
With quick " Da Capos " of self-praise,
Till the tree rings again.

M. B. Smedley.

THE ROBIN PURSUING A BUTTERFL~~Y~~

CAN this be the bird tc man so good,
That, after their bewildering,
Did cover with leaves the little children
So painfully in the wood ?
What ailed thee, Robin, that thou couldst ~~p~~
A beautiful creature
That is gentle by nature ?
Beneath the summer sky,
From flower to flower let him fly ;
'Tis all that he wishes to do.

The cheerer thou of our in-door sadness,
He is the friend of our summer gladness ;
What hinders then that ye should be
Playmates in the sunny weather,
And fly about in the air together ?
His beautiful wings in crimson are drest,
A crimson as bright as thine own :
If thou wouldst be happy in thy nest,
O pious bird ! whom man loves best,
Love him, or leave him alone !

Word~~s~~

"EVERY LITTLE HELPS."

WHAT, if a drop of rain should plead—
" So small a drop as I
Can ne'er refresh the thirsty mead ;
I'll tarry in the sky."

What, if the shining beam of noon
Should in its fountain stay;
Because its feeble light alone
Cannot create a day ?

Does not each rain-drop help to form
The cool refreshing shower ?
And every ray of light, to warm
And beautify the flower ?

THE PRIEST AND THE MULBERRY-TREE.

DID you hear of the curate who mounted his mare,
And merrily trotted along to the fair ?
Of creature more tractable none ever heard ;
In the height of her speed she would stop at a word ;
But again with a word, when the curate said
    "Hey ! "
She put forth her mettle and gallop'd away.

As near to the gates of the city he rode,
While the sun of September all brilliantly glow'd,
The good priest discover'd, with eyes of desire,
A mulberry-tree in a hedge of wild brier ;
On boughs long and lofty, in many a green shoot,
Hung, large, black, and glossy, the beautiful fruit.

The curate was hungry and thirsty to boot ;
He shrunk from the thorns, though he long'd for the
    fruit ;
With a word he arrested his courser's keen speed,
And he *stood up erect* on the back of his steed ;

P

On the saddle he stood while the creature stood stil
And he gather'd the fruit till he took his good fill.

" Sure never," he thought, " was a creature so rare
So docile, so true, as my excellent mare;
Lo, here now I stand," and he gazed all around,
" As safe and as steady as if on the ground;
Yet how had it been, if some traveller this way,
Had, dreaming no mischief, but chanced to cɪ
    ' Hey ' ? "

He stood with his head in the mulberry-tree,
And he spoke out aloud in his fond reverie.
At the sound of the word the good mare made a pusl
And down went the priest in the wild-brier bush,
He remember'd too late, on his thorny green bed,
MUCH THAT WELL MAY BE THOUGHT CANNOT WISEI
    BE SAID.

                        T. L. Peacoc

BIRDS IN SUMMER.

How pleasant the life of a bird must be,
Flitting about in each leafy tree;
In the leafy tree, so broad and tall,
Like a green and beautiful palace-hall,
With its airy chambers, light and boon,[1]
That open to sun, and stars, and moon,
That open unto the bright blue sky,
And the frolicsome winds as they wander by.

They have left their nests in the forest bough;
Those homes of delight they need not now;

---

     [1] *Boon*—gay, cheerful.

And the young and the old they all wander out,
And traverse their green world round about :
And hark ! at the top of this leafy hall,
How one to the other they lovingly call ;
" Come up, come up ! " they seem to say,
" Where the topmost twigs in the breezes sway ! "

" Come up, come up, for the world is fair,
Where the merry leaves dance in the summer air ! "
And the birds below give back the cry,
" We come, we come, to the branches high ! "
How pleasant the life of a bird must be,
Flitting about in a leafy tree ;
And away through the air what joy to go,
And to look on the bright, green earth below.

How pleasant the life of a bird must be,
Skimming about on the breezy sea,
Cresting the billows like silvery foam,
And then wheeling away to its cliff-built home !
What joy it must be to sail, upborne
By a strong free wing, through the rosy morn,
To meet the young sun face to face,
And pierce like a shaft[1] the boundless space !

How pleasant the life of a bird must be,
Wherever it listeth,[2] there to flee ;
To go, when a joyful fancy calls,
Dashing adown 'mong the waterfalls,
Then wheeling about with its mates at play,
Above and below, and among the spray,
Hither and thither, with screams as wild
As the laughing mirth of a rosy child !

[1] *Shaft*—arrow.   [2] *Listeth*—chooses, pleases.

What joy it must be, like a living breeze,
To flutter about 'mong the flowering trees;
Lightly to soar, and to see beneath
The wastes of the blossoming purple heath,
And the yellow furze, like fields of gold,
That gladden some fairy regions old!
On mountain tops, on the billowy sea,
On the leafy stems of the forest tree,
How pleasant the life of a bird must be!

Mary Hor

THE STRID;

OR, THE FOUNDING OF BOLTON PRIORY! [1]

YOUNG Romilly through Barden woods
Is ranging high and low,
And holds a greyhound in a leash,[2]
To let slip on buck or doe.

The pair have reached that fearful chasm,
How tempting to bestride!
For lordly Wharf is there pent in
With rocks on either side.

This striding place is called " the Strid,"
A name which it took of yore;
A thousand years hath it borne that name
And shall a thousand more.

And hither is young Romilly come;
And what may now forbid

---

[1] *Bolton Priory*—a celebrated Abbey, now in ruins, mantically situated on the banks of the Wharf, in Yorks!
[2] *Leash*—a leathern thong.

That he, perhaps for the hundredth time
　Should bound across the Strid?

He sprang in glee—for what cared he
　That the river was strong, and the rocks
　　were steep?
But the greyhound in the leash hung back,
　And checked him in his leap!

The boy is in the arms of Wharf!
　And strangled with a merciless force—
For never more was young Romilly seen
　Till he rose a lifeless corse!

Long, long in darkness his mother sat,
　And her first words were, "Let there be
In Bolton, on the field of Wharf,
　A stately Priory!"

The stately Priory was reared,
　And Wharf, as he moved along,
To matins[1] joined a mournful voice,
　Nor failed at even-song.[2]

And the lady prayed in heaviness
　That looked not for relief;
But slowly did her succour come,
　And patience to her grief.

Oh! there is never sorrow of heart
　That shall lack a timely end,
If but to God we turn, and ask
　Of Him to be our Friend.　　*Wordsworth.*

[1] *Matins*—morning prayers, as performed or chanted in Roman Catholic churches.
[2] *Even-song*—evening service, corresponding to that of the morning.

THE CAMP.

You know we French stormed Ratisbon ;—
    A mile or so away,
On a little mound Napoleon
    Stood on our storming day ;
With neck out-thrust—you fancy how—
    Legs wide, arms locked behind,
As if to balance the prone brow
    Oppressive with its mind.

Just as perhaps he mused, " My plans,
    That soar, to earth may fall,
Let once my army-leader, Lannes,
    Waver at yonder wall ; "
And 'twixt the battery smokes there flew
    A rider, bound on bound
Full-galloping ; nor bridle drew
    Until he reached the mound.

Then off there flung in smiling joy,
    And held himself erect
By just his horse's mane, a boy :
    You hardly could suspect,—
So tight he kept his lips compressed,
    Scarce any blood came through,—
You looked twice ere you saw his breast
    Was all but shot in two.

" Well," cried he, "Emperor ! by God's grace
    We've got you Ratisbon !
The Marshal's in the market-place,
    And you'll be there anon
To see your flag-bird flap his vans
    Where I, to heart's desire,

Perched him !" The chief's eye flashed : his plans
Soared up again like fire.

The chief's eye flashed ; but presently
   Softened itself as sheathes
A film the mother eagle's eye,
   When her bruised eaglet breathes :
" You're wounded ! " " Nay," his soldier's pride
   Touched to the quick, he said :
" I'm killed, Sire ! "   And his chief beside,
   Smiling, the boy fell dead.
R. Browning.

THE EXAMPLE OF BIRDS.

RING-DOVE ! resting benignly calm,
Tell my bosom thy secret balm ;
Blackbird ! straining thy tuneful throat,
Teach my spirit thy thankful note ;
Small Wren ! building thy happy nest,
Where shall I find a home of rest ?
Eagle ! cleaving the vaulted sky,
Teach my nature to soar as high ;
Sky-lark ! winging thy way to heaven,
Be thy track to my footsteps given !

FRIENDSHIP.

SMALL service is true service, while it lasts :
   Of friends, however humble, spurn not one ;
The daisy, by the shadow that it casts,
   Protects the lingering dew-drop from the sun.
Wordsworth

GOD PROVIDETH FOR THE MORROW.

Lo the lilies of the field,
How their leaves instruction yield !
Hark to Nature's lesson, given
By the blessed birds of heaven !
Every bush and tufted tree
Warbles sweet philosophy :—
" Mortal, fly from doubt and sorrow :
God provideth for the morrow !

" Say, with richer crimson glows
The kingly mantle, than the rose ?
Say, have kings more wholesome fare
Than we poor citizens of air ?
Barns nor hoarded grain have we,
Yet we carol merrily ;
Mortal, fly from doubt and sorrow :
God provideth for the morrow !

" One there lives whose guardian eye
Guides our humble destiny ;
One there lives, who, Lord of all,
Keeps our feathers, lest they fall.
Pass we blithely, then, the time,
Fearless of the snare and lime,[1]
Free from doubt and faithless sorrow,
God provideth for the morrow ! "　　*Heb*

----&----

THE WORM AND THE SNAIL;

OR, BE CONTENT WITH YOUR LOT.

A LITTLE worm, too close that played
In contact with a gardener's spade,

[1] *Lime*—birdlime, a substance used by birdcatch

Writhing about in sudden pain,
Perceived that he was cut in twain ;
His nether half left short and free,
Much doubting its identity.
However, when the shock was past,
New circling rings were formed so fast
By Nature's hand, which fails her never,
That soon he was as long as ever ;
But yet the insult and the pain
This little reptile did retain,
In what, in man, is called the brain.
One fine spring evening, bright and wet,
Ere yet the April sun was set,
When slimy reptiles crawl and coil
Forth from the soft and humid soil,
He left his subterranean clay,
To move along the gravelly way ;
Where suddenly his course was stopt
By something on the path that dropt ;
When, with precaution and surprise,
He straight shrunk up to half his size.
That 'twas a stone was first his notion,
But soon discovering locomotion,
He recognized the coat of mail
And horny antlers of a snail,
Which some young rogue (we beg his pardon)
Had flung into his neighbour's garden.
The snail, all shattered and infirm,
Deplored his fate, and told the worm :—
" Alas ! " says he, " I know it well,
All this is owing to my shell ;
They could not send me up so high,
Describing circles in the sky,

But that, on this account, 'tis known
I bear resemblance to a stone :
Would I could rid me of my case,
And find a tenant for the place !
I'll make it known to all my kin ;—
This house to let—inquire within ! "
" Good ! " says the worm, " the bargain's strucl
I take it, and admire my luck !
That shell, from which you'd fain be free,
Is just the very thing for me.
Oft have I wished, when danger calls,
For such impervious [1] castle walls,
Both for defence and shelter made,
From greedy crow, and murderous spade :
Yes, neighbour snail, I'll hire the room,
And pay the rent when strawberries come."
" Do," says the snail, " and I'll declare
You'll find the place in good repair ;
With winding ways, that will not fail
To accommodate your length of tail."
(This fact the wily rogue concealing—
The fall had broken in his ceiling.)
" Oh," says the sanguine worm, " I knew
That I might safely deal with you ; "
Thus was the tenement transferred,
And that without another word.
    Off went the snail in houseless plight ;
Alas ! it proved a frosty night,
And ere a peep of morning light,
One wish supreme he found prevail ;
In all the world this foolish snail

---

[1] *Impervious*—that cannot be passed through.

Saw nothing he should like so well—
Which was—that he had got a shell.
But soon for this he ceased to sigh;
A little duck came waddling by,
Who, having but a youthful bill,
Had ventured not so large a pill,
(E'en at imperious hunger's call)
As this poor reptile, house and all;
But finding such a dainty bite
All ready to his appetite,
Down went the snail, whose last lament
Mourned his deserted tenement.
   Meantime the worm had spent his strength
In vain attempts to curl his length
His small apartment's space about,
For head or tail must needs stick out.
Now, if this last was left, 'twas more
Exposed to danger than before,
And " 'twould be vastly strange," he said,
" To sit in-doors without one's head."—
Alas ! he now completely bears
The unknown weight of household cares,
And wishes much some kind beholder
Would take the burden off his shoulder.
Now broke the dawn ; and soon with fear,
Feeling the shock of footsteps near,
He tried to reach that wished-for goal,
The shelter of a neighbouring hole,
Which proved, when danger threatened sore,
A certain refuge heretofore.
But failed him now this last resort ;
His new appendage stopped him short ;

For all his efforts would not do
To force it in, or drag it through.
Oh then, poor worm ! what words can say
How much he wished his shell away !
But wishes all were vain, for oh !
The garden roller, dreaded foe,
Came growling by, and did not fail
To crush our hero head and tail,
—Just when the duck devoured the snail.

Thus says the fable :—"Learn from hence
It argues want of common sense
To think our trials and our labours
Harder and heavier than our neighbours';
Or that 'twould lighten toils and cares,
To give them ours in change for theirs :
For whether man's appointed lot
Be really equalized or not,
(A point we need not now discuss,)
Habit makes ours the best to us."

Jane T

THE INNOCENT THIEF.

FROM THE LATIN OF VINCENT BOURNE.

NOT a flower can be found in the fields,
    Or the spot that we till for our pleasure
From the largest to least, but it yields
    The bee, never wearied, a treasure.

Scarce any she quits unexplored,
    With a diligence truly exact ;
Yet steal what she may for her hoard,
    Leaves evidence none of the fact.

Her lucrative task she pursues,
    And pilfers with so much address,
That none of their odour they lose,
    Nor charm by their beauty the less.

Not thus inoffensively preys
    The canker-worm, indwelling foe !
His voracity not thus allays
    The sparrow, the finch, or the crow.

The worm, more expensively fed,
    The pride of the garden devours :
And birds peck the seed from the bed,
    Still less to be spared than the flowers.

But she, with such delicate skill,
    Her pillage so fits for her use,
That a chemist in vain with his still [1]
    Would labour the like to produce.

Then grudge not her temperate meals,
    Nor a benefit blame as a theft,
Since, stole she not [2] all that she steals,
    Neither honey nor wax would be left.

                             Cowper.

GOOD NIGHT AND GOOD MORNING.

A FAIR little girl sat under a tree,
Sewing as long as her eyes could see ;
Then smoothed her work, and folded it right,
And said, " Dear work ! Good night ! Good night ! "

---

[1] *Still*—a vessel used in distillation, or the process of extracting the spirit from liquids.

[2] *Stole she not*—if she did not steal.

Q

Such a number of rooks came over her head,
Crying " Caw ! caw ! " on their way to bed ;
She said, as she watched their curious flight,
" Little black things ! Good night ! Good night ! "

The horses neighed and the oxen lowed ;
The sheeps' " Bleat ! bleat ! " came over the road ;
All seeming to say, with a quiet delight,
" Good little girl ! Good night ! Good night ! "

She did not say to the sun " Good night ! "
Though she saw him there, like a ball of light ;
For she knew that he had God's time to keep
All over the world, and never could sleep.

The tall pink foxglove bowed his head ;
The violets curtsied, and went to bed ;
And good little Lucy tied up her hair,
And said, on her knees, her favourite prayer.

And while on her pillow she softly lay,
She knew nothing more till again it was day ;
And all things said to the beautiful sun,
" Good morning ! Good morning ; our work is
    begun ! "

Lord Houghton.

QUESTIONS TO BIRDS AND THEIR ANSWERS.

CUCKOO.

WHY art thou always welcome, lonely bird ?
—" The heart grows young again when I am heard ;
Not in my double note the magic lies,
But in the fields, the woods, the streams and skies."

KINGFISHER.

Why dost thou hide thy beauty from the sun ?
—" The eye of men, but not of heaven, I shun ;
Beneath the rushy bank, with alders crowned,
I build and brood where running waters sound ;
There, there the halcyon [1] peace may still be found."

PHEASANT.

Pheasant, forsake the country ; come to town !
I'll warrant thee a place beneath the crown.
—" No ; not to roost upon the throne would I
Renounce the woods, the mountains, and the sky."

STORK.

Stork, why were human virtues given to thee ?
—" That human beings might resemble me ;
Kind to my offspring, to my partner true,
And duteous to my parents—what are you ? "
                                    Montgomery.

THE COTTAGER AND HIS LANDLORD.

FROM THE LATIN OF MILTON.

A PEASANT to his lord paid yearly court,
Presenting pippins of so rich a sort,
That he, displeased to have a part alone,
Removed the tree, that all might be his own.
The tree, too old to travel, though before
So fruitful, withered, and would yield no more.

[1] *Halcyon*—the Greek name for the Kingfisher. The word
generally means, as in this place, quiet and placid, from the
retiring *and peaceful habits* of the bird.

The squire, perceiving all his labour void,
Cursed his own pains, so foolishly employed;
And, " Oh ! " he cried, " that I.had lived cor
With tribute, small indeed, but kindly mean
My avarice has expensive proved to me,
And cost me both my pippins and my tree."

Co

THE PARROT.

THE deep affections of the breast,
 That Heaven to living things imparts,
Are not exclusively possessed
 . By human hearts.

A Parrot, from the Spanish main,
 Full young, and early caged, came o'er,
With bright wings, to the bleak domain
 Of Mulla's ¹ shore.

To spicy groves, where he had won
 His plumage of resplendent hue,
His native fruits, and skies, and sun,
 He bade adieu.

For these he changed the smoke of turf,
 A heathery land and misty sky,
And turned on rocks and raging surf
 His golden eye.

But, petted, in our climate cold
 He lived and chattered many a day ;
Until with age, from green and gold,
 His wings grew grey.

¹ *Mulla*—the island of Mull, one of the Hebrides, si
in the north-west of Scotland.

At last, when blind and seeming dumb,
  He scolded, laughed, and spoke no more,
A Spanish stranger chanced to come
  To Mulla's shore;

He hailed the bird in Spanish speech,
  The bird in Spanish speech replied,
Flapped round his cage with joyous screech,
  Dropt down, and died.

Campbell.

A FAIRY'S SONG.[1]

COME, follow, follow me,
Ye fairy elves that be ;
Light tripping o'er the green,
Come follow Mab, your queen !
Hand in hand we'll dance around,
For this place is fairy ground.

When mortals are at rest,
And snoring in their nest
Unheard and unespied
Through key-holes we do glide ;
Over tables, stools, and shelves,
We trip it with our fairy elves.

And if the house is swept,
And from uncleanness kept,
We praise the household maid,
And duly she is paid;

[1] This song, which is taken, with little alteration, from Percy's *Reliques*, appears to have been first published in the year *1658.*

For every night before we go,
We drop a tester[1] in her shoe.

Then o'er the mushroom's head
Our table-cloth we spread;
A grain of rye or wheat,
The manchet[2] that we eat;
Pearly drops of dew we drink
In acorn-cups filled to the brink.

The grasshopper, gnat, and fly
Serve for our minstrelsy;
Grace said, we dance awhile,
And so the time beguile;
And if the moon doth hide her head,
The glow-worm lights us home to bed.

O'er tops of dewy grass ·
So nimbly do we pass,
The young and tender stalk
Ne'er bends where we do walk;
Yet in the morning may be seen
Where we the night before have been,

AN ITALIAN SONG.

DEAR is my little native vale;
    The ring-dove builds and murmurs there :
Close by my cot she tells her tale
    To every passing villager.
The squirrel leaps from tree to tree,
And shells his nuts at liberty.

[1] *Tester*—a sixpence.
[2] *Manchet*—a small white loaf—food.

In orange groves and myrtle bowers,
   That breathe a gale of fragrance round,
I charm the fairy-footed hours
   With my loved lute's romantic sound;
Or crowns of living laurel weave
For those that win the race at eve.

The shepherd's horn at break of day,
   The ballet danced in twilight glade,
The canzonet [1] and roundelay
   Sung in the silent greenwood shade;
These simple joys that never fail,
Shall bind me to my native vale.
                      Rogers.

THE DOG OF ST. BERNARD'S.

THEY tell that on St. Bernard's [2] mount.
   Where holy monks abide,
Still mindful of misfortune's claim,
   Though dead to all beside;

The weary, way-worn traveller
   Oft sinks beneath the snow;
For, where his faltering steps to bend
   No track is left to show.

'Twas here, bewildered and alone,
   A stranger roamed at night;

[1] *Canzonet*—a little song, sometimes sung in parts.
[2] *St. Bernard's*—a lofty mountain, one of the Alps, in Switzerland, on the summit of which is a monastery, whose inmates are accustomed to give hospitable shelter to the weary traveller.

His heart was heavy as his tread,
　His scrip alone was light.

Onward he pressed, yet many an hour
　He had not tasted food;
And many an hour he had not known
　Which way his footsteps trod;

And if the convent's bell had rung
　To hail the pilgrim near,
It still had rung in vain for him—
　He was too far to hear;

And should the morning light disclose
　Its towers amid the snow,
To him 'twould be a mournful sight—
　He had not strength to go.

Valour could arm no mortal man
　That night to meet the storm—
No glow of pity could have kept
　A human bosom warm.

But obedience to a master's will
　Had taught the Dog[1] to roam,
And through the terrors of the waste,
　To fetch the wanderer home.

And if it be too much to say
　That pity gave him speed,
'Tis sure he not unwillingly
　Performed the generous deed.

[1] The hospitable monks keep a number of wild-lookin
sagacious dogs, which they send forth in stormy weath
rescue travellers.

For now he listens—and anon
 He scents the distant breeze,
And casts a keen and anxious look
 On every speck he sees.

And now deceived, he darts along,
 As if he trod the air—
Then disappointed, droops his head
 With more than human care.

He never loiters by the way,
 Nor lays him down to rest,
Nor seeks a refuge from the shower
 That pelts his generous breast.

And surely 'tis not less than joy
 That makes it throb so fast,
When he sees, extended on the snow,
 The wanderer found at last?

'Tis surely he—he saw him move,
 And at the joyful sight
He tossed his head with a prouder air,
 His fierce eye grew more bright;

Eager emotion swelled his breast
 To tell his generous tale—
And he raised his voice to its loudest tone
 To bid the wanderer hail.

The pilgrim heard—he raised his head,
 And beheld the shaggy form—
With sudden fear, he seized the gun
 That rested on his arm;

" Ha ! art thou come to rend alive
    What dead thou mightst devour ?
And does thy savage fury grudge
    My one remaining hour ! "

Fear gave him back his wasted strength,
    He took his aim too well—
The bullet bore the message home—
    The injured mastiff fell.

His eye was dimmed, his voice was still,
    And he tossed his head no more—
But his heart, though it ceased to throb with joy,
    Was generous as before !

For round his willing neck he bore
    A store of needful food,[1]
That might support the traveller's strength
    On the yet remaining road.

Enough of parting life remained
    His errand to fulfil—
One painful, dying effort more
    Might save the murderer still.

So he heeded not his aching wound,
    But crawled to the traveller's side,
Marked with a look the way he came,
    Then shuddered, groaned and died ! " [2]

                      Miss Fry.

[1] A bottle of wine and a loaf are tied round the necks of *these dogs* when they are sent forth.

[2] *It is* said that the traveller, tracing the dog's footsteps *in the* snow, reached the convent in safety.

SUMMER.

'Tis June—the merry, smiling June—
'Tis blushing summer now;
The rose is red, the bloom is dead,
The fruit is on the bough.

The bird-cage hangs upon the wall,
Amid the clustering vine;
The rustic seat is in the porch,
Where honeysuckles twine.

The rosy, ragged urchins play
Beneath the glowing sky;
They scoop the sand, or gaily chase
The bee that buzzes by.

The household spaniel flings his length
Beneath the sheltering wall;
The panting sheep-dog seeks the spot
Where leafy shadows fall.

The petted kitten frisks among
The bean-flowers' fragrant maze;
Or, basking, throws her dappled form
To catch the warmest rays.

The opened casements, flinging wide,
Geraniums give to view;
With choicest posies ranged between,
Still wet with morning dew.

The mower whistles o'er his toil,
The emerald grass must yield;
The scythe *is out*, the swath is down,
There's incense in the field.

Oh ! how I love to calmly muse,'
   In such an hour as this !
To nurse the joy creation gives,
   In purity and bliss.   *Eliza Cook.*

——— ◆◇◆ ———

MY HEART'S IN THE HIGHLANDS.

My heart's in the Highlands, my heart is not here;
My heart's in the Highlands a-chasing the deer,
Chasing the wild deer, and following the roe,
My heart's in the Highlands wherever I go.

Farewell to the Highlands, farewell to the north,
The birthplace of valour, the country of worth ;
Wherever I wander, wherever I rove,
The hills of the Highlands for ever I love.

Farewell to the mountains high covered with snow ;
Farewell to the straths [1] and green valleys below;
Farewell to the forests and wild-hanging woods;
Farewell to the torrents and loud-pouring floods.

My heart's in the Highlands, my heart is not here ;
My heart's in the Highlands, a-chasing the deer;
Chasing the wild deer, and following the roe,
My heart's in the Highlands wherever I go!
                                        Burns.

——— ◆◇◆ ———

INCIDENT,

CHARACTERISTIC OF A FAVOURITE DOG.

On his morning rounds, the master
   Goes to learn how all things fare;

[1] *Straths*—strath means generally a wide valley with a
large *river* running through it.

Searches pasture after pasture,
 Sheep and cattle eyes with care:
And for silence or for talk,
 He hath comrades in his walk;
Four dogs, each pair of different breed,
Distinguished two for scent, and two for speed.

See a hare before him started!
 Off they fly in earnest chase;
Every dog is eager-hearted;
 All the four are in the race:
And the hare whom they pursue
 Hath an instinct what to do;
Her hope is near; no turn she makes;
But, like an arrow, to the river takes.

Deep the river was, and crusted
 Thinly by a one night's frost,
But the nimble hare hath trusted
 To the ice, and safely crossed;
She hath crossed, and without heed
 All are following at full speed;
When lo! the ice, so thinly spread,
Breaks—and the greyhound, Dart, is over-head!

Better fate have Prince and Swallow—
 See them cleaving to the sport!
Music hath no heart to follow,
 Little Music she stops short,
She hath neither wish nor heart;
 Hers is now another part—
A loving creature she, and brave!
And fondly strives her struggling friend to save.

R

From the brink her paw she stretches,
　　Very hands, as you would say,
And afflicting moans she fetches
　　As he breaks the ice away.
For herself she hath no fears—
　　Him alone she sees and hears,
Makes efforts and complainings, nor gives o'er
Until her fellow sank, and re-appeared no more.
                                        Wordsworth.

THE STAR OF THE EAST.

BRIGHTEST and best of the sons of the morning !
　　Dawn on our darkness and lend us thine aid !
Star of the East, the horizon adorning,
　　Guide where our infant Redeemer is laid !

Cold on His cradle the dew-drops are shining,
　　Low lies His head with the beasts of the stall ;
Angels adore Him in slumber reclining,
　　Maker and Monarch and Saviour of all !

Say, shall we yield Him, in costly devotion,
　　Odours of Edom and offerings divine ?
Gems of the mountains and pearls of the ocean,
　　Myrrh from the forest or gold from the mine ?

Vainly we offer each ample oblation :
　　Vainly with gifts would His favour secure :
Richer by far is the heart's adoration ;
　　Dearer to God are the prayers of the poor.

Brightest and best of the sons of the morning !
Dawn on our darkness and lend us thine aid !

Star of the East, the horizon adorning,
Guide where our infant Redeemer is laid !
Heber.

THE TRAVELLER IN AFRICA.[1]

A NEGRO SONG.

THE loud wind roared, the rain fell fast,
The white man yielded to the blast;
He sat him down beneath our tree,
For weary, sad, and faint was he :
And, ah ! no wife nor mother's care
For him the milk and corn prepare.

CHORUS.

The white man shall our pity share;
Alas ! no wife nor mother's care
For him the milk and corn prepare.

The storm is o'er, the tempest past,
And mercy's voice has hushed the blast;
The wind is heard in whispers low,
The white man far away must go :
But ever in his heart will bear
Remembrance of the negro's care.

CHORUS.

Go ! white man, go ! but with thee bear
The negro's wish, the negro's prayer,
Remembrance of the negro's care.
Duchess of Devon.

[1] These lines were suggested by an affecting incident told
in *the travels of Mungo* Park in Africa.

LINES WRITTEN IN MARCH.

THE cock is crowing,
The stream is flowing,
The small birds twitter,
The lake doth glitter,
The green field sleeps in the sun :
The oldest and youngest
Are at work with the strongest ;
The cattle are grazing,
Their heads never raising—
There are forty feeding like one !

Like an army defeated
The snow hath retreated,
And now doth fare ill,
On the top of the bare hill.
The plough-boy is whooping—anon—anon :
There's joy in the mountains,
There's life in the fountains ;
Small clouds are sailing,
Blue sky prevailing ;
The rain is over and gone !

Wordsworth.

THE HAREBELL AND THE FOXGLOVE.

IN a valley obscure, on a bank of green shade,
A sweet little Harebell her dwelling had made :
Her roof was a woodbine, that tastefully spread
Its close-woven tendrils, o'er-arching her head ;
Her bed was of moss, that each morning made new ;
She dined on a sunbeam, and supped on the dew ;

Her neighbour, the Nightingale, sung her to rest,
And care had ne'er planted a thorn in her breast.

One morning she saw, on the opposite side,
A Foxglove displaying his colours of pride;
She gazed on his form, that in stateliness grew,
And envied his height and his beautiful hue;
She marked how the flowerets all gave way before
him,
While they pressed round her dwelling with far
less decorum.
Dissatisfied, jealous, and peevish she grows,
And the sight of this Foxglove destroys her repose;
She tires of her vesture, and, swelling with spleen,
Cries, " Ne'er such a dowdy blue mantle was seen ! "
Nor keeps to herself any longer her pain,
But thus to a Primrose begins to complain :
" I envy your mood, that can patient abide
The respect paid that Foxglove, his airs and his
pride:
There you sit, still the same, with your colourless
cheek;
But you have no spirit—would I were as meek ! "

The Primrose, good-humoured, replied, " If you
knew
More about him—(remember I'm older than you,
And, better instructed, can tell you his tale)—
You would envy him least of all flowers in this vale;
With all his fine airs and his dazzling show,
No flower more baneful and odious can blow;
And the reason the others before him gave way,
Is because *they all hate* him, and shrink from his
sway.

To stay near him long would be fading or death,
For he scatters a pest with his venomous breath ;
While the flowers that you fancy are crowding you
    there,
Spring round you delighted your converse to share ;
His flame-coloured robe is imposing, 'tis true ;
Yet who likes it so well as your mantle of blue ?
For we know that of innocence one is the vest,
The other the cloak of a treacherous breast.
I see your surprise—but I know him full well,
And have numbered his victims as fading they fell ;
He blighted twin violets that under him lay,
And poisoned a sister of mine the same day."

The Primrose was silent ; the Harebell, 'tis said,
Inclined for a moment her beautiful head,
But quickly recovered her spirits, and then
Declared that she ne'er would feel envy again.

THE DAWNING DAY.

So here hath been dawning
    Another blue day :
Think, wilt thou let it
    Slip useless away ?

Out of Eternity
    This new day is born ;
Into Eternity
    At night doth return.

Behold it aforetime
    No eyes ever did :
So soon it for ever
    From all eyes is hid.

Here hath been dawning
Another blue day :
Think, wilt thou let it
Slip useless away ?

Carlyle.

———◦◦———

THE CICADA [1] OR TREEHOPPER.

. FROM THE GREEK OF ANACREON.

HAPPY insect ! what can be
In happiness compared to thee?
Fed with nourishment divine,
The dewy morning's gentle wine ;
Nature waits upon thee still,
And thy verdant cup does fill.
Thou dost drink, and dance, and sing
Happier than the happiest king !
All the fields which thou dost see,
All the plants belong to thee ;
All that summer hours produce,
Fertile made with early juice ;
Man for thee does sow and plough,
Farmer he, and landlord thou !
Thou dost innocently enjoy,
Nor does thy luxury destroy ;
Thee country hinds with gladness hear,
Prophet of the ripened year !
To thee, of all things upon earth,
Life is no longer than thy mirth,
Happy insect ! happy thou
Dost neither age nor winter know ;

[1] *The cicada is* sometimes confounded with the grass-
pper, to which family, however, it does not belong.

But when thou'st drunk, and danced and sung
Thy fill, the flowery leaves among,
Sated with the summer feast
Thou retirest to endless rest.

Cowley.

———•◦•———

THE CRICKET.

FROM THE LATIN OF VINCENT BOURNE.

LITTLE inmate, full of mirth,
Chirping on my kitchen hearth,
Wheresoe'er be thine abode,
Always harbinger of good:[1]
Pay me for thy warm retreat
With a song more soft and sweet;
In return thou shalt receive
Such a strain as I can give.

Thus thy praise shall be expressed,
Inoffensive, welcome guest!
While the rat is on the scout,
And the mouse with curious snout,
With what vermin else[2] infest
Every dish and spoil the best;
Frisking thus before the fire
Thou hast all thy heart's desire.

Though in voice and shape they be
Formed as if akin to thee,

[1] The cricket, being attracted by the warmth and comfort
of the hearth, is to be regarded rather as the attendant than
the harbinger of plenty and abundance.
[2] *With what vermin else*—and other vermin besides.

Thou surpassest, happier far,
Happiest grasshoppers [1] that are ;
Theirs is but a summer song,
Thine endures the winter long,
Unimpaired, and shrill and clear
Melody throughout the year.   *Cowper.*

THE LOCUST.

THE locust is fierce, and strong, and grim,
And an armed man is afraid of him :
He comes like a winged shape of dread,
With his shielded back and his armed head,
And his double wings for hasty flight,
And a keen, unwearying appetite.

He comes with famine and fear along,
An army a million million strong ;
The Goth and the Vandal, and dwarfish Hun,[2]
With their swarming people, wild and dun,
Brought not the dread that the locust brings,
When is heard the rush of their myriad wings.

From the deserts of burning sand they speed,
Where the lions roam and the serpents breed, ·
Far over the sea, away, away !
And they darken the sun at noon of day.

[1] In allusion to the insect which is the subject of the preceding poem.
[2] *Goths, Vandals, and Huns*—barbarian nations of the north, celebrated in history as the invaders, and at last the destroyers, of the *Roman* empire.

Like Eden the land before them they find,
But they leave it a desolate waste behind.[1]

The peasant grows pale when he sees them come,
And standeth before them weak and dumb;
For they come like a raging fire in power,
And eat up a harvest in half an hour;
And the trees are bare, and the land is brown,
As if trampled and trod by an army down.

There is terror in every monarch's eye,
When he hears that this terrible foe is nigh;
For he knows that the might of an armed host
Cannot drive the spoiler from out his coast,
That terror and famine his land await,
And from north to south 'twill be desolate.

Thus, the ravening locust is strong and grim;
And what were an armed man to him ?
Fire turneth him not, nor sea prevents,
He is stronger by far than the elements !

[1] The prophet Joel (ii. 3, 7, 8), referring to the invasion
of locusts, thus writes:—

A fire devoureth before them,
And behind them a flame burneth :
The land is as the Garden of Eden before them,
And behind them a desolate wilderness ;
Yea, and nothing shall escape them.

*   *   *   *   *

And they shall march every one on his way,
And they shall not break their ranks ;
Neither shall one thrust another ;
They shall walk every one in his path ;
And when they fall on the sword, they shall not be
wounded.

The broad green earth is his prostrate prey,
And he darkens the sun at the noon of day !
Mary Howitt.

----◦◦◦----

BRUCE AND THE SPIDER.

For Scotland's and for freedom's right,
   The Bruce his part had played,
In five successive fields of fight
   Been conquered and dismayed :
Once more against the English host
His band he led, and once more lost
   The meed for which he fought ;
And now from battle, faint and worn,
The homeless fugitive forlorn
   A hut's lone shelter sought.

And cheerless was that resting place
   For him who claimed a throne :
His canopy, devoid of grace,
   The rude, rough beams alone ;
The heather couch his only bed—
   Yet well I ween [1] had slumber fled [2]
From couch of eider down !
Through darksome night till dawn of day,
Absorbed in wakeful thought he lay
   Of Scotland and her crown.

The sun rose brightly and its gleam
   Fell on that hapless bed,

----

[1] *Ween*—think or imagine.
[2] *Had slumber fled*—slumber would have fled.

And tinged with light each shapeless beam
　Which roofed the lowly shed;
When, looking up with wistful [1] eye,
The Bruce beheld a spider try
　His filmy thread to fling
From beam to beam of that rude cot;
And well the insect's toilsome lot
　Taught Scotland's future king.

Six times his gossamery [2] thread
　The wary spider threw;
In vain the filmy line was sped,
　For powerless or untrue
Each aim appeared, and back recoiled
The patient insect, six times foiled,
　And yet unconquered still;
And soon the Bruce, with eager eye,
Saw him prepare once more to try
　His courage, strength, and skill.

One effort more, his seventh and last!
　The hero hailed the sign!
And on the wished-for beam hung fast
　That slender, silken line;
Slight as it was, his spirit caught
The more than omen, for his thought
　The lesson well could trace,
Which even " he who runs may read,"
That Perseverance gains its meed,
　And Patience wins the race.

　　　　　　　　　　　Bernard Barton.

[1] *Wistful*—attentive, full of thought.
[2] *Gossamery*—light, flimsy.

THE FOUNTAIN.

INTO the sunshine,
  Full of the light,
Leaping and flashing
  From morn till night!—

Into the moonlight,
  Whiter than snow,
Waving so flower-like
  When the winds blow!—

Into the starlight
  Rushing in spray,
Happy at midnight,
  Happy by day!—

Ever in motion,
  Blithesome and cheery,
Still climbing heavenward,
  Never a-weary;—

Glad of all weathers,
  Still seeming best,
Upward or downward,
  Motion thy rest;—

Full of a nature
  Nothing can tame,
Changed every moment,
  Ever the same;—

Ceaseless aspiring,
  Ceaseless content,
Darkness or sunshine
  Thy element:—

s

Glorious fountain !
Let my heart be
Fresh, changeful, constant,
Upward, like thee !

Lowell.

TO' A SPANIEL ON HIS KILLING. A BIRD.

A SPANIEL, Beau, that fares like you,
  Well fed, and at his ease,
Should wiser be than to pursue
  Each trifle that he sees.

But you have killed a tiny bird,
  Which flew not till to-day,
Against my orders, whom you heard
  Forbidding you the prey.

Nor did you kill that you might eat,
  And ease a doggish pain,
For him, though chased with furious heat,
  You left where he was slain.

Nor was he of the thievish sort,
  Or one whom blood allures,
But innocent was all his sport
  Whom you have torn for yours.

My dog ! what remedy remains,
  Since, teach you all I can,
I see you after all my pains,
  So much resemble man?

Sir, when I flew to seize the bird
   In spite of your command,
A louder voice than yours I heard,
   And harder to withstand.

You cried—forbear !—but in my breast
   A mightier cried—proceed !
'Twas Nature, Sir, whose strong behest
   Impelled me to the deed.

Yet, much as Nature I respect,
   I ventured once to break
(As you, perhaps, may recollect)
   Her precept for your sake ;

And when your linnet, on a day,
   Passing his prison door,
Had fluttered all his strength away,
   And, panting, pressed the floor ;

Well knowing him a sacred thing,
   Not destined to my tooth,
I only kissed his ruffled wing,
   And licked his feathers smooth.

Let my obedience then excuse
   My disobedience now,
Nor some reproof yourself refuse
   From your aggrieved bow-wow ;

If killing birds be such a crime
   (Which I can hardly see),
What think you, Sir, of killing time
   With verse addressed to me ?   Cowper.

INDIA.

Where sacred Ganges pours along the plain,
And Indus rolls to swell the eastern main,
What awful scenes the curious mind delight,
What wonders burst upon the dazzled sight !
There giant palms lift high their tufted heads,
The plantain wide his graceful foliage spreads,
Wild in the woods the active monkey springs,
The chattering parrot claps his painted wings ;
'Mid tall bamboos lies hid the deadly snake,
The tiger couches in the tangled brake ;
The spotted axis bounds in fear away,
The leopard darts on his defenceless prey.
'Mid reedy pools and ancient forests rude,
Cool peaceful haunts of awful solitude !
The huge rhinoceros rends the crashing boughs,
And stately elephants untroubled browse.
Two tyrant seasons rule the wide domain,
Scorch with dry heat, or drench with floods of rain :
Now, feverish herds rush madding o'er the plains,
And cool in shady streams their throbbing veins;
The birds drop lifeless from the silent spray,
And nature faints beneath the fiery day ;
Then bursts the deluge on the sinking shore,
And teeming plenty empties all her store.   *Aikin.*

TO THE BLACKBIRD.
IN THE MORNING.[1]

Golden Bill ! Golden Bill !
Lo ! the peep of day ;

[1] The Blackbird's is the earliest note heard in the morning. In the evening he takes his part with his minstrel brethren, chiming in at intervals.

All the air is cool and still,
From the elm-tree on the hill
    Chant away;
While the moon drops down the west,
And the stars before the sun
Melt, like snow-flakes, one by one,
Ere the lark has left his nest,
Let thy loud and welcome lay
    Pour along
    Few notes, but strong.

IN THE EVENING.

Jet-bright wing! Jet-bright wing!
Flit across the sunset glade,
Lying there in wait to sing;
Listen, with thine head awry,
Keeping time with twinkling eye,
While from all the woodland shade,
Birds of every plume and note
    Strain the throat,
Till both hill and valley ring;
And the warbled minstrelsy
Ebbing, flowing, like the sea,
Claims brief interludes from thee;
Then, with simple swell and fall,
Breaking beautiful through all,
Let thy pure, clear pipe repeat
Few notes, but sweet.   *Montgomery.*

THE PEARL.

LITTLE particle of rain,
That from a passing cloud descended,
s 2

Was heard thus idly to complain :—
" My brief existence now is ended ;
Outcast alike of earth and sky,
Useless to live, unknown to die."

It chanced to fall into the sea—
    And there an open shell received it ;—
And, after years, how rich was he
    Who from its prison-house relieved it !
That drop of rain had formed a gem,
Fit for a monarch's diadem.

S. C. Hall.

THE FLY.

Prithee,[1] little buzzing fly,
Eddying round my taper, why
Is it that its quivering light,
Dazzling, captivates your sight ?
Bright my taper is, 'tis true,
Trust me, 'tis too bright for you ;
'Tis a flame—vain thing, beware !
'Tis a flame you cannot bear.

Touch it, and 'tis instant fate ;
Take my counsel ere too late :
Buzz no longer round and round,
Settle on the wall or ground :
Sleep till morn ; at daybreak rise ;
Danger then you may despise,
Enjoying in the sunny air
The life your caution now may spare.

[1] *Prithee*—I pray thee.

Lo ! my counsel nought avails ;
Round and round and round it sails,
Sails with idle unconcern—
Prithee, trifler, *canst* thou burn ?
Madly heedless as thou art,
Know thy danger, and depart :
Why persist ?—I plead in vain,
Singed it falls and writhes in pain.

Is not this—deny who can—
Is not this a type of man ?
Like the fly, he rashly tries
Pleasure's burning sphere, and dies.
Vain the friendly caution, still
He rebels, alas ! and will.
What I sing let all apply ;
Flies are weak, and *man's* a fly.

Bruce.

THE SWALLOW AND RED-BREAST.

THE swallows, at the close of day,
When autumn shone with fainter ray,
Around the chimney circling flew,
Ere yet they bade a long adieu
To climes, where soon the winter drear
Should close the unrejoicing year.
Now with swift wing they skim aloof,
Now settle on the crowded roof,
As counsel and advice to take,
Ere they the chilly north forsake ;—
Then *one, disdainful,* turned his eye
Upon a red-breast twittering nigh,

And thus began with taunting scorn :—
" Thou household imp, obscure, forlorn,
Through the deep winter's dreary day,
Here, dull and shivering, shalt thou stay,
Whilst we, who make the world our home,
To softer climes impatient roam,
Where summer still on some green isle
Rests, with her sweet and lovely smile.
Thus, speeding far and far away,
We leave behind the shortening day."

" 'Tis true," the red-breast answered meek,
" No other scenes I ask, or seek ;
To every change alike resigned,
I fear not the cold winter's wind.
When spring returns, the circling year
Shall find me still contented here ;
But whilst my warm affections rest
Within the circle of my nest,
I learn to pity those that roam,
And love the more my humble home."

W. L. Bowles.

"MY FATHER'S AT THE HELM."

THE curling waves, with awful roar,
  A little boat assailed ;
And pallid fear's distracting power
  O'er all on board prevailed—

Save one, the captain's darling child,
  Who steadfast viewed the storm ;
And cheerful, with composure, smiled
  At danger's threatening form.

" And sport'st thou thus," a seaman cried,
  " While terrors overwhelm ? "
" Why should I fear ? " the boy replied;
  " My father's at the helm ! "

So when our worldly all is reft—
  Our earthly helper gone,
We still have one true anchor left—
  God helps, and He alone.

He to our prayers will bend an ear,
  He gives our pangs relief;
He turns to smiles each trembling tear,
  To joy each torturing grief.

Then turn to Him, 'mid sorrows wild,
  When want and woes o'erwhelm;
Remembering, like the fearless child,
  Our Father's at the helm.

———◦◦◦———

THE UNREGARDED TOILS OF THE POOR.

Alas ! what secret tears are shed,
  What wounded spirits bleed ;
What loving hearts are sundered,
  And yet man takes no heed !

He goeth in his daily course,
  Made fat with oil and wine,
And pitieth not the weary souls
  That in his bondage pine,
That turn for him the mazy wheel,
  That delve [1] for him the mine\

  [1] *Delve*—dig.

And pitieth not the children small
　　In noisy factories dim,
That all day long, lean, pale, and faint,
　　Do heavy tasks for him !

To him they are but as the stones
　　Beneath his feet that lie :
It entereth not his thoughts that they
　　From him claim sympathy :
It entereth not his thoughts that God
　　Heareth the sufferer's groan,
That in His righteous eye, their life
　　Is precious as his own.
　　　　　　　　　　　　　Mary Howitt.

THE DIVERTING HISTORY OF JOHN GILPIN.

SHOWING HOW HE WENT FURTHER THAN HE INTENDED, AND CAME SAFE HOME AGAIN.

JOHN GILPIN was a citizen
　　Of credit and renown ;
A train-band [1] captain eke [2] was he
　　Of famous London town.

John Gilpin's spouse said to her dear,
　　" Though wedded we have been
These twice ten tedious years, yet we
　　No holiday have seen.

---

[1] *Train-band*—a company of men, not soldiers by profession, trained to martial exercise in times of emergency.
[2] *Eke*—also.

" To-morrow is our wedding-day,
    And we will then repair
Unto the Bell at Edmonton,[1]
    All in a chaise and pair.

" My sister, and my sister's child,
    Myself, and children three,
Will fill the chaise, so you must ride
    On horseback *after we*."

He soon replied, " I do admire
    Of womankind but one ;
And you are she, my dearest dear,
    Therefore it shall be done.

" I am a linen-draper bold,
    As all the world doth know ;
And my good friend, the calender,[2]
    Will lend his horse to go."

Quoth [3] Mistress Gilpin, " That's well said ;
    And for that [4] wine is dear,
We will be furnished with our own,
    Which is both bright and clear."

John Gilpin kissed his loving wife ;
    O'erjoyed was he to find,
That, though on pleasure she was bent,
    She had a frugal mind.

[1] *Edmonton*—a village in the northern suburbs of London.
[2] *Calender*—put for calenderer—one whose trade it is to give cloth a smooth and glossy surface.
[3] *Quoth*—says, or said.
[4] *For that*—because.

The morning came, the chaise was brought,
But yet was not allowed
To drive up to the door, lest all
Should say that she was proud.

So three doors off the chaise was stayed,
Where they did all get in ;
Six precious souls, and all agog [1]
To dash through thick and thin.

Smack went the whip, round went the wheels,
Were never folks so glad ;
The stones did rattle underneath,
As if Cheapside were mad.

John Gilpin, at his horse's side,
Seized fast the flowing mane,
And up he got in haste to ride,
But soon came down again ;

For saddle-tree scarce reached had he
His journey to begin,
When, turning round his head, he saw
Three customers come in.

So down he came ; for loss of time,
Although it grieved him sore,
Yet loss of pence, full well he knew,
Would trouble him much more.

'Twas long before the customers
Were suited to their mind,
When Betty, screaming, came down stairs,—
" *The wine* is left behind ! "

[1] *Agog*—in a state of desire.

" Good lack ! " quoth he ; " yet bring it me,
 My leathern belt likewise,
In which I bear my trusty sword
 When I do exercise ! " [1]

Now Mistress Gilpin—careful soul !—
 Had two stone bottles found,
To hold the liquor that she loved,
 And keep it safe and sound.

Each bottle had a curling ear,
 Through which the belt he drew ;
And hung a bottle on each side,
 To make his balance true.

Then over all, that he might be
 Equipped from top to toe,
His long red cloak, well brushed and neat,
 He manfully did throw.

Now see him mounted once again
 Upon his nimble steed,
Full slowly pacing o'er the stones,
 With caution and good heed.

But finding soon a smoother road
 Beneath his well-shod feet,
The snorting beast began to trot,
 Which galled him in his seat.

So, " Fair and softly ! " John he cried,
 But John he cried in vain ;
That trot became a gallop soon,
 In spite of curb and rein.

[1] *When I do exercise*—as captain of one of the train-
bands.

T

So stooping down, as needs he must
  Who cannot sit upright,
He grasped the mane with both his hands,
  And eke with all his might.

His horse, who never in that sort
  Had handled been before,
What thing upon his back had got
  Did wonder more and more.

Away went Gilpin, neck or nought;
  Away went hat and wig;
He little dreamt, when he set out,
  Of running such a rig.[1]

The wind did blow, the cloak did fly,
  Like streamer long and gay,
Till, loop and button failing both,
  At last it flew away.

Then might all people well discern
  The bottles he had slung;
A bottle swinging at each side,
  As hath been said or sung.

The dogs did bark, the children screamed,
  Up went the windows all,
And every soul cried out, " Well done ! "
  As loud as he could bawl.

Away went Gilpin—who but he ?
  His fame soon spread around,—

---

[1] *Running a rig*—an inelegant expression for getting
trouble.

" He carries weight ![1] he rides a race !
'Tis for a thousand pound ! "

And still, as fast as he drew near,
   'Twas wonderful to view,
How in a trice the turnpike-men
   Their gates wide open threw.

And now, as he went bowing down
   His reeking [2] head full low,
The bottles twain behind his back
   Were shattered at a blow.

Down ran the wine into the road,
   Most piteous to be seen,
Which made his horse's flanks to smoke
   As they had basted been.

But still he seemed to carry weight,
   With leathern girdle braced ;
For all might see the bottle necks
   Still dangling at his waist.

Thus all through merry Islington
   These gambols he did play ;
Until he came unto the Wash [3]
   Of Edmonton so gay ;

And there he threw the wash about
   On both sides of the way ;
Just like unto a trundling mop
   Or a wild goose at play.

[1] *He carries weight*—an expression used in horse-racing, when the rider carries something with him to make his weight on the horse equal to that of a heavier man.
[2] *Reeking*—smoking, steaming.
[3] *The Wash*—the horse-pond, lying partly in the road.

At Edmonton his loving wife
   From the balcony spied
Her tender husband, wondering much
   To see how he did ride.

" Stop, stop, John Gilpin ! Here's the hou
   They all at once did cry ;
" The dinner waits, and we are tired ! "
   Said Gilpin, " So am I."

But yet his horse was not a whit
   Inclined to tarry there ;
For why ?—his owner had a house,
   Full ten miles off, at Ware.

So like an arrow swift he flew,
   Shot by an archer strong ;
So did he fly—which brings me to
   The middle of my song.

Away went Gilpin, out of breath,
   And sore against his will ;
Till, at his friend the calender's
   His horse at last stood still.

The calender, amazed to see,
   His neighbour in such trim,
Laid down his pipe, flew to the gate,
   And thus accosted him :—

" What news ? what news ? your tidings
   Tell me you must, and shall—
Say why bare-headed you are come,
   Or why you come at all ? "

Now Gilpin had a pleasant wit
  And loved a timely [1] joke ;
And thus unto the calender,
  In merry guise,[2] he spoke :—

" I came because your horse would come ;
  And, if I well forebode,
My hat and wig will soon be here;
  They are upon the road."

The calender, right glad to find
  His friend in merry pin,[3]
Returned him not a single word,
  But to the house went in :

Whence straight he came with hat and wig,
  A wig that flowed behind,
A hat not much the worse for wear,
  Each comely in its kind.

He held them up, and in his turn
  Thus showed his ready wit,—
" My head is twice as big as yours,
  They therefore needs must fit.

" But let me scrape the dirt away
  That hangs upon your face ;
And stop and eat, for well you may
  Be in a hungry case."

Said John, " It is my wedding-day,
  And all the world would stare,

[1] *Timely*—at the right time, seasonable.
[2] *Guise*—manner, mood.
[3] *Pin*—mood, humour.
[4] *Case*—condition, state.

If wife should dine at Edmonton,
  And I should dine at Ware."

So turning to his horse, he said,
  " I am in haste to dine ;
'Twas for your pleasure you came here,
  You shall go back for mine."

Ah ! luckless speech, and bootless [1] boast
  For which he paid full dear ;
For, while he spoke, a braying ass
  Did sing most loud and clear ;

Whereat his horse did snort, as he
  Had heard a lion roar,
And galloped off with all his might,
  As he had done before.

Away went Gilpin, and away
  Went Gilpin's hat and wig ;
He lost them sooner than at first,
  For why ?—they were too big.

Now Mistress Gilpin, when she saw
  Her husband posting down
Into the country far away,
  She pulled out half-a-crown ;

And thus unto the youth she said
  That drove them to the Bell—
" This shall be yours, when you bring bacl
  My husband safe and well."

The youth did ride, and soon did meet
  John coming back amain,[2]

    [1] *Bootless*—useless, unavailing.
    [2] *Amain*—with vehemence, vigorously.

Whom in a trice he tried to stop,
  By catching at his rein;

But not performing what he meant,
  And gladly would have done;
The frighted steed he frighted more,
  And made him faster run.

Away went Gilpin, and away
  Went postboy at his heels,
The postboy's horse right glad to miss
  The rumbling of the wheels.

Six gentlemen upon the road,
  Thus seeing Gilpin fly,
With postboy scampering in the rear,
  They raised the hue-and-cry :—[1]

" Stop thief! stop thief!"—"a highwayman !"
  Not one of them was mute;
And all and each that passed that way
  Did join in the pursuit.

And now the turnpike gates again
  Flew open in short space;
The toll-men thinking as before,
  That Gilpin rode a race.

And so he did, and won it too,
  For he got first to town;
Nor stopped till where he had got up
  He did again get down.

---

[1] *Hue-and-cry*—properly, the term used in law to express *the pursuit of a thief,* or other delinquent.

Now let us sing, " Long live the king ! [1]
And Gilpin long live he ! "
And when he next doth ride abroad,
May I be there to see !

Cou

———◆◇◆———

A SONG OF SEVEN YEARS OLD.

THERE'S no dew left on the daisies and clover,
    There's no rain left in heaven :
I've said my " seven times " over and over ;
    Seven times one are seven.

I am old, so old, I can write a letter ;
    My birthday lessons are done ;
The lambs play always, they know no better ;
    They are only one times one.

O moon ! in the night I have seen you sailing
    And shining so round and low ;
You were bright ! ah, bright ! but your light is
        ing—
    You are nothing now but a bow.

You moon, have you done something wrong
        heaven,
    That God has hidden your face ?—
I hope if you have you will soon be forgiven,
    And shine again in your place.

O velvet bee, you're a dusty fellow,
    You've powdered your legs with gold !
O brave marsh marybuds, rich and yellow,
    Give me your money to hold !

    [1] This was written in George the Third's reign.

O columbine, open your folded wrapper,
  Where two twin turtle-doves dwell !
O cuckoopint, toll me the purple clapper
  That hangs in your clear green bell !
And show me your nest with the young ones in it ;
  I will not steal them away !
I am old ! you may trust me, linnet, linnet—
  I am seven times one to-day.

Jean Ingelow.

THE CAPTIVE SQUIRREL'S PETITION:

ADDRESSED TO THE LITTLE GIRL WHO KEPT HIM.

AH ! little maiden, do you love in the summer woods
    to rove,
When the gay lark's song is in the cloud, the black-
    bird's in the grove ;
When the cowslip hangs her golden bells like jewels
    in the grass,
And each cup sends forth a tender sound as your
    bounding footsteps pass ;
When the dew is on the willow-leaf and the sun
    looks o'er the hill,
And Nature's loveliness with joy your inmost soul
    can thrill—
If songs of birds and summer flowers e'er filled your
    heart with glee,
Oh ! think upon my hapless fate, and set your captive
    free !
A native of the dark green woods, my home is far
    away,
*Where gaily 'mid the giant oaks, my bright-eye
offspring play ;*

Their couch is lined with softest moss, within an
    tree;
The wind that sweeps the forest boughs is not
    blithe than we;
And oft beneath our nimble feet the old
    branches shake,
As lightly through the beechen groves our
    way we take;
The boundless forest was my home—how hard
    fate must be,
Confined within this narrow cage—oh! set
    captive free!

Oh! if you love the pleasant woods, when si
    reigns around,
When the mighty shadows calmly sleep, like g
    on the ground;
When the glow-worm sports her fairy lamp b
    the moonlit stream,
And the lofty trees in solemn state frown darkl
    the beam;
When the blossomed thorn flings out its sweets,
    the minstrel nightingale
Pours forth his lay, and echo tells to distant hill
    tale;
And the soft mists hang a crown of gems on e
    bush and tree;
Oh! if you love the beauteous sight, then set
    captive free!

Oh! think how hard your lot would be, in
    dark room confined,
Without a single friend to cheer the anguish of
    mind;

            [1] *Sear*—dry and withered.

Severed from every kindred tie, and left alone to
   weep
O'er perished joys, when every eye is closed in
   tranquil sleep!
The glorious sunbeams to your heart no cheering
   light would bring,
But heaviness and gloom would rest on every
   pleasant thing:
If freedom to your soul is dear, have pity then on
   me,
Unbar the narrow cage, and set your hapless
   prisoner free!

Susanna Strickland.

EPITAPH ON A TAME HARE.[1]

HERE lies whom hound did ne'er pursue,
   Nor swifter greyhound follow;
Whose foot ne'er tainted morning's dew.
   Nor ear heard huntsman's halloo;

Old Tiney, surliest of his kind,
   Who, nursed with tender care,
And to domestic bounds confined,
   Was still a wild Jack-hare.

Though duly from my hand he took
   His pittance every night,
He did it with a jealous look,
   And, when he could, would bite.

[1] Tiney and Puss were the names of two tame hares kept
many years by the poet Cowper:—on the death of Tiney he
wrote these lines as a memorial.

His diet was of wheaten bread,
  And milk, and oats, and straw,
Thistles, or lettuces instead,
  With sand to scour his maw.[1]

On twigs of hawthorn he regaled,
  Or pippin's russet peel ;
And when his juicy salads failed,
  Sliced carrots pleased him well.

A Turkey carpet was his lawn,
  Whereon he loved to bound,
To skip and gambol like a fawn,
  And swing his rump around.

His frisking was at evening hours,
  For then he lost his fear,
But most before approaching showers
  Or when a storm drew near.

Eight years and five round rolling m(
  He thus saw steal away ;
Dozing out all his idle noons,
  And every night at play.

I kept him for his humour's sake,
  For he would oft beguile
My heart of thoughts that made it ac]
  And force me to a smile.

But now beneath this walnut shade,
  He finds his long last home,
And waits, in snug concealment laid,
  Till gentler Puss shall come.

    [1] *Maw*—stomach.

She, still more aged, feels the shocks
From which no care can save;
And, partner once of Tiney's box,
Must soon partake his grave.
                                Cowper.

———◦◦◦———

THE REVEILLÉ.[1]

Up ! quit thy bower, late wears the hour,
Long have the rooks cawed round the tower;
O'er flower and tree loud hums the bee,
And the wild-kid sports merrily :—
The sun is bright, the skies are clear;
Wake, lady ! wake, and hasten here.

Up! maiden fair, and bind thy hair,
And rouse thee in the breezy air;
The lulling stream that soothed thy dream
Is dancing in the sunny beam;
Waste not these hours, so fresh, so gay,
Leave thy soft couch and haste away.

Up ! time will tell, the morning bell
Its service-sound[2] has chimed well;
The aged crone[3] keeps house alone,
The reapers to the fields are gone.
Lose not these hours, so cool, so gay,
Lo ! whilst thou sleep'st they haste away.
                                Miss Baillie.

[1] *Reveillé*—the notice that it is time to rise; properly
used as a military term.
[2] *Service-sound*—sound for matins, or morning prayers.
[3] *Crone*—an old woman.

U

GOOD NIGHT.

THE sun is down, the day gone by,
The stars are twinkling in the sky.
Nor torch nor taper longer may
Eke out[1] a blithe but stinted[2] day !
The hours have passed with stealthy flight;
We needs must part; good night, good night !

The lady in her curtained bed,
The herdsman in his wattled shed,[3]
The clansman[4] in the heathered hall,[5]
Sweet sleep be with you, one and all ;
We part in hopes of days as bright
As this gone by; good night, good night !

Sweet sleep be with us one and all !
And if upon its stillness fall
The visions of a busy brain,
We'll have our pleasure o'er again,
To warm the heart, to charm the sight !
Gay dreams to all ! good night ! good night !

Miss Baillie.

CONSTANTINOPLE.

WHERE the Thracian channel[6] roars
On lordly Europe's eastern shores,

[1] *Eke out*—lengthen.
[2] *Stinted*—limited—too short.
[3] *Wattled shed*—a shed, the walls of which are made of twigs and sticks twisted or woven together.
[4] *Clansman*—a member of a clan or family—here a dependent member, whose place is in the hall.
[5] *Heathered hall*—strewn with heath to lie on.
[6] *Thracian channel*—the Straits of Constantinople.

Where the proudly jutting land
Frowns on Asia's western strand,
High on seven hills is seen to shine
The second Rome of Constantine.
Beneath her feet, with graceful pride,
Propontis[1] spreads his ample tide;
His fertile banks profusely pour
Of luscious fruits a varied store;
Rich with a thousand glittering dyes,
His flood a finny shoal supplies;
While crowding sails on rapid wing
The rifled south's bright treasures bring.
With crescents gleaming to the skies,
Mosques and minarets[2] arise;
Mounted on whose topmost wall,
The turban'd priests to worship call.
The mournful cypress rises round,
Tapering from the burial-ground;
Olympus, ever capped with snow,
Crowns the busy scene below.

Miss Aikin.

SONG OF THE NORTH WIND.

I am here from the north, the frozen north,
'Tis a thousand leagues away!
And I left, as I came from my cavern forth,
The streaming lights[3] at play.

---

[1] *Propontis*—the Sea of Marmora.
[2] *Minarets*—high, slender turrets.
[3] *The streaming lights*—the northern lights, or aurora realis.

From the deep sea's verge to the zenith high,
   At one vast leap they flew,
And kindled a blaze in the midnight sky,
   O'er the glittering icebergs blue.

The frolicsome waves they shouted to me,
   As I swept their thousands past,
" Where are the chains that can fetter the sea? "—
   But I bound the boasters fast.

In their pride of strength, the pine trees tall
   Of my coming took no heed ;
But I bowed the proudest of them all,
   As if it had been a reed.

I found the tops of the mountains bare,
   And I gave them a crown of snow,
And roused the hungry wolf from his lair,
   To hunt the Esquimaux.

I saw where lay in the forest spent
   The fire of the embers white ;
And I breathed on the lordly element,
   And nursed it into might.

It floateth amain, my banner red,
   With a proud and lurid glare ;
And the fir-clad hills, as torches dread,
   Flame in the wintry air.

O'er valley and hill and mere[1] I range,
   And, as I sweep along,
Gather all sounds that are wild and strange,
   And mingle them in my song.

[1] *Mere*—a large lake.

My voice hath been uttered everywhere,
  And the sign of my presence seen ;
But the eye of man the form I wear
Hath never beheld, I ween !

KING COPHETUA AND THE BEGGAR MAID.

HER arms across her breast she laid ;
She was more fair than words can say ;
Barefooted came the beggar maid
Before the King Cophetua.
In robe and crown the king stepped down,
To meet and greet her on her way ;
" It is no wonder," said the lords,
" She is more beautiful than day."

As shines the moon in clouded skies,
She in her poor attire was seen:
One praised her ankles, one her eyes,
One her dark hair and lovesome mien.
So sweet a face, such angel grace,
In all that land had never been ;
Cophetua swore a royal oath :
" This beggar maid shall be my queen."

Tennyson.

THE AMBITIOUS WEED.

OR, THE DANGER OF SELF-CONFIDENCE.

AN idle weed that used to crawl
Unseen behind the garden wall,
  (Its *most* becoming station,)
At last, refreshed by sun and showers,

Which nourish weeds as well as flowers,
Amused its solitary hours
  With thoughts of elevation.

These thoughts encouraged day by day,
It shot forth many an upward spray,
  And many a tendril band ;
. But as it could not climb alone,
It uttered oft a lazy groan
To moss and mortar, stick and stone,
  To lend a helping hand.

At length, by friendly arms sustained,
The aspiring vegetable gained
  The object of its labours :
That which had cost her many a sigh,
And nothing else would satisfy—
Which was not only being *high*,
  But *higher* than her neighbours.

And now this weed, though weak, and spent
With climbing up the steep ascent,
  Admired her figure tall :
And then (for vanity ne'er ends
With that which it at first intends)
Began to laugh at those poor friends
  Who helped her up the wall.

But by and by my lady spied
The garden on the other side :
  And fallen was her crest,
To see, in neat array below,
A bed of all the flowers that blow—
Lily and rose—a goodly show,
  In fairest colours drest.

Recovering from her first surprise,
She soon began to criticise :—
" A dainty sight, indeed !
I'd be the meanest thing that blows
Rather than that affected rose ;
So much perfume offends my nose,"
Exclaimed the vulgar weed.

" Well, 'tis enough to make one chilly,
To see that pale consumptive Lily
Among these painted folks.
Miss Tulip, too, looks wondrous odd,
She's gaping like a dying cod ;—
What a queer stick is Golden-Rod !
And how the Violet pokes !

" Not for the gayest tint that lingers
On Honeysuckle's rosy fingers,
Would I with her exchange :
Since this, at least, is very clear,
Since they are there, and I am here
I occupy a higher sphere—
Enjoy a wider range."

Alas ! poor envious weed !—for lo,
That instant came the gardener's hoe
And lopped her from her sphere :
But none lamented when she fell ;
No passing Zephyr sighed, " Farewell ; "
No friendly bee would hum her knell ;
No fairy dropt a tear ;—

While those sweet flowers of genuine worth,
Inclining toward the modest earth,
Adorn the vale below ;

Content to hide in sylvan dells
Their rosy buds and purple bells ;
Though scarce a rising Zephyr tells
   The secret where they grow.
                  Jane Tt

THE GLORY OF GOD.

I PRAISED the earth, in beauty seen,
With garlands gay of various green ;
I praised the sea, whose ample field
Shone glorious as a silver shield :
But earth and ocean seemed to say,
" Our beauties are but for a day."

I praised the sun, whose chariot rolled
On wheels of amber and of gold ;
I praised the moon, whose softer eye
Smiled sweetly through the summer sky :
But moon and sun in answer said,
" Our days of light are numbered."

O God ! O good beyond compare,
If these thy meaner works are fair,
If these thy bounties gild the span
Of ruined earth and sinful man,
How glorious must those mansions be
Where thy redeemed ones dwell with thee.
                             L

A LULLABY.

SWEET and low, sweet and low,
Wind of the western Sea,

Low, low, breathe and blow,
  Wind of the western Sea !
Over the rolling waters go,
  Come from the dying moon, and blow,
Blow him again to me;
While my little one, while my pretty one, sleeps.

Sleep and rest, sleep and rest,
  Father will come to thee soon;
Rest, rest on mother's breast,
  Father will come to thee soon:
Father will come to his babe in the nest,
Silver sails all out of the west
  Under the silver moon:
Sleep, my little one, sleep, my pretty one, sleep.
Tennyson.

ST. PHILIP NERI [1] AND THE YOUTH.

St. Philip Neri, as old writers say,
Met a young stranger in Rome's streets one day :
And, being ever courteously inclined
To give young folks a sober turn of mind,
He fell into discourse with him; and thus
The dialogue they held comes down to us :—

St. P. N. Tell me what brings you, gentle youth,
    to Rome?
Youth. To make myself a scholar, sir, I come.
St. P. N. And, when you are one, what do you
    intend ?
Youth. To be a priest, I hope, sir, in the end.

[1] *St. Philip Neri*—an eminent Roman Catholic priest who
flourished in the 16th century.

St. P. N. Suppose it so—what have you next
    view ?
Youth. That I may get to be a canon, too.
St. P. N. Well : and how then ?
    Youth. Why then, for aught I k
I may be made a bishop.
    St. P. N. Be it so—
What then ?
    Youth. Why, Cardinal's a high degree,
And yet my lot it possibly may be.
St. P. N. Suppose it was—what then ?
    Youth. Why, who can say
But I've a chance of being Pope one day ?
St. P. N. Well, having worn the mitre and
    hat,
And triple crown, what follows after that ?
Youth. Nay, there is nothing further, to be s
Upon this earth, that wishing can procure :
When I've enjoyed a dignity so high
As long as God shall please, then—I must die.
St. P. N. What ? *must* you die ! fond youth,
    at the best
But *wish,* and *hope,* and *may be* all the rest ?
Take my advice—whatever may betide,
For that which must be, first of all provide,
Then think of that which may be : and, indee
When well prepared, who knows what
    succeed ?
But you may be, as you are pleased to hope,
Priest, canon, bishop, cardinal, and pope.
                        By

THE DOG AND THE WATER-LILY.

THE noon was shady, and soft airs
  Swept Ouse 's [1] silent tide,
When, 'scaped from literary cares,
  I wandered by its side.

My dog, now [2] lost in flags and reeds,
  Now starting into sight,
Pursued the swallow o'er the meads
  With scarce a slower flight.

It was the time when Ouse displayed
  Its lilies newly blown;
Their beauties I intent surveyed,
  And one I wished my own.

With cane extended far, I sought
  To steer it close to land!
But still the prize, though nearly caught,
  Escaped my eager hand.

Beau marked my unsuccessful pains
  With fixed, considerate face,
And puzzling set his puppy brains
  To comprehend the case.

But with a cherup clear and strong,
  Dispersing all his dream,
I thence withdrew, and followed long
  The windings of the stream.

My ramble ended, I returned;
  Beau, trotting far before,
The floating wreath again discerned,
  And plunging left the shore.

[1] *Ouse*—a river in Buckinghamshire.
[2] *Now lost, &c.*—the first *now* means at one time, the second, at another time.

I saw him with that lily cropt
  Impatient swim to meet
My quick approach, and soon he dropt
  The treasure at my feet.

Charmed with the sight—" The world,"]
" Shall hear of this thy deed :
My dog shall mortify the pride
  Of man's superior breed.

" But chief myself I will enjoin,
  Awake at duty's call,
To show a love as prompt as thine
  To Him who gives me all."

THE SOLDIER'S DREAM.

OUR bugles sang truce, for the night-clc
  lower'd,
  And the sentinel stars set their watch in t
And thousands had sunk on the ground, over
  The weary to sleep, and the wounded to (

When reposing that night on my pallet of st
  By the wolf-scaring fagot that guarded th
At the dead of the night a sweet vision I sav
  And thrice ere the morning I dreamt it ag

Methought, from the battle-field's dreadful a
  Far, far I had roamed on a desolate track
'Twas autumn—and sunshine arose on the w
  To the home of my fathers, that welcoi
  back.

I flew to the pleasant fields traversed so oft
In life's morning march, when my bosom was
young ;
I heard my own mountain-goats bleating aloft,
And knew the sweet strain that the corn-reapers
sung.

Then pledged we the wine-cup, and fondly I swore,
From my home and my weeping friends never to
part,
My little ones kissed me a thousand times o'er,
And my wife sobb'd aloud in her fulness of heart.

"Stay, stay with us,—rest, thou art weary and worn !"
And fain was their war-broken soldier to stay ;
But sorrow returned with the dawning of morn,
And the voice in my dreaming ear melted away.

Campbell.

———◆◇◆———

THE ARAB TO HIS FAVOURITE STEED.[1]

MY beautiful ! my beautiful ! that standest meekly
by,
With thy proudly arched and glossy neck, and dark
and fiery eye,
Fret not to roam the desert now, with all thy winged
speed,
I may not mount on thee again—thou'rt sold, my
Arab steed !
Fret not with that impatient hoof—snuff not the
breezy wind—
The farther that thou fliest now, so far am I be-
hind ;

———

[1] These lines represent the grief of an Arab, who had
been induced by poverty to sell his favourite horse.

X

The stranger hath thy bridle-rein—thy mas
   his gold—
Fleet-limbed and beautiful, farewell; thou'rt
   steed, thou'rt sold.

Farewell ! those free, untired limbs full man
   must roam,
To reach the chill and wintry sky which cl
   stranger's home ;
Some other hand, less fond, must now thy c
   bed prepare,
Thy silky mane, I braided once, must be a
   care !
The morning sun shall dawn again, but nev
   with thee
Shall I gallop through the desert paths, w
   were wont to be ;
Evening shall darken on the earth, and o'er th
   plain
Some other steed, with slower step, shall b
   home again.

Yes, thou must go ! the wild, free breeze, t
   liant sun and sky,
Thy master's house—from all of these my exi
   must fly ;
Thy proud dark eye will grow less proud, t
   become less fleet,
And vainly shalt thou arch thy neck, thy
   hand to meet.
Only in sleep shall I behold that dark eye, g
   bright ;—
Only in sleep shall hear again that step so fi
   light :

And when I raise my dreaming arm to check or
    cheer thy speed,
Then must I, starting, wake to feel,—thou'rt *sold*, my
    Arab steed!

Ah! rudely, then, unseen by me, some cruel hand
    may chide,
Till foam-wreaths lie, like crested waves, along thy
    panting side:
And the rich blood that's in thee ' swells, in thy
    indignant pain,
Till careless eyes, which rest on thee, may count
    each starting vein.
Will they ill-use thee? If I thought—but no, it
    cannot be—
Thou art so swift, yet easy curbed; so gentle, yet so free:
And yet, if haply, when thou'rt gone, my lonely heart
    should yearn—
Can the hand which cast thee from it now command
    thee to return?

Return! alas! my Arab steed! what shall thy
    master do,
When thou, who wast his all of joy, hast vanished
    from his view?
When the dim distance cheats mine eye, and through
    the gathering tears,
Thy bright form, for a moment, like the false mirage [1]
    appears;
Slow and unmounted shall I roam, with weary step
    alone,
Where with fleet step, and joyous bound, thou oft
    hast borne me on;

    [1] *Mirage*—a deception of the sight, by which objects or
the earth appear raised into the air.

And sitting down by that green well, I'll pause and
    sadly think,
" It was here he bowed his glossy neck when last I
    saw him drink ! "

When last I saw thee drink !—Away ! the fevered
    dream is o'er—
I could not live a day, and *know* that we should meet
    no more !
They tempted me, my beautiful !—for hunger's power
    is strong—
They tempted me, my beautiful !—but I have loved
    too long.
Who said that I had given thee up ? who said that
    thou wast sold ?
'Tis false—'tis false, my Arab steed ! I fling them
    back their gold !
Thus, *thus,* I leap upon thy back, and scour the
    distant plains ;
Away ! who overtakes us now shall claim thee for
    his pains !

                Mrs. Norton.

THE SILK-WORM.

FROM THE LATIN OF VINCENT BOURNE.

THE beams of April, ere it goes,
A worm, scarce visible, disclose ;
All winter long content to dwell
The tenant of his native shell.
The same prolific season gives
The sustenance by which he lives,

The mulberry-leaf, a simple store,
That serves him—till he needs no more !
For, his dimensions once complete,
Thenceforth none ever sees him eat;
Though, till his growing-time be past,
Scarce ever is he seen to fast.
That hour arrived, his work begins ;
He spins and weaves, and weaves and spins ;
Till circle upon circle wound
Careless around him and around,
Conceals him with a veil, though slight,
Impervious [1] to the keenest sight.
Thus self-enclosed, as in a cask,[2]
At length he finishes his task :
And, though a worm when he was lost,
Or caterpillar at the most,
When next we see him, wings he wears,
And in papilio [3] pomp appears ;
Becomes oviparous ; [4] supplies
With future worms and future flies
The next ensuing year !—and dies.

Well were it for the world, if all
Who creep about this earthly ball—
Though shorter-lived than most he be—
Were useful in their kind as he.

Cowper.

[1] *Impervious*—that cannot be passed through or pene-
trated.
[2] In allusion to the cocoon or web, in which the silk-worm
envelopes himself.
[3] *Papilio*—butterfly.
[4] *Oviparous*—bringing forth eggs.

A WISH.

MINE be a cot beside the hill ;
  A beehive's hum shall soothe my ear ;
A willowy brook, that turns the mill,
  With many a fall shall linger near.

The swallow oft beneath my thatch
  Shall twitter from her clay-built nest ;
Oft shall the pilgrim lift the latch,
  And share my meal, a welcome guest.

Around my ivied porch shall spring
  Each fragrant flower that drinks the dew ;
And Lucy at her wheel shall sing
  In russet gown and apron blue.

Rogers.

THE DAISY.

ON FINDING ONE IN BLOOM ON CHRISTMAS-DAY.

THERE is a flower, a little flower,
  With silver crest and golden eye,
That welcomes every changing hour,
  And weathers every sky ;
The prouder beauties of the field
  In gay but quick succession shine ;
Race after race their honours yield,
  They flourish and decline.

But this small flower, to Nature dear,
  While moons and stars their courses run,
Wreathes the whole circle of the year,
  Companion of the sun.

It smiles upon the lap of May
  To sultry August spreads its charms,
Lights pale October on its way,
  And twines December's arms.

The purple heath, and golden broom,
  On moory mountains catch the gale,
O'er lawns the lily sheds perfume,
  The violet in the vale;
But this bold floweret climbs the hill,
  Hides in the forest, haunts the glen,
Plays on the margin of the rill,
  Peeps round the fox's den.

Within the garden's cultured round,
  It shares the sweet carnation's bed;
And blooms on consecrated ground,
  In honour of the dead.
The lambkin crops its crimson gem,[1]
  The wild bee murmurs on its breast,
The blue fly bends its pensile[2] stem
  Light o'er the sky-lark's nest.

'Tis Flora's[3] page:[4]—In every place,
  In every season, fresh and fair,
It opens with perennial[5] grace,
  And blossoms everywhere.
On waste and woodland, rock and plain,
  Its humble buds unheeded rise;
The rose has but a summer reign,
  The Daisy never dies.   *Montgomery.*

[1] *Gem*—the first bud of the flower.
[2] *Pensile*—hanging, bending.
[3] *Flora*—the Goddess of Flowers.
[4] *Page*—an attendant.
[5] *Perennial*—perpetual.

THE RETIRED CAT.

A POET's cat, sedate and grave
As poet well could wish to have,
Was much addicted to inquire
For nooks to which she might retire,
And where, secure as mouse in chink,
She might repose, or sit and think.
Sometimes ascending, with an air,
An apple-tree, or lofty pear,
Lodged with convenience in the fork,
She watched the gardener at his work ;
Sometimes her ease and solace sought
In an old empty watering-pot ;
There, wanting nothing but a fan,
To seem some nymph in her sedan,
In ermine dressed, of finest sort,
And ready to be borne to court.

But love of change it seems has place
Not only in our wiser race ;
Cats also feel, as well as we,
That passion's force, and so did she.
Her climbing, she began to find,
Exposed her too much to the wind,
And the old watering-pot of tin
Was cold and comfortless within :
She therefore wished, instead of those,
Some place of more secure repose,
Where neither cold might come, nor air
Too rudely wanton with her hair,
And sought it in the likeliest mode
Within her master's snug abode.

A drawer, it chanced, at bottom lined
With linen of the softest kind—
A drawer was hanging o'er the rest,
Half open, in the topmost chest,
Of depth enough, and none to spare,
Inviting her to slumber there.
Puss, with delight beyond expression,
Surveyed the scene and took possession.
Then resting at her ease, ere long,
And lulled by her own hum-drum song,
She left the cares of life behind,
And slept as she would sleep her last;
When in came, housewifely inclined,
The chambermaid, and shut it fast;
By no ill-natured thought impelled,
But quite unconscious whom it held.
    Awakened by the shock, cried Puss,
" Was ever cat attended thus !
The open drawer was left, I see,
Merely to prove a nest for me ;
For soon as I was well composed,
Then came the maid, and it was closed.
How smooth these kerchiefs and how sweet;
Oh ! what a delicate retreat.
I will resign myself to rest,
Till the sun, sinking in the west,
Shall call to supper, when, no doubt,
Susan will come and let me out."

The evening came, the sun descended,
And Puss remained still unattended.
The night rolled tardily away,
(*With her, indeed, 'twas never day,*)

The sprightly moon her course renewed,
The evening grey again ensued ;
And Puss came into mind no more
Than if entombed the day before.
With hunger pinched, and pinched for room,
She now presaged approaching doom,
Nor slept a single wink or purred,
Feeling the risk she had incurred.

That night, by chance, the poet watching,
Heard an inexplicable scratching ;
His noble heart went pit-a-pat,
And to himself he said, " What's that ? "
He drew the curtain at his side,
And forth he peeped, but nothing spied ;
Yet, by his ear directed, guessed
Something imprisoned in the chest,
And doubtful what, with prudent care,
Resolved it should continue there.
At length a voice which well he knew,
A long and melancholy mew,
Saluting his poetic ears,
Consoled him and dispelled his fears.
He left his bed, he trod the floor,
And 'gan ¹ in haste the drawers explore,
The lowest first, and without stop
The rest in order, to the top ;
For 'tis a truth well known to most,
That whatsoever thing is lost,
We seek it ere it come to light
In every corner but the right.

¹ *'Gan*—began.

Forth skipped the cat, not now replete,
As erst, with airy self-conceit,
Nor in her own fond apprehension
A theme for all the world's attention :
But sober, modest, cured of all
Her notions so fantastical ;
And wishing for her place of rest
Anything rather than a chest.
Then stepped the poet into bed
With this reflection in his head :—

MORAL.

Beware of too sublime a sense
Of your own worth and consequence !
The man who dreams himself so great,
And his importance of such weight,
That all around in all that's done,
Must move and act for *him* alone,
Will learn in school of tribulation,
The folly of his expectation.

Cowper.

REASONS FOR MIRTH.

THE sun is careering in glory and might,
'Mid the deep blue sky and the clouds so bright ;
The billow is tossing its foam on high,
And the summer breezes go lightly by ;
The air and the water dance, glitter, and play—
And why should not I be as merry as they ?

The linnet is singing the wild wood through,
The fawn's bounding footsteps skim over the dew,
The butterfly flits round the blossoming tree,
And the cowslip and blue-bell are bent by the bee :

All the creatures that dwell in the forest are
And why should not I be as merry as they ?
Miss M₁

———✦———

NAPOLEON AND THE YOUNG ENGLISH SA

I LOVE contemplating—apart
From all his homicidal ¹ glory—
The traits that soften to our heart
      Napoleon's story.

'Twas when his banners at Boulogne
Armed in our island every freeman,
His navy chanced to capture one
      Poor British seaman.

They suffered him, I know not how,
Unprisoned on the shore to roam ;
And aye was bent his youthful brow
      On England's home.

His eye, methinks, pursued the flight
Of birds to Britain, half-way over,
With envy—*they* could reach the white,
      Dear cliffs of Dover.

A stormy midnight watch, he thought,
Than this sojourn would have been dearer
If but the storm his vessel brought
      To England nearer.

At last, when care had banished sleep,
He saw one morning, dreaming, doating,
An empty hogshead from the deep
      Come shoreward floating.

¹ *Homicidal*—man-killing, murderous.

He hid it in a cave, and wrought
The live-long day, laborious, lurking,
Until he launched a tiny boat,
    By mighty working.

Oh dear me! 'twas a thing beyond
Description !—Such a wretched wherry,
Perhaps ne'er ventured on a pond,
    Or crossed a ferry.

For ploughing in the salt-sea field,
It would have made the boldest shudder;
Untarred, uncompassed, and unkeeled,—
    No sail—no rudder.

From neighbouring woods he interlaced
His sorry skiff with wattled willows;
And thus equipped he would have passed
    The foaming billows.

A French guard caught him on the beach,
His little Argo [1] sorely jeering,
Till tidings of him chanced to reach
    Napoleon's hearing.

With folded arms Napoleon stood,
Serene alike in peace and danger,
And in his wonted attitude,
    Addressed the stranger.

" Rash youth, that wouldst yon Channel pass
On twigs and staves so rudely fashioned,
Thy heart with some sweet English lass
    Must be impassioned."

[1] *Argo*—the name of an ancient ship; a ship in general.

Y

" I have no sweetheart," said the lad ;
" But absent years from one another,
  Great was the longing that I had
            To see my mother."

" And so thou shalt," Napoleon said,
" You've both my favour justly won,
  A noble mother must have bred
            So brave a son."

He gave the tar a piece of gold,
And, with a flag of truce, commanded
He should be shipped to England Old,
            And safely landed.

Our sailor oft could scantly shift
To find a dinner, plain and hearty,
But never changed the coin and gift
            Of Buonaparte.

Campbell.

———◦◇◦———

SONG OF THE STRAWBERRY GIRL.

IT is summer ! it is summer ! how beautiful it
    looks ;
There is sunshine on the old grey hills, and sunshine
    on the brooks ;
A singing-bird on every bough, soft perfumes on the
    air,
A happy smile on each young lip, and gladness
    everywhere !

Oh ! is it not a pleasant thing to wander through the
    woods,
To look upon the painted flowers, and watch the
    opening buds ;

Or seated in the deep cool shade, at some tall ash-
   tree's root,
To fill my little basket with the sweet and scented
   fruit?

They tell me that my father's poor—that is no grief
   to me
When such a blue and brilliant sky my upturned eye
   can see;
They tell me, too, that richer girls can sport with toy
   and gem;
It may be so—and yet, methinks, I do not envy
   them.

When forth I go upon my way, a thousand toys are
   mine,
The clusters of dark violets, the wreaths of the wild
   vine;
My jewels are the primrose pale, the bind-weed, and
   the rose;
And show me any courtly gem more beautiful than
   those.

And then the fruit! the glowing fruit, how sweet the
   scent it breathes!
I love to see its crimson cheek rest on the bright
   green leaves!
Summer's own gift of luxury, in which the poor may
   share,
The wild-wood fruit my eager eye is seeking everywhere.

Oh! summer is a pleasant time, with all its sounds
   and sights;
Its dewy mornings, balmy eves, and tranquil calm
   delights;

I sigh when first I see the leaves fall yellow on the
plain,
And all the winter long I sing—"Sweet summer come
again ! "

---◆◇●---

THE GLOW-WORM.

FROM THE LATIN OF VINCENT BOURNE.

BENEATH the hedge, or near the stream,
    A worm is known to stray,
That shows by night a lucid beam,
    Which disappears by day.

Disputes have been, and still prevail,
    From whence its rays proceed ;
Some give that honour to his tail,
    And others to his head.

But this is sure,—the hand of Night,
    That kindles up the skies,
Gives *him* a modicum of light,
    Proportioned to his size.

Perhaps indulgent nature meant,
    By such a lamp bestowed,
To bid the traveller, as he went,
    Be careful where he trod ;

Nor crush a worm whose useful light
    Might serve, however small,
To show a stumbling-stone by night,
    And save him from a fall.

Whate'er she meant, this truth divine
    Is legible and plain,

'Tis power Almighty bids him shine,
Nor bids him shine in vain.

Cowper.

———◆◇◆———

THE SANDS OF DEE.

', MARY, go and call the cattle home,
   And call the cattle home,
   And call the cattle home
  Across the sands of Dee ; "
he western wind was wild and dark with foam,
  And all alone went she.

he western tide crept up along the sand,
   And o'er and o'er the sand,
   And round and round the sand,
  As far as eye could see,
he rolling mist came down and hid the land :
  And never home came she.

! is it weed, or fish, or floating hair—
   A tress of golden hair,
   A drownèd maiden's hair,
  Above the nets at sea ?
ʳas never salmon yet that shone so fair,
  Among the stakes on Dee."

hey rowed her in across the rolling foam,
   The cruel, crawling foam,
   The cruel, hungry foam,
  To her grave beside the sea :
ut still the boatmen hear her call the cattle home,
  Across the sands of Dee.

Kingsley.

x 2

THE MOTHER AND BABE IN THE SNOW.[1]

THE cold winds swept the mountain height,
   And pathless was the dreary wild,
And 'mid the cheerless hours of night
   A mother wandered with her child;
As through the drifting snow she pressed,
The babe was sleeping on her breast.

And colder still the winds did blow,
   And darker hours of night came on,
And deeper grew the drifts of snow—
   Her limbs were chilled, her strength was gone,
" Oh God ! " she cried, in accents wild,
" If *I* must perish—save my child ! "

She stripped her mantle from her breast,
   And bared her bosom to the storm,
And round the child she wrapped the vest,
   And smiled to think her babe was warm ;
One kiss she gave, one tear she shed,
Then sank upon the snowy bed.

At dawn, a traveller, passing by,
   Saw her beneath the fleecy veil ;
The frost of death was in her eye,
   Her cheek was cold, and hard, and pale ;
He moved the robe from off the child—
The babe looked up and sweetly smiled.

Thus answered was the mother's prayer,
Thus saved, the object of her care.

[1] The circumstances alluded to in these lines (which ar
taken from an American newspaper) occurred a few yea
ago in Vermont, United States.

THE CHAFFINCH'S·NEST AT SEA.

In Scotland's realm, forlorn and bare,
   The history chanced of late—
The history of a wedded pair,
   A chaffinch and his mate.

The spring drew near, each felt a breast
   With genial instinct filled;
They paired, and would have built a nest,
   But found not where to build.

The heaths uncovered, and the moors,
   Except with snow and sleet,
Sea-beaten rocks and naked shores,
   Could yield them no retreat.

Long time a breeding-place they sought,
   Till both grew vexed and tired;
At length a ship arriving brought
   The good so long desired.

A ship! could such a restless thing
   Afford them place of rest?
Or was the merchant charged to bring
   The homeless birds a nest?

Hush;—silent readers profit most—
   This racer of the sea
Proved kinder to them than the coast,—
   It served them with a tree.

But such a tree! 'twas shaven deal,
   The tree they call a mast;
And had a hollow with a wheel,[1]
   Through which the tackle passed.

[1] *Hollow with a wheel*—a block or pulley.

Within that cavity, aloft,
　　Their roofless home they fixed;
Formed with materials neat and soft,
　　Bents,[1] wool, and feathers mixed.

Four ivory eggs soon pave its floor,
　　With russet specks bedight: [2]
The vessel weighs,[3] forsakes the shore,
　　And lessens to the sight.

The mother-bird is gone to sea,
　　As she had changed her kind;
But goes the male? Far wiser, he
　　Is doubtless left behind.

No :—soon as from ashore he saw
　　The winged mansion move,
He flew to reach it, by a law
　　Of never-failing love;

Then perching at his consort's side,
　　Was briskly borne along;
The billows and the blasts defied,
　　And cheered her with a song.

The seaman, with sincere delight,
　　His feathered shipmate eyes,
Scarce less exulting in the sight
　　Than when he tows a prize.

For seamen much believe in signs,
　　And, from a chance so new,
Each some approaching good divines; [4]
　　And may his hopes be true!

[1] *Bents*—the stalks of a species of grass.
[2] *Bedight*—decked, ornamented.
[3] *Weighs*—weighs *anchor*—sets sail.
[4] *Divines*—guesses, foretells.

Hail, birds ! who, rather than resign
  Your matrimonial plan,
Were not afraid to plough the brine,
  In company with man.

Be it your fortune, year by year,
  The same resource to prove ;
And may ye, sometimes landing here,
  Instruct us how to love !   *Cowper.*

THE MAZE.

FROM THE LATIN OF VINCENT BOURNE.

FROM right to left, and to and fro,
Caught in a labyrinth, you go,
And turn, and turn, and turn again,
To solve the mystery, but in vain ;—
Stand still and breathe, and take from me
A clue that soon shall set you free !
Not Ariadne, if you met her,
Herself could serve you with a better.
You entered easily—find where—
And make with ease your exit there.
                              Cowper.

THE BETTER LAND.

" I HEAR thee speak of the better land ;
Thou call'st its children a happy band ;
Mother ! oh where is that radiant shore ?—
Shall we not seek it, and weep no more ?
Is it where the flower of the orange blows,
And the fire-flies dance through the myrtle boughs?"
  "*Not there, not there, my child.*"

" Is it where the feathery palm-trees rise,
And the date grows ripe under sunny skies?
Or 'midst the green islands of glittering seas,
Where fragrant forests perfume the breeze,
And strange bright birds, on their starry wings,
Bear the rich hues of all glorious things? "
    " Not there, not there, my child."

" Is it far away, in some region old,
Where the rivers wander o'er sands of gold?—
Where the burning rays of the ruby shine,
And the diamond lights up the secret mine,
And the pearl gleams forth from the coral strand?—
Is it there, sweet mother, that better land?"
    " Not there, not there, my child."

" Eye hath not seen it, my gentle boy!
Ear hath not heard its deep songs of joy,
Dreams cannot picture a world so fair,—
Sorrow and death may not enter there;
Time doth not breathe on its fadeless bloom,
For beyond the clouds, and beyond the tomb,
    It is there, it is there, my child."
                Mrs. Hemans.

TIME.

Time that is passed, thou never canst recall;
Of time to come, thou art not sure at all;
Time present, only, is within thy power,
And therefore NOW improve the present hour.
                Byrom.

THE SPARROWS AT COLLEGE.

FROM THE LATIN OF VINCENT BOURNE.

NONE ever shared the social feast,
Or as an inmate or a guest,
Beneath the celebrated dome,
Where once Sir Isaac had his home,[1]
Who saw not (and with some delight
Perhaps reviewed the novel sight)
How numerous, at the tables there,
The sparrows beg their daily fare.
For there, in every nook and cell,
Where such a family may dwell,
Sure as the vernal season comes
Their nest they weave in hope of crumbs,
Which, kindly given, may serve with food
Convenient their unfeathered brood!
And oft, as with its summons clear
The warning bell salutes their ear,
Sagacious listeners to the sound,
They flock from all the fields around,
To reach the hospitable hall,
None more attentive to the call.
Arrived, the pensionary[2] band,
Hopping and chirping close at hand
Solicit what they soon receive,
The sprinkled, plenteous donative.[3]
Thus is a multitude, though large,
Supported at a trivial charge;

[1] Sir Isaac Newton studied at Trinity College, Cambridge.
[2] *Pensionary*—depending on a pension, or stated allowance.
[3] *Donative*—gift.

A single doit[1] would overpay
The expenditure of every day,
And who can grudge so small a grace
To suppliants, natives of the place ?

Cowper.

THE WOODMAN AND HIS DOG.

FORTH goes the woodman, leaving unconcerned
The cheerful haunts of man to wield the axe,
And drive the wedge in yonder forest drear—
From morn to eve his solitary task.
Shaggy, and lean, and shrewd, with pointed ears,
And tail cropped short, half lurcher and half cur,
His dog attends him.   Close behind his heel
Now creeps he slow ; and now, with many a frisk
Wide scampering, snatches up the drifted snow
With ivory teeth, or ploughs it with his snout,
Then shakes his powdered coat and barks for joy.
Heedless of all his pranks, the sturdy churl
Moves right towards his work, nor stops for aught,
But now and then, with pressure of his thumb,
To adjust the fragrant charge[2] of a short tube
That fumes beneath his nose ; the trailing cloud
Streams far behind him, scenting all the air.

Cowper.

THE SQUIRREL.

THE squirrel, flippant, pert, and full of play,
Drawn from his refuge in some lonely elm

[1] *Doit*—a small coin, no longer in use.
[2] *Charge*—load, contents. The *charge* in this case was
he tobacco that filled the pipe.

That age or injury hath hollowed deep,
Where, in his bed of wool and matted leaves,
He has outslept the winter, ventures forth
To frisk awhile, and bask in the warm sun :
He sees me, and at once, swift as a bird,
Ascends the neighbouring beech: there whisks his
    brush,
And perks[1] his ears, and stamps and cries aloud,
With all the prettiness of feigned alarm
And anger insignificantly fierce.

                  Cowper.

CASABIANCA, THE HEROIC BOY.[2]

THE boy stood on the burning deck,
  Whence all but he had fled ;
The flame that lit the battle's wreck
  Shone round him o'er the dead ;
Yet beautiful and bright he stood
  As born to rule the storm ;
A creature of heroic blood,
  A proud though child-like form !

The flames rolled on—he would not go
  Without his father's word ;
That father, faint in death below,
  His voice no longer heard.

[1] *Perks*—raises, tosses up.
[2] Young Casabianca, a boy about thirteen years old, son of the admiral of the *Orient*, a French ship of war, remained at his post in the battle of the Nile after the ship had taken fire, and all the guns had been abandoned ; and perished in the explosion of the vessel when the flames reached the powder.

He called aloud—" Say, father, say,
  If yet my task is done ! "
He knew not that the chieftain lay
  Unconscious of his son.

" Speak, father ! " once again he cried,
  " If I may yet be gone !
And "—but the booming[1] shots replied,
  And fast the flames rolled on.
Upon his brow he felt their breath,
  And in his waving hair ;
And looked from that lone post of death,
  In still yet brave despair !

He shouted yet once more aloud,
  " My father ! must I stay ? "
While o'er him fast, through sail and shroud,
  The wreathing fires made way :
They wrapped the ship in splendour wild,
  They caught the flag on high,
And streamed above the gallant child,
  Like banners in the sky.

Then came a burst of thunder sound—
  The boy—oh ! where was he ?
Ask of the winds, that far around
  With fragments strewed the sea,
With mast and helm and pennon[2] fair,
  That well had borne their part—
But the noblest thing that perished there
  Was that young, faithful heart.
                   Mrs. Hemans.

---

[1] *Booming*—rushing with great noise and tumult.
[2] *Pennon*—a small flag or banner.

THE LAND OF CONTRADICTIONS.

THERE is a land in distant seas
Full of all contrarieties.
There beasts have mallards' bill and legs,
Have spurs like cocks, like hens lay eggs.
There parrots walk upon the ground,
And grass upon the trees is found;
On other trees—another wonder—
Leaves without upper side or under.
There pears you'll scarce with hatchet cut;
Stones are outside the cherries put;
Swans are not white, but black as soot;
There neither leaf, nor root, nor fruit
Will any Christian palate suit;
Unless in desperate need you'll fill ye
With root of fern and stalk of lily.
There missiles to far distance sent
Come whizzing back from whence they went.
There a voracious ewe-sheep crams
Her paunch with flesh of tender lambs;
While, 'stead of bread, and beef, and broth,
Men feast on many a roasted moth.
There quadrupeds go on two feet,
And yet few quadrupeds so fleet.
There birds, although they cannot fly,
In swiftness with the greyhound vie.
With equal wonder you may see
The foxes fly from tree to tree;
And what they value most, so wary,
These foxes in their pockets carry.
The sun when you to face him turn ye,
From right to left performs his journey.

The north winds scorch; but when the breeze is
Full from the south, why then it freezes.
Now of what place can such strange tales
Be told with truth but New South Wales.[1]

———◆◇◆———

UNDER THE GREENWOOD TREE.

Under the greenwood tree,
Who [2] loves to lie with me,
And tune his merry note
Unto the sweet bird's throat;
Come hither, come hither, come hither,
  Here shall he see
    No enemy
But winter and rough weather.

Who [2] doth ambition shun,
And loves to live i' the sun,
Seeking the food he eats,
And pleased with what he gets;
Come hither, come hither, come hither,
  Here shall he see
    No enemy
But winter and rough weather.

Shakspere.

———◆◇◆———

THE DAME SCHOOLMISTRESS.

IN yonder cot, along whose mouldering walls,
In many a fold, the mantling woodbine falls,

[1] The remarkable animals, trees, and plants referred to in
this poem are not all found in New South Wales, but in
various parts of the great continent of Australia. Specimens
of them may be seen in most large museums of England.
[2] *Who*—he who.

The village matron kept her little school—
Gentle of heart, yet knowing well *to* rule;
Staid was the dame, and modest was her mien;
Her garb was coarse, yet whole, and nicely clean :
Her neatly-bordered cap, as lily fair,
Beneath her chin was pinned, with decent care,
And pendent ruffles of the whitest lawn,
Of ancient make, her elbows did adorn.
Faint with old age, and dim were grown her eyes,
A pair of spectacles their want supplies;
These does she guard secure in leathern case
From thoughtless wights in some unweeted [1] place.
Here first I entered, though with toil and pain,
The lowly vestibule [2] of learning's fane; [3]
Entered with pain, yet soon I found the way,
Though sometimes toilsome, many a sweet display.

Much did I grieve, on that ill-fated morn,
When I was first to school reluctant borne;
Severe I thought the dame, though oft she tried
To soothe my swelling spirits when I sighed;
And oft, when harshly she reproved, I wept,
To my lone corner, broken-hearted, crept,
And thought of tender home, where anger never
     kept.
But soon, enured to alphabetic toils,
Alert I met the dame with jocund smiles;
First at the form, my task for ever true,
A little favourite rapidly I grew :
And oft she stroked my head with fond delight,
Held me a pattern to the dunce's sight;

[1] *Unweeted*—unknown.
[2] *Vestibule*—porch, entrance. 　　[3] *Fane—temple.*

And as she gave my diligence its praise,
Talked of the honours of my future days
                                    Kirke

THE KITTEN AND THE FALLING LEA\

SEE the kitten on the wall
Sporting with the leaves that fall—
Withered leaves—one—two—and three—
From the lofty elder-tree !
Through the calm and frosty air
Of this morning, bright and fair,
Eddying round and round they sink
Softly, lowly : one might think,
From the motions that are made,
Every little leaf conveyed
Sylph or fairy hither tending—
To this lower world descending,
Each invisible and mute,
In his wavering parachute.[1]
—But the kitten, how she starts,
Crouches, stretches, paws, and darts !
First at one, and then its fellow,
Just as light and just as yellow ;
There are many now—now one—
Now they stop, and there are none.
What intenseness of desire
In her up-turned eye of fire !
With a tiger-leap, half-way,
Now she meets the coming prey,

[1] *Parachute*—a machine, in form resembling a la
brella, by which persons may descend from a great h
the air; generally used in connection with a balloon

Lets it go as fast, and then
Has it in her power again :
Now she works with three or four,
Like an Indian conjuror ; [1]
Quick as he in feats of art,
Far beyond in joy of heart.
Were her antics played in the eye
Of a thousand standers-by,
Clapping hands, with shout and stare,
What would little Tabby care
For the plaudits of the crowd ?
Far too happy to be proud ;
Over-wealthy in the treasure
Of her own exceeding pleasure !
                            Wordsworth.

THE SANDAL-TREE.

THE best revenge is love :—disarm
Anger with smiles ; heal wounds.with balm ;
  Give water to thy thirsting foe ;
The sandal-tree, as if to prove
How sweet to conquer hate by love,
  Perfumes the axe that lays it low.
                            S. C. Wilkes.

RAIN IN SUMMER.

How beautiful is the rain !
After the dust and the heat,

[1] *Indian conjuror.*—The Indian conjurors perform asto-
nishing feats with balls, keeping several in motion above, and
even *around, them* at the same time.

In the broad and fiery street,
In the narrow lane,
How beautiful is the rain !

How it clatters along the roofs,
Like the tramp of hoofs !
How it gushes and struggles out
From the throat of the overflowing spout !
Across the window-pane
It pours and pours;
And swift and wide,
With a muddy tide,
Like a river down the gutter roars
The rain, the welcome rain !

The sick man from his chamber looks
At the twisted brooks;
He can feel the cool
Breath of each little pool;
His fevered brain
Grows calm again,
And he breathes a blessing on the rain.

From the neighbouring school
Come the boys,
With more than their wonted noise
And commotion;
And down the wet streets
Sail their mimic fleets,
Till the treacherous pool
Engulfs them in its whirling
And turbulent ocean.

In the country on every side,
Where, far and wide,
Like a leopard's tawny and spotted hide,

Stretches the plain,
To the dry grass and the drier grain
How welcome is the rain !

In the furrowed land
The toilsome and patient oxen stand :
Lifting the yoke-encumbered head;
With their dilated nostrils spread,
They silently inhale
The clover-scented gale,
And the vapours that arise
From the well-watered and smoking soil.
For this rest in the furrow after toil
Their large and lustrous eyes
Seem to thank the Lord,
More than man's spoken word.

Near at hand,
From under the sheltering trees,
The farmer sees
His pastures and his fields of grain,
As they bend their tops
To the numberless beating drops
Of the incessant rain.
He counts it as no sin
That he sees therein
Only his own thrift and gain.   *Longfellow.*

----◦----

THE CHILD AND HIND.

Come, maids and matrons, to caress
Wiesbaden's [1] gentle hind;

[1] *Wiesbaden*—the capital of the Duchy of Nassau, in
Germany, near which city occurred the incident narrated in
the poem.

And, smiling, deck its glossy neck
With forest flowers entwined.

'Twas after church—on Ascension day—
When organs ceased to sound,
Wiesbaden's people crowded gay
The deer-park's pleasant ground.

Here came a twelve years' married pair—
And with them wandered free
Seven sons and daughters, blooming fair,
A gladsome sight to see !

Their Wilhelm, little innocent,
The youngest of the seven,
Was beautiful as painters paint
The cherubim of heaven.

By turns he gave his hand, so dear,
To parent, sister, brother ;
And each,[1] that he was safe and near,
Confided in the other.

But Wilhelm loved the field-flowers bright,
With love beyond all measure ;
And culled them with as keen delight
As misers gather treasure.

Unnoticed, he contrived to glide
Adown a greenwood alley,
By lilies lured—that grew beside
A streamlet in the valley ;

[1] *And each &c.*—As they wandered along, a scattered ban
each one thought that some other of the party was taki
care of him.

And there, where under beech and birch
    The rivulet meandered,
He strayed, till neither shout nor search
    Could track where he had wandered.

Still louder, with increasing dread,
    They called his darling name :
But 'twas like speaking to the dead—
    An echo only came.

Hours passed till evening's beetle roams
    And blackbird's songs begin ;
Then all went back to happy homes,
    Save Wilhelm's kith and kin.[1]

The night came on—all others slept
    Their cares away till morn ;
But, sleepless, all night watched and wept
    That family forlorn.

Betimes the town-crier had been sent
    With loud bell up and down ;
And told the afflicting accident
    Throughout Wiesbaden's town.

The news reached Nassau's Duke—ere earth
    Was gladdened by the lark,
He sent a hundred soldiers forth
    To ransack all his park.

But though they roused up beast and bird
    From many a nest and den,
No signal of success was heard
    From all the hundred men.

[1] *Kith and kin*—friends and relations.

A second morning's light expands,
  Unfound the infant fair ;
And Wilhelm's household wring their ha
  Abandoned to despair.

But, haply, a poor artisan
  Searched ceaselessly, till he
Found safe asleep the little one
  Beneath a beechen tree.

His hand still grasped a bunch of flowers
  And—true, though wondrous—near,
To sentry his reposing hours,
  There stood a female deer,

Who dipped her horns at all that passed
  The spot where Wilhelm lay ;
Till force was had to hold her fast,
  And bear the boy away.

Hail ! sacred love of childhood—hail !
  How sweet it is to trace
Thine instinct in Creation's scale,
  Even 'neath the human race !

To this poor wanderer of the wild,
  Speech, reason were unknown—
And yet she watched a sleeping child,
  As if it were her own !

Oa

THE BIRDS OF PASSAGE.

Birds, joyous birds of the wandering wing !
Whence is it ye come with the flowers of spri

—" We come from the shores of the green old Ni
?rom the land where the roses of Sharon smile,
?rom the palms that wave through the Indian sky
?rom the myrrh-trees of glowing Araby.

? We have swept o'er cities in song renowned,
?ilent they lie with the desert round !
?e have crossed proud rivers whose tide hath rollec
?ll dark with the warrior-blood of old ;
?nd each worn wing hath regained its home
?nder peasant's roof or monarch's dome."

?nd what have ye found in the monarch's dome,
?ince last ye traversed the blue sea's foam ?
—" We have found a change ;—we have found a
    pall,
?nd a gloom o'ershadowing the banquet hall ;
?nd a mark on the floor as of life-drops spilt :—
?ought looks the same save the nest we built."

? ! joyous birds, it hath ever been so ;
?rough the halls of kings doth the tempest go,
?t the huts of hamlets lie still and deep,
?l the hills o'er their quiet a vigil keep :—
?, what have ye found in the peasant's cot
?e last ye parted from that sweet spot ?

?change we have found there, and many a change,
?? and footsteps, and all things strange ;
?are the heads of the silvery hair,
?he young that were have a brow of care ;
?he place is hushed where the children played ;
?t looks the same save the nest we made."

?your tale of the beautiful earth,
?at o'ersweep it in power and mirth ;

A A

Yet through the wastes of the track
Ye have a guide, and shall *we* desp
Ye over desert and deep have pass
So may *we* reach our bright home

$\qquad\qquad\qquad\qquad\qquad$ A

————◆◇◆————

THE DOVE.

I HAD a dove, and the sweet dove die
And I have thought it died of grie
Oh ! what could it grieve for ? Its fee
With a silken thread of my own hai
Sweet little Red-Feet ! why should j
Why would you leave me, sweet bird
You lived alone in the forest tree ;
Why, pretty thing, would you not li
I kiss'd you oft, and gave you white
Why not live sweetly, as in the greer

————◆◇◆————

THE MOTHER AND HER CH

As to her lips the mother lifts her bo
What answering looks of sympathy a
He walks, he speaks.　In many a bro
His wants, his wishes, and his griefs
And ever, ever to her lap he flies,
When rosy sleep comes on with swee
Locked in her arms, his arms across l
(That name most dear for ever on his
As with soft accents round her neck h
And, cheek to cheek, her lulling son

How blest to feel the beatings of his heart,
Breathe his sweet breath, and kiss for kiss impart;
Watch o'er his slumbers like the brooding dove,
And, if she can, exhaust a mother's love !

But soon a nobler task demands her care :
Apart she joins his little hands in prayer,
Telling of Him who sees in secret there !—
And now the volume on her knee has caught
His wandering eye—now many a written thought
Never to die, with many a lisping sweet,
His moving, murmuring lips endeavour to repeat.
Released, he chases the bright butterfly;
Oh, he would follow—follow through the sky !
Climbs the gaunt mastiff slumbering in his chain,
And chides and buffets, clinging by the mane;
Then runs, and, kneeling by the fountain side,
Sends his brave ship in triumph down the tide,—
A dangerous voyage ! or if now he can,
If now he wears the habit of a man,
Flings off the coat, so long his pride and pleasure,
And, like a miser digging for his treasure,
His tiny spade in his own garden plies,
And in green letters sees his name arise !
Where'er he goes, for ever in her sight,
She looks, and looks, and still with new delight !

Rogers.

———◦◦◦———

LUCY.

SHE dwelt among the untrodden ways,
   Beside the springs of Dove ;
A maid whom there were none to praise,
   And very few to love.

A violet by a mossy stone,
  Half hidden from the eye !
—Fair as a star, when only one
  Is shining in the sky.

She lived unknown, and few could
  When Lucy ceased to be ;
But she is in her grave, and, oh,
  The difference to me !

                              W

SELF-EXAMINATION.

FROM THE GREEK OF PYTHAGORAS.

LET not soft slumbers close my eyes,
Before I've recollected thrice
The train of actions through the day :
Where have my feet marked out thei:
What have I learnt where'er I've beei
From all I've heard—from all I've se(
What know I more, that's worth the :
What have I done, that's worth the d
What have I sought, that I should sh\
What duties have I left undone ?
Or into what new follies run ?
These self-inquiries are the road
That leads to virtue and to God.

THE BREAD-FRUIT TREE.

THERE is an island where no peasants
To drive the ploughshare in the fertil\

No seed is sown, no corn-fields deck the plain,
No ponderous millstones bruise the ripened grain;
Their mellow harvest ripens overhead,
Their groves supply them with abundant bread;
On stately trees, the sun and genial air,
Without man's aid, unceasing food prepare.
Still further benefits these trees bestow;
The stem is felled, behold! the light canoe;
From the tough fibres of the bark proceeds
Such simple clothing as the climate needs.
Delightful clime! where flowers perpetual grow,
Unchecked by winter's frost, or showers of snow.

THE PIOUS WISH.

OH that mine eye might closed be
To what becomes me not to see!
That deafness might possess mine ear
To what concerns me not to hear!
That truth my tongue might closely tie
From ever speaking foolishly!
That no vain thought might ever rest,
Or be conceived within my breast!
That by each word, each deed, each thought,
Glory may to my God be brought.

Ellwood.

THE NAUTILUS.

WHERE southern suns and winds prevail,
And undulate the summer seas,[1]

[1] *The Nautilus* is found in the Mediterranean Sea.

A A 2

The Nautilus expands his sail,
And scuds before the freshening breeze.

Oft is a little squadron seen
Of mimic ships, all rigged complete;
Fancy might think the fairy-queen
Was sailing with her elfin fleet.

With how much beauty is designed
Each channeled bark of purest white!
With orient pearl each cabin [1] lined,
Varying with every change of light;

While with his little slender oars,
His silken sail and tapering mast,
The dauntless mariner explores
The dangers of the watery waste;

Prepared, should tempests rend the sky,
From harm his fragile bark to keep,
He furls [2] his sail, his oars lays by,
And seeks his safety in the deep.

Then safe on ocean's shelly bed,
He hears the storm above him roar,
'Mid groves of coral glowing red,
And rocks o'erhung with madrepore.

So let us catch life's favouring gale;
But, if fate's adverse winds be rude,
Take calmly in the adventurous sail,
And find repose in solitude.

Charlotte Smi

[1] *Cabin*—in allusion to the chambers or compartments the shell.
[2] *Furls*—takes in.

THE LESSONS TAUGHT BY NATURE.

'Twas thus to man the voice of Nature spake :—
" Go, from the creatures thy instruction take :
Learn from the birds what food the thickets yield ;
Learn from the beasts the physic of the field ;
The arts of building from the bee receive ;
Learn of the mole to plough, the worm to weave ;
Learn of the little Nautilus to sail,
Spread the thin oar, and catch the driving gale."

Pope.

HUMILITY.

The bird that soars on highest wing
  Builds on the ground her lowly nest ;
And she that doth most sweetly sing,
  Sings in the shade when all things rest :
In lark and nightingale we see
What honour hath humility.

THE INCHCAPE ROCK; [1]

OR, THE ROVER'S FATE.

No stir in the air, no stir in the sea,
The ship was as still as she could be ;
Her sails from heaven received no motion,
Her keel was steady in the ocean.

[1] The Inchcape Rock is a dangerous sunken rock off the coast of Forfarshire, Scotland, on which the Bell-rock Lighthouse now stands.

Without either sign or sound of their shock,
The waves floated over the Inchcape Rock ;
So little they rose, so little they fell,
They did not move the Inchcape bell.

The good old abbot of Aberbrothock
Had floated that bell on the Inchcape Rock ;
On the waves of the storm it floated and swun
And louder and louder its warning rung.

When the rock was hid by the surge's swell,
The mariners heard the warning bell ;
And then they knew the perilous rock,
And blessed the priest of Aberbrothock.

The sun in heaven was shining gay,
All things were joyful on that day ;
The sea-birds screamed, as they wheeled arou
And there was pleasure in the sound.

The float of the Inchcape bell was seen,
A darker speck on the ocean green ;
Sir Ralph the rover [1] walked the deck,
And he fixed his eye on the darker speck.

He felt the cheering power of spring ;
It made him whistle, it made him sing ;
His heart was mirthful to excess—
But the rover's mirth was wickedness.

His eye was on the bell and float ;
Quoth he, " My men, put out the boat,
And row me to the Inchcape Rock,
And I'll plague the priest of Aberbrothock."

[1] *Rover*—wanderer, pirate.

The boat is lowered, the boatmen row,
And.to the Inchcape Rock they go ;
Sir Ralph bent over from the boat,
And cut the warning-bell from the float !

Down sank the bell with a gurgling sound :
The bubbles arose and burst around ;
Quoth Sir Ralph, " The next who comes to the rock,
Will not bless the priest of Aberbrothock."

Sir Ralph the rover sailed away ;
He scoured the seas for many a day ;
And now, grown rich with plundered store,
He steers his course for Scotland's shore.

So thick a haze o'erspread the sky,
They could not see the sun on high ;
The wind had blown a gale all day,
At evening it had died away.

On deck the rover takes his stand ;
So dark it is, they see no land ;
Quoth Sir Ralph, " It will be lighter soon,
For there is the dawn of the rising moon."

" Canst hear," said one, " the breakers roar ?
Yonder, methinks, should be the shore ;
Now, where we are, I cannot tell,
But I wish we could hear the Inchcape bell."

They hear no sound, the swell is strong,
Though the wind has fallen, they drift along,
Till the vessel strikes with a shivering shock—
" Alas ! it is the Inchcape Rock ! "

Sir Ralph the rover tore his hair,
He *beat himself* in wild despair ;

But the waves rush in on every sid
And the vessel sinks beneath the ti(

─────◆─────

THE DESTROYER.

I saw the Memphian [1] pyramid
　In awful grandeur rise,
Which, like a mighty pillar, seemed
　To prop the lofty skies.

An old man, with a snow-white beard
　Across the desert came,
With a long grey robe thrown loosely
　His breast and withered frame.

He stood beside the pyramid,
　And laid his hand thereon,
When, lo! the pile fell crumbling dov
　Till every stone was gone.

There was a city vast and great,
　The world's imperial queen,
Whose lofty towers and palaces
　On every side were seen ;

The hum of busy multitudes,
　The shout of armèd bands,
The song of triumph, and the clash
　Of shields and glittering brands ;

With every sound of revelry,
　That from the banquet flows,
From out that city's crowded streets,
　In mingled discord, rose.

[1] *Memphian*—belonging to Memphis, a celebra
ancient Egypt, situated on the western bank of th

I looked, and, lo! that same old man,
  With a visage pale and grim,
Passed through those streets, observing none,
  And none observing him;

Yet as he paced those crowded streets,
  Quick hurrying to and fro,
All sounds of revelry were changed
  To the bitter wails of woe.

Still on he went without a stop,
  Till every sound had fled;
And nought within those walls was heard
  But the echo of his tread.

Still on he went, still on he went,
  Till palace, tower, and wall,
Sank down in one unseemly mass,
  And ruin covered all.

Who art thou, stern destroyer? say—
" I'm known in every clime—
Man and his works all pass away
  Beneath the hand of TIME! "

                              Hudson.

GRATITUDE TO GOD.

How cheerful along the gay mead
The daisy and cowslip appear!
The flocks, as they carelessly feed,
Rejoice in the spring of the year;
The myrtles that deck the gay bowers,
The herbage that springs from the sod,
Trees, plants, cooling fruits, and sweet flowers
All rise to the praise of my God!

Shall man, the great master of all,
The only insensible prove ?
Forbid it, fair gratitude's call;
Forbid it, devotion and love !
The Lord who such wonders could raise,
And still can destroy with a nod,
My lips shall incessantly praise ;
My soul shall rejoice in my God.

                                        A(

———◦◇◦———

THE SEA.

BEAUTIFUL, sublime, and glorious;
    Mild, majestic, foaming, free—
Over time itself victorious,
    Image of eternity !

Sun, and moon, and stars shine o'er thee,
    See thy surface ebb and flow ;
Yet attempt not to explore thee
    In thy soundless[1] depths below.

Whether morning's splendours steep thee
    With the rainbow's glowing grace,
Tempests rouse, or navies sweep thee,
    'Tis but for a moment's space.

Earth—her valleys and her mountains,
    Mortal man's behests obey ;
Thy unfathomable fountains
    Scoff his search, and scorn his sway.

Such art thou—stupendous ocean !
    But, if overwhelmed by thee,

Soundless—that cannot be fathomed or measu

Can we think, without emotion,
What must thy Creator be ?
Bernard Barton.

BIRDS.

Say, who the various nations can declare
That plough with busy wing the peopled air ?
These cleave the crumbling bark for insect food ;
Those dip their crooked beak in kindred blood ;
Some haunt the rushy moor, the lonely woods ;
Some bathe their silver plumage in the floods ;
Some fly to man, his household gods implore,
And gather round his hospitable door ;
Wait the known call, and find protection there
From all the lesser tyrants of the air.

The tawny Eagle seats his callow brood
High on the cliff, and feasts his young with blood.
On Snowdon's rocks, or Orkney's wide domain,
Whose beetling cliffs o'erhang the western main,
The Royal bird his lonely kingdom forms
Amidst the gathering clouds and sullen storms ;
Through the wide waste of air he darts his sight,
And holds his sounding pinions poised for flight :
With cruel eye premeditates the war,
And marks his destined victim from afar :
Descending in a whirlwind to the ground,
His pinions like the rush of waters sound ;
The fairest of the fold he bears away,
And to his nest compels the struggling prey.
He scorns the game that meaner hunters tore,
And *dips his talons* in no vulgar gore.

B B

With lovelier pomp, along the grassy plain,
The silver pheasant draws his shining train :
Once on the painted banks of Ganges' stream
He spread his plumage to the sunny gleam :
But now the wiry net his flight confines,
He lowers his purple crest, and inly pines.

To claim the verse unnumbered tribes appea
That swell the music of the vernal year : ·
Seized with the spirit of the kindly spring,
They tune the voice, and sleek the glossy wi
With emulative strife the notes prolong,
And pour out all their little souls in song.
When winter bites upon the naked plain,
Nor food nor shelter in the groves remain,
By instinct led, a firm, united band,
Is marshalled by some skilful general's hand
The congregated nations wing their way
In dusky columns o'er the trackless sea ;
In clouds unnumbered annual hover o'er
The craggy Bass,[1] or Kilda's[2] utmost shore ;
Thence spread their sails to meet the s
        wind,
And leave the gathering tempest far behind ;
Pursue the circling sun's indulgent ray,
Course the swift seasons, and o'ertake the da
                              Mrs. Barl

————◦◇•————

INSECTS.

OBSERVE the insect race, ordained to ke
The lazy sabbath [3] of a half-year's sleer

[1] *Bass*—an island in the Frith of Forth, Scotla
[2] *Kilda*—one of the Hebrides, west of Scotlanc
[3] *Sabbath*—rest.

Entombed beneath the filmy web they lie,
And wait the influence of a kinder sky.
When vernal sunbeams pierce their dark retreat,
The heaving tomb distends with vital heat;
The full-formed brood, impatient of their cell,
Start from their trance and burst their silken shell;
Trembling awhile they stand, and scarcely dare
To launch at once upon the untried air;
At length assured, they catch the favouring gale,
And leave their sordid spoils, and high in ether [1]
    sail.

Lo! the bright train their radiant wings unfold,
With silver fringed and freckled o'er with gold.
On the gay bosom of some fragrant flower
They, idly fluttering, live their little hour;
Their life all pleasure, and their task all play,
All spring their age, and sunshine all their day.

What atom forms of insect life appear!
And who can follow Nature's pencil here?
Their wings with azure, green, and purple glossed,
Studded with coloured eyes, with gems embossed,
Inlaid with pearl, and marked with various stains
Of lively crimson through their dusky veins.
Some shoot like living stars athwart the night
And scatter from their wings a vivid light, [2]
To guide the Indian to his tawny loves,
As through the wood with cautious steps he moves.

See the proud giant of the beetle race;
What shining arms his polished limbs enchase!

[1] *Ether*—the upper region of the air.
[2] *Some shoot, &c.*—the fireflies, which are very abundant *in South America* and the West Indies.

Like some stern warrior, formidably bright,
His steely sides reflect a gleaming light;
On his large forehead spreading horns he w
And high in air the branching antlers bears
O'er many an inch extends his wide domaii
And his rich treasury swells with hoarded

Mrs. Barba

THE KID.

A TEAR bedews my Delia's eye
To think yon playful kid must die;
From crystal spring and flowery mead
Must, in his prime of life, recede.

Erewhile,[1] in sportive circles, round
She saw him wheel, and fris', and boun(
From rock to rock pursue his way,
And on the fearful margin play.

Pleased on his various freaks to dwell,
She saw him climb my rustic cell;
Thence eye my lawns with verdure brigl
And seem all ravished at the sight.

She tells with what delight he stood
To trace his features in the flood:
Then skipped aloof with quaint amaze;
And then drew near again to gaze.

She tells me how, with eager speed,
He flew to hear my vocal reed;
And how, with critic face profound,
And steadfast ear, devoured the sound.

[1] *Erewhile*—a little while ago.

His every frolic, light as air,
Deserves the gentle Delia's care;
And tears bedew her tender eye
To think the playful kid must die.

Shenstone.

DAY-BREAK.

SEE the day begins to break,
And the light shoots like a streak
Of subtle fire; the wind blows cold
While the morning doth unfold;
Now the birds begin to rouse,
And the squirrel from the boughs
Leaps, to get him nuts and fruit;
The early lark, that erst[1] was mute,
Carols in the rising day
Many a note and many a lay.

Beaumont and Fletcher.

UNFOLDING THE FLOCKS.

SHEPHERDS, rise, and shake off sleep—
See the blushing morn doth peep
Through your windows, while the sun
To the mountain-tops has run,
Gilding all the vales below
With the rising flames, which grow
Brighter with his climbing still.—
Up! ye lazy swains! and fill
Bag and bottle for the field;
Clasp your cloaks fast, lest they yield

[1] *Erst*—formerly, before.

B B 2

From the mountain, and ere day
Bear a lamb or kid away ;
Or the crafty, thievish fox
Break upon your simple flocks.
To secure yourself from these
Be not too secure in ease ;
So shall you good shepherds prove,
And deserve your master's love.
Now, good night! may sweetest slumbers
And soft silence fall in numbers
On your eye-lids! so farewell ;
Thus I end my evening knell.
                    Beaumont and Fletcher.

———◆◆———

SWISS HOME-SICKNESS.

WHEREFORE so sad and faint my heart?
    The stranger's land is fair ;
Yet, weary, weary, still thou art—
    What find'st thou wanting there ?

What wanting?—All, oh ! all I love !
    Am I not lonely here ?
Through a fair land in sooth, I rove,
    But what like *home* is dear ?

My home ! oh ! thither would I fly,
    Where the free air is sweet,
My father's voice, my mother's eye,
    My own wild hills to greet ;

My hills, with all their soaring steeps,
    With all their glaciers[1] bright,

Glaciers—fields of ice, such as are met with in the
lows of the Alps.

Where in his joy the chamois sleeps,
  Mocking the hunter's might.

Here no familiar look I trace,
  I touch no friendly hand;
No child laughs kindly in my face,
  As in my own sweet land.

Mrs. Hema

———◦◦◦———

A HAWKING PARTY IN THE OLDEN TI

HARK! hark! the merry warder's horn
Far o'er the wooded hills is borne,
Far o'er the slopes of ripening corn,
    On the free breeze away!
The bolts are drawn, the bridge is o'er
The sullen moat—and steeds a score
Stand saddled at the castle door,
    For 'tis a merry day!

With braided hair of gold or jet,
There's many a May and Margaret
Before her stately mirror set,
    With waiting woman by;
There's scarlet cloak, and hat and hood
And riding dress of camlet good,
Green as the leaf within the wood,
    To shroud those ladies high.

And then into the castle-hall
Come crowding gallant knights and tall
Equipped as for a festival,
    For they will hawk to-day;—

And then out breaks a general din
From those without, as those within
Upon the terrace steps are seen
 In such a bright array !

The kenneled hounds' long bark is heard,
The falconer talking to his bird,
The neighing steeds, the angry word
 Of grooms impatient there.
But soon the bustle is dismissed,
The falconer sets on every wrist
A hooded hawk,[1] that's stroked and kissed
 By knight and lady fair.

And sitting in their saddles free,
The brave, the fair of high degree,
Forth rides that gallant company,
 Each with a bird on hand ;
And falconers with their hawking gear,[2]
And other birds, bring up the rear,
And country-folk from far and near
 Fall in and join the band.

And merrily thus in shine and shade,
Gay glancing through the forest glade,
On rides the noble cavalcade,
 To moorlands wild and grey ;
And then the noble sport is high ;
The jess[3] is loosed, the hood thrown by ;

[1] *Hooded hawk.*—The falcon's head was kept covered until
he moment that he was let loose after his prey.
[2] *Hawking gear*—the apparatus used in hawking.
[3] *Jess*—one of the short straps round the leg of a hawk
by which it was held on the wrist.

And " *leurre !* " the jolly falconers cry,
And wheeling round the falcons fly
   Impatient of their prey.

A moment and the quarry's[1] ta'en,
The falconer's cry sounds forth amain,
The true hawk soars and soars again,
   Nor once the game is missed !
And thus the jocund day is spent,
In joyous sport and merriment ;
And baron old were well content
To fell his wood, and pawn his rent,
   For the hawk upon his wrist.

Oh, falcon proud, and goshawk gay,
Your pride of place has passed away,
The lone wood is your home by day,
   Your resting perch by night ;
The craggy rock your castle-tower,
The gay green wood your " ladies' bow
Your own wild will the master power
   That can control your flight !

Yet, noble bird, old fame is thine,
Still liv'st thou in the minstrel's line ;
Still in old pictures art the sign
   Of high and pure degree ;
And still, with kindling hearts we read,
How barons came to Runnymede,
Falcon on wrist, to do the deed
   That made all England free !

                         Mary H

   [1] Quarry—prey.

UNKIND REFLECTIONS.

OH! never let us lightly fling
A barb[1] of woe to wound another;
Oh! never let us haste to bring
The cup of sorrow to a brother.

Each has the power to wound; but he
Who wounds that he may witness pain,
Has spurned the law of charity,
Which ne'er inflicts a pang in vain.

'Tis godlike to awaken joy,
Or sorrow's influence to subdue—
But not to wound, or to annoy,
Is part of virtue's lesson too.

Peace, winged in fairer worlds above,
Shall lend her dawn to brighten this;
Then all man's labour shall be love,
And all his aim his brother's bliss.

Gisborne.

———◦◦◦———

THE LOSS OF THE ROYAL GEORGE.[2]

TOLL for the brave!
The brave that are no more!
All sunk beneath the wave,
Fast by their native shore!

[1] *Barb*—an arrow.
[2] *The Royal George*—a vessel of war of 100 guns, commanded by Admiral Kempenfelt, which went down in Spithead harbour, August 29, 1782, with 800 men on board, who were all *lost.*

Eight hundred of the brave,
  Whose courage well was tried,
Had made the vessel heel,[1]
  And laid her on her side;

A land breeze shook the shrouds,
  And she was overset;
Down went the Royal George,
  With all her crew complete.

Toll for the brave!
  Brave Kempenfélt is gone;
His last sea fight is fought;
  His work of glory done.

It was not in the battle;
  No tempest gave the shock;
She sprang no fatal leak;
  She ran upon no rock:

His sword was in his sheath,
  His fingers held the pen,
When Kempenfelt went down,
  With twice four hundred men.

Weigh the vessel up,
  Once dreaded by our foes!
And mingle with our cup
  The tear that England owes.

Her timbers yet are sound,
  And she may float again,

---

[1] *Heel*—lean on one side.

Full-charged with England's thunder,
And plough the distant main.[1]

But Kempenfelt is gone;
His victories are o'er;
And he and his eight hundred
Shall plough the wave no more.

Cowper.

LESSONS TO BE DERIVED FROM BIRDS.

WHAT is that, mother?
    The lark, my child!—
The morn has but just looked out, and smiled,
When he starts from his humble grassy nest,
And is up and away with the dew on his breast,
And a hymn in his heart, to yon pure bright sphere,
To warble it out in his Maker's ear.
    Ever, my child! be thy morn's first lays
    Tuned, like the lark's, to thy Maker's praise?

What is that, mother?
    The dove, my son!
And that low, sweet voice, like a widow's moan,
Is flowing out from her gentle breast,
Constant and pure by that lonely nest,

[1] This hope was never realised. The vessel remained in the spot where it had sunk for more than fifty years; but in the course of the last few years, Colonel Pasley, a celebrated engineer, succeeded, by means of the diving-bell, in recovering several of the guns and other stores, and in bursting asunder, with charges of gunpowder, the timbers of the hulk, which still held firmly together.

C C

As the wave is poured from some crystal urn,
For her distant dear one's quick return.
Ever, my son, be thou like the dove—
In friendship as faithful, as constant in love.

What is that, mother?
The eagle, boy!
Proudly careering his course of joy,
Firm on his own mountain vigour relying,
Breasting the dark storm, the red bolt defying;
His wing on the wind, and his eye on the sun,
He swerves not a hair, but bears onward, right on
Boy! may the eagle's flight ever be thine,
Onward and upward, true to the line.

What is that, mother?
The swan, my love!
He is floating down from his native grove;
No loved one, now, no nestling nigh,
He is floating down by himself to die;
Death darkens his eye, and unplumes his wings,
Yet the sweetest song is the last he sings.[1]
Live so, my love, that when death shall come,
Swan-like and sweet, it may waft thee home.

G. W. Doa

---◆◇◆---

SABBATH MORNING.

How still the morning of the hallowed day!
Mute is the voice of rural labour, hushed

---

[1] The notion of the swan's singing before its death, a
indeed of its singing at all, must be reckoned amongst t
fictions of the poets.

The ploughboy's whistle and the milkmaid's song ;
The scythe lies glittering in the dewy wreath
Of tedded grass,[1] mingled with fading flowers,
That yestermorn bloomed waving in the breeze :
Sounds the most faint attract the ear—the hum
Of early bee, the rustling of the leaves,
The distant bleating, midway up the hill.
To him who wanders o'er the upland leas,[2]
The blackbird's note comes mellower from the dale,
And sweeter from the sky the gladsome lark
Warbles his heaven-tuned song : the lulling brook
Murmurs more gently down the deep-worn glen,
While from yon lowly roof, whose curling smoke
O'ermounts the mist, is heard at intervals
The voice of psalms, the simple song of praise.

Grahame.

MORAL MAXIMS

FROM VARIOUS AUTHORS.

Trust not yourself, but, your defects to know,
Make use of every friend, of every foe.

Pope.

Avoid extremes ; and shun the fault of such,
Who still are pleased too little, or too much :
At every trifle scorn to take offence—
That always shows great pride, or little sense.

Id.

---

[1] *Tedded grass*—newly-mown grass, laid in rows.
[2] *Lea*—enclosed pasture land.

By ignorance is pride increased ;
Those most assume who know the least.

Gay.

Cowards are cruel, but the brave
Love mercy, and delight to save.

Id.

Distrust mankind, with your own heart confer,
And dread even *there* to find a flatterer.

Young.

Duty by habit is to pleasure turned;
He is content who to obey has learned.

Sir Egerton Brydges.

To thine own woes be not thy thoughts confined;
But go abroad and think of all mankind.

Id.

Firm in resolve by sterling worth to gain
Love and respect, thou shalt not strive in vain.

Id.

The skies, the air, the morning's breezy call,
Alike are free, and full of health, to all.

Id.

He fails who pleasure makes his prime pursuit
For pleasure is of duty done the fruit.

———◦◦◦———

It is a virtue to improve the mind;
And if for truth we labour we shall find.

I

———◦◦◦———

By exercise our skill and courage grows
And that which once was scanty, overflows.

Id.

———◦◦◦———

That thou mayst injure no man, dove-like be;
And serpent-like, that none may injure thee.

Cowper.

———◦◦◦———

Absence of occupation is not rest :—
A mind quite vacant is a mind distrest.

Id.

———◦◦◦———

No wealth into this world we brought,
  And none can take away;
The blind in mind, the poor in thought,
  How blind! how poor are they!

C. D. Sillery.

———◦◦◦———

A very little satisfies
  An honest and a grateful heart;

c c 2

And who would [1] more than will suffice,
Does covet more than is his part.

If happiness has not her seat
  And centre in the breast,
We may be wise, or rich, or great,
  But never can be blest.

Burns.

———◆◆◆———

Trust not to each accusing tongue,
  As most weak persons do ;
But still believe that story false
  Which *ought not* to be true.

Sheridan.

———◆◆◆———

On folly's lips eternal tattlings dwell ;
Wisdom speaks little, but that little well ;
So lengthening shades the sun's decline betray,
But shorter shadows mark meridian day.

Bishop.

———◆◆◆———

Virtue's a fund of unexhausted store,
For there the very *wish* for more *is* more.

Id.

———◆◆◆———

Go to the bee ! and thence bring home,
(Worth all the treasures of her comb)
  An antidote against rash strife ;
She, when her angry flight she wings,
But once, and at her peril, *stings ;*
  But *gathers* honey—all her life.

Id.

1 *Would*—wishes for.

How sharper than a serpent's tooth it is
To have a thankless child !

Shakspeare.

———◆◆———

Poor and content is rich, and rich enough;
But riches, endless, are as poor as winter,
To him that ever fears he shall be poor.

Id.

———◆◆———

——————Who best
Can suffer, best can do ; best reign, who first
Well hath obeyed.

Milton.

———◆◆———

THE NOBLE NATURE.

It is not growing like a tree
In bulk, doth make man better be;
Or standing long an oak three hundred year,
To fall a log at last, dry, bald, and sere;
A lily of a day
Is fairer far in May,
Although it fall and die that night
It was the plant and flower of sight.
In small proportions we just beauty see;
And in short measures life may perfect be.

Ben Jonson.

———◆◆———

THE WREN'S NEST.

Among the dwellings framed by birds
In field or forest with nice care,

Is none that with the little wren's
  In snugness may compare.

No door the tenement requires,
  And seldom needs a laboured roof;
Yet is it to the fiercest sun
  Impervious and storm-proof.

So warm, so beautiful withal,
  In perfect fitness for its aim,
That to the kind [1] by special grace
  Their instinct surely came.

And when from their abode they seek
  An opportune recess,
The hermit has no finer eye
  For shadowy quietness.

These find, mid ivied abbey walls,
  A canopy in some still nook;
Others are penthoused [2] by a brae [3]
  That overhangs a brook.

There to the brooding bird, her mate
  Warbles by fits his low clear song;
And by the busy streamlet, both
  Are sung to all day long.

Or in sequestered lanes they build,
  Where, till the flitting bird's return,
Her eggs within the nest repose
  Like relics in an urn.

---

[1] *The kind*—the wren kind, wrens in general.
[2] *Penthoused*—covered by a penthouse or shed.
[3] *Brae*—a Scottish word signifying a declivity.

But still, where general choice is good,
  There is a better and a best:
And, among fairest objects, some
  Are fairer than the rest.

This one of those small builders proved
  In a green covert, where, from out
The forehead of a pollard oak,[1]
  The leafy antlers sprout;

For she who planned the mossy lodge,
  Mistrusting her evasive skill,
Had to a primose looked for aid
  Her wishes to fulfil.

High on the trunk's projecting brow
  And fixed an infant's span above
The budding flowers, peeped forth the nest,
  The prettiest of the grove!

The treasure proudly did I show
  To some whose minds without disdain
Can turn to little things; but once
  Looked up for it in vain;

'Tis gone—a ruthless spoiler's prey,
  Who heeds not beauty, love, or song;
'Tis gone! (so seemed it) and we grieved
  Indignant at the wrong.

Just three days after, passing by,
  In clearer light the moss-built cell
I saw, espied its shaded mouth,
  And felt that all was well.

[1] *Pollard oak*—an oak that has had its head lopped or oped.

The primrose for a veil had spread
  The largest of her upright leaves:
And thus, for purposes benign,
  A simple flower deceives.

Concealed from friends who might disturb
  Thy quiet with no ill intent,
Secure from evil eyes and hands,
  On barbarous plunder bent,

Rest, mother-bird! and when thy young
  Take flight, and thou art free to roam,
When withered is the guardian flower
  And empty thy late home,

Think how ye prospered, thou and thine,
  Amid the unviolated grove,
Housed near the growing primrose tuft,
  In foresight, or in love.

Wordsworth

OH SPARE MY FLOWER.

Oh spare my flower! my gentle flower,
  The slender creature of a day!
Let it bloom out its little hour,
  And pass away.

Too soon its fleeting charms must lie
  Decayed, unnoticed, overthrown;
Oh hasten not its destiny,
  So like my own.

The breeze will roam this way to-morrow,
  And sigh to find its playmate gone;

The bee will come its sweets to borrow,
  And meet with none.

Oh spare ! and let it still outspread
  Its beauties to the passing eye,
And look up from its lowly bed
  Upon the sky.

Oh spare my flower ! Thou know'st not what
  Thy undiscerning hand would tear ;
A thousand charms thou notest not
  Lie treasured there.

Not Solomon, in all his state,
  Was clad like Nature's simplest child,
Nor could the world combined create
  One floweret wild.

Spare, then, this humble monument
  Of the Almighty's power and skill ;
And let it at his shrine present
  Its homage still.

He made it who makes nought in vain ;
  He watches it who watches thee ;
And He can best its date ordain,
  Who bade it be.

Lyte.

———◦◇◦———

LAMBS AT PLAY.

What know, ye who have felt and seen
morning smiles and soul-enlivening green,
you give the thrilling transport way ?
eye brighten, when young lambs at play
r your path with animated pride,
merry clusters by your side ?

Ye who can smile—to wisdom no disgrace—
At the arch meaning of a kitten's face;
If spotless innocence, and infant mirth,
Excites to praise or gives reflection birth;
In shades like these pursue your favourite joy,
'Midst Nature's revels, sports that never cloy.
A few begin a short but vigorous race,
And Indolence, abashed, soon flies the place:
Thus challenged forth, see thither, one by one,
From every side assembling playmates run;
A thousand wily antics mark their stay,
A starting crowd, impatient of delay :
Like the fond dove from fearful prison freed,
Each seems to say, " Come, let us try our speed,"
Away they scour, impetuous, ardent, strong,
The green turf trembling as they bound along;
Adown the slope, then up the hillock climb,
Where every molehill is a bed of thyme ;
There, panting, stop; yet scarcely can refrain,
A bird, a leaf, will set them off again :
Or, if a gale with strength unusual blow,
Scattering the wild-briar roses into snow,
Their little limbs increasing efforts try,
Like the torn flower, the fair assemblage fly.
Ah, fallen rose ! sad emblem of their doom ;
Frail as thyself, they perish while they bloom !

Bloomfield

THE AFFECTION OF A DOG.

WHEN wise Ulysses,[1] from his native coast
Long kept by wars, and long by tempest tost,

---

[1] *Ulysses*—king of Ithaca (an island in the Mediterranean) and celebrated as a leader in the Trojan war.

ived at last, poor, old, disguised, alone,
all his friends, and e'en his queen, unknown,
nged as he was, with age, and toils, and cares,
rowed his reverend face, and white his hairs,
iis own palace forced to ask his bread,
rned by those slaves his former bounty fed;
got of all his own domestic crew,
faithful dog alone his master knew!
ed, unhoused, neglected, on the clay,
a an old servant, now cashiered,[1] he lay:
l, though e'en then expiring on the plain,
ched with resentment of ungrateful man,
l longing to behold his ancient lord again,
l when he saw, he rose, and crawled to meet—
as all he could—and fawned and kissed his feet,
ed with dumb joy; then falling by his side,
ed his returning lord, looked up, and died!

THE ROSE.

Rose had been washed (just washed in a
ower,)
ch Mary to Anna conveyed;
entiful moisture encumbered the flower,
weighed down its beautiful head.

was all filled, and the leaves were all wet,
t seemed, to a fanciful view,
for the buds it had left with regret
flourishing bush where it grew.

[1] *Cashiered*—discarded, turned off.

D D

I hastily seized it, unfit as it was
  For a nosegay, so dripping and drowned :
And, swinging it rudely, too rudely, alas !
  I snapped it—it fell to the ground !

And such, I exclaimed, is the pitiless part
  Some act by the delicate mind ;
Regardless of wringing and breaking a heart
  Already to sorrow resigned.

This elegant rose, had I shaken it less,
  Might have bloomed with its owner awhile ;
And the tear that is wiped with a little address,
  May be followed perhaps by a smile.

Cowper.

SUNSHINE AFTER A SHOWER.

Ever after summer shower,
When the bright sun's returning power
With laughing beam has chased the storm,
And cheered reviving Nature's form :
By sweet-briar hedges bathed in dew,
Let me my wholesome path pursue ;
There, issuing forth, the frequent snail
Wears the dank [1] way with slimy trail ; [2]
While as I walk, from pearled bush
The sunny, sparkling drop I brush,
And all the landscape fair I view
Clad in a robe of fresher hue ;
And so loud the blackbird sings,
That far and near the valley rings ;

Dank—damp, moist.   [2] Trail—track.

From shelter deep of shaggy rock
The shepherd drives his joyful flock ;
From bowering beech the mower blithe
With new-born vigour grasps the scythe ;
While o'er the smooth unbounded meads
Its last faint gleam the rainbow spreads.

Thomas Warton.

NOW AND THEN.

In distant days of wild romance,
　Of magic mist and fable,
When stones could argue, trees advance,
　And brutes to talk were able ;
When shrubs and flowers were said to preach,
And manage all the parts of speech ;—

'Twas then, no doubt, if 'twas at all,
　(But doubts we need not mention,)
That THEN and NOW, two adverbs small,
　Engaged in sharp contention ;
But how they made each other hear,
Tradition doth not make appear.

THEN was a sprite of subtle frame,
　With rainbow tints invested,
On clouds of dazzling light she came,
　And stars her forehead crested ;
Her sparkling eye of azure hue
Seemed borrowed from the distant blue.

Now rested on the solid earth,
　And sober was her vesture ;
She seldom either grief or mirth
　Expressed by word or gesture ;

Composed, sedate, and firm she stood,
And looked industrious, calm, and good.

THEN sang a wild, fantastic song,
 Light as the gale she flies on ;
Still stretching, as she sailed along,
 Towards the fair horizon,
Where clouds of radiance, fringed with gold,
O'er hills of emerald beauty rolled.

Now rarely raised her sober eye
 To view that golden distance :
Nor let one idle minute fly
 In hope of THEN's assistance ;
But still, with busy hands, she stood,
Intent on doing *present* good.

She ate the sweet but homely fare
 That passing moments brought her :
While THEN, expecting dainties rare,
 Despised such bread and water ;
And waited for the fruits and flowers
Of future, still receding hours.

Now, venturing once to ask her why,[1]
 She answered with invective ;
And pointed as she made reply,
 Towards that long perspective
Of years to come, in distant blue,
Wherein she meant to *live* and *do.*

"Alas ! " says she, "how hard you toil,
 With undiverted sadness !

[1] *To ask her why*—that is, to ask her why she waited f
the fruits and flowers of the future, instead of enjoying t
present.

Behold yon land of wine and oil—
  Those sunny hills of gladness;
Those joys I wait with eager brow "—
" And so you always will," said NOW.

" That fairy land that looks so real,
  Recedes as you pursue it;
Thus while you wait for times ideal,
  I take my work and do it;
Intent to form, when time is gone,
A pleasant past to look upon."

" Ah, well," said THEN, " I envy not
  Your dull fatiguing labours;
Aspiring to a brighter lot,
  With thousands of my neighbours;
Soon as I reach that golden hill "—
" But that," says NOW, " you never will."

" And e'en suppose you should," said she,
  " (Though mortal ne'er attained it,)
Your nature you must change with me,
  The moment you had gained it:
Since hope fulfilled, you must allow,
Turns NOW to THEN, and THEN to NOW."

Jane Taylor.

A FAREWELL.

My fairest child, I have no song to give you;
  No lark could pipe to skies so dull and grey:
Yet ere we part, one lesson I can give you
  For every day.

D D 2

Be good, sweet maid, and let who will be clever
Do noble things, not dream them, all day lon[
And so make life, death, and that vast for ever,
One grand, sweet song.

Kingsle

THE WOOD-LANE IN SPRING.

I KNOW a lane, thick set with golden broom,
Where the pale primrose and tall orchis bloom;
And azure violets, lowly drooping, shed
Delicious perfume round their mossy bed;
And all the first-born blossoms of the year,
That spring uncultured, bud and blossom here.
Oh! 'tis a lovely spot! high overhead
Gigantic oaks their lofty branches spread;
The glossy ivy, the rich eglantine,
The rambling briony, and sweet woodbine,
Fling their fantastic wreaths from spray to spray,
And shower their treasures on the lap of May.
Here, the blithe blackbird trills his matin song,
Till woodland dells his bugle notes prolong;
And the gay linnet and the airy thrush
Responsive whistle from the hawthorn bush;
Near, though unseen, the lonely cuckoo floats,
And wakes the morn with his complaining notes;
Here the shy partridge leads her yellow brood,
And the majestic pheasant from the wood
No longer dreads the cruel fowler's gun,
But sports his gorgeous plumage in the sun.
'Tis passing sweet to rove these woodland bowers,
When the young sun has shed on leaves and flower

A tender glory, and the balmy thorn
Spreads his white banner to the breath of morn—
Sporting a coronal of living light,
Strung from the dew-drops of the weeping night.
'Tis sweet to trace the footsteps of the spring
O'er the green earth—to see her lightly fling
Her flowery wreaths on Nature's breathing shrine,
And round the hoary woods her garlands twine;
To hear her voice in every passing breeze
That stirs the new-born foliage on the trees.
'Tis sweet to hear the song of birds arise
At early dawn, to gaze on cloudless skies,
To scatter round you, as you lightly pass,
A shower of diamonds from each blade of grass;
And while your footsteps press the dewy sod,
" To look through Nature up to Nature's God."

———◆◆———

THE GRASSHOPPER AND THE CRICKET.

THE poetry of earth is never dead:
  When all the birds are faint with the hot sun,
  And hide in cooling trees, a voice will run
From hedge to hedge about the new-mown mead:
That is the grasshopper's—he takes the lead
  In summer luxury—he has never done
  With his delights, for when tired out with fun,
He rests at ease beneath some pleasant weed.
The poetry of earth is ceasing never:
  On a lone winter evening, when the frost
Has wrought a silence, from the stove there shrills
The Cricket's song, in warmth increasing ever,
  And seems to one in drowsiness half lost,
The *grasshopper's* among the grassy hills.   Keats

THE HOMES OF ENGLAND.

THE stately Homes of England,
How beautiful they stand!
Amidst their tall ancestral trees,
O'er all the pleasant land.
The deer across their greensward bound
Through shade and sunny gleam,
And the swan glides past them with the sound
Of some rejoicing stream.

The merry Homes of England!
Around their hearths by night,
What gladsome looks of household love
Meet in the ruddy light!
There woman's voice flows forth in song,
Or childish tale is told;
Or lips move tunefully along
Some glorious page of old.

The blessed Homes of England!
How softly on their bowers
Is laid the holy quietness
That breathes from Sabbath hours!
Solemn, yet sweet, the church bell's chime
Floats through their woods at morn;
All other sounds, in that still time,
Of breeze and leaf are born.

The cottage Homes of England!
By thousands on her plains,
They are smiling o'er the silvery brooks,
And round the hamlet-fanes.
Through glowing orchards forth they peep,
Each from its nook of leaves;

And fearless there the lowly sleep,
As the bird beneath their eaves.

The free, fair Homes of England!
Long, long in hut and hall,
May hearts of native proof be reared
To guard each hallowed wall!
And green for ever be the groves,
And bright the flowery sod,
Where first the child's glad spirit loves
Its country and its God!

Mrs. Hemans.

WISHES.

AID in my quiet bed, in study as I were,
saw within my troubled head a heap of thoughts
    appear,
nd every thought did show so lively in mine eyes,
hat now I sighed, and then I smiled, as cause of
    thoughts did rise.
saw the little boy, in thought how oft that he
id wish of God, to 'scape the rod, a tall young man
    to be;
he young man eke that feels his bones with pain
    opprest,
ow he would be a rich old man, to live and lie at
    rest!
he rich old man, that sees his end draw on so sore,
ow would he be a boy again to live so much the
    more.
hereat full oft I smiled to see how all those three,
om boy to man, from man to boy, would chop and
    change degree.

Earl of Surrey.

THE FROST SPIRIT.

HE comes—he comes—the frost spirit comes!
  You may trace his footsteps now
On the naked woods, and the blasted fields,
  And the broad hill's withered brow.
He has smitten the leaves of the grey old trees,
  Where their pleasant green came forth,
And the winds which follow wherever he goes,
  Have shaken them down to earth.

He comes—he comes—the frost spirit comes!
  From the frozen Labrador—
From the icy bridge of the Northern Seas,
  Which the white bear wanders o'er—
Where the fisherman's sail is stiff with ice,
  And the luckless forms below
In the sunless cold of the atmosphere
  Into marble statues grow !

He comes—he comes—the frost spirit comes!
  On the rushing northern blast,
And the dark Norwegian pines have bowed
  As his fearful breath went past.
With an unscorched wing he has hurried on,
  Where the fires of Hecla glow
On the darkly beautiful sky above
  And the ancient ice below.

He comes—he comes—the frost spirit comes!
  And the quiet lake shall feel
The torpid touch of his glazing breath,
  And ring to the skater's heel ;
And the streams which danced on the broken rock
  Or sang to the leaning grass,

>ow again to the winter's chain,
. in mournful silence pass.

nes—he comes—the frost spirit comes!
us meet him as we may,
irn with the light of the parlour fire
evil power away ;
ither closer the circle round,
in that fire-light dances high,
ugh at the shriek of the baffled fiend
iis sounding wing goes by !

Mellen.

THE FAIRIES.

Up the airy mountain,
Down the rushy glen,
We daren't go a-hunting
For fear of little men ;
Wee folk, good folk,
Trooping all together ;
Green jacket, red cap,
And white owl's feather !

Down along the rocky shore
Some make their home,
They live on crispy pancakes
Of yellow tide-foam ;
Some in the reeds
Of the black mountain-lake,
With frogs for their watch-dogs,
All night awake.

High on the hill-top
The old king sits ;

He is now so grey and old
He's nigh lost his wits.
With a bridge of white mist
Columbkill he crosses,
On his stately journeys
From Slieveleague to Rosses;
Or going up with music
On cold starry nights
To sup with the queen
Of the gay Northern Lights.

They stole little Bridget
For seven years long;
When she came down again,
Her friends were all gone.
They took her lightly back,
Between the night and morrow,
They thought that she was fast asleep,
But she was dead with sorrow.
They have kept her ever since
Deep within the lakes,
On a bed of flag-leaves,
Watching till she wakes.

By the craggy hill-side,
Through the mosses bare,
They have planted thorn-trees
For pleasure here and there.
Is any man so daring
As dig them up in spite,
He shall find their sharpest thorns
In his bed at night.

Up the airy mountain,
Down the rushy glen,

We daren't go a-hunting
For fear of little men ;
Wee folk, good folk,
Trooping all together;
Green jacket, red cap,
And white owl's feather !

Allingham.

U BEN ADHEM AND THE ANGEL.

en Adhem (may his tribe increase)
one night from a deep dream of peace,
r, within the moonlight in his room,
it rich, and like a lily in bloom,
el writing in a book of gold :—
ng peace had made Ben Adhem bold,
the presence in the room he said,
writest thou ? "—The vision raised its head,
;h a look made of all sweet accord,
ed, " The names of those who love the
."
s mine one ? " said Abou.   " Nay, not so,"
the Angel.   Abou spoke more low,
erly still, and said, " I pray thee then
ie as one that loves his fellow-men."

gel wrote, and vanish'd.   The next night
again with a great wakening light,
iow'd the names whom love of God had
'd,
! Ben Adhem's name led all the rest.

Leigh Hunt.

E E

THE DISPUTED CASE.

BETWEEN Nose and Eyes a strange contest arose;
The spectacles set them unhappily wrong:
The point in dispute was, as all the world knows,
To which the said spectacles ought to belong.

So Tongue was the lawyer, and argued the cause
With a great deal of wit, and a wig full of learning,
While chief baron Ear sat to balance the laws,
So famed for his talent in nicely discerning.

" In behalf of the Nose it will quickly appear,
And your lordship," he said, " will undoubtedly find,
That the Nose has had spectacles always in wear,
Which amounts to possession time out of mind."

Then holding the spectacles up to the court—
" Your lordship observes they are made with a
    straddle,
As wide as the ridge of the Nose is, in short,
Designed to sit close to it, just like a saddle.

" Again; would your lordship a moment suppose
('Tis a case that has happened, and may be again)
That the visage or countenance had not a nose,
Pray who would, or who could, wear spectacles then?

" On the whole it appears, and my argument shows,
With a reasoning the court will never condemn,
That the spectacles plainly were made for the nose,
And the nose was as plainly intended for them."

Then shifting his side (as the lawyer knows how)
He pleaded again in behalf of the Eyes;
But what were his arguments few people know,
For the court did not think they were equally wise.

So his lordship decreed, with a grave solemn tone,
Decisive and clear, without one " if " or " but,"
That, whenever the Nose put his spectacles on,
By day-light, or candle-light, Eyes should be shut.

Cowper.

A SONG OF A BOAT.

I.

THERE was once a boat on a billow:
Lightly she rocked to her port remote,
And the foam was white in her wake like snow,
And her frail mast bowed when the breeze would
blow,
And bent like a wand of willow.

II.

I shaded mine eyes one day when the boat
Went curtseying over the billow;
I marked her course till, a dancing mote,
She faded out on the moonlit foam,
And I stayed behind in the dear loved home;
And my thoughts all day were about the boat,
And my dreams upon the pillow.

III.

I pray you hear my song of a boat,
For it is but short:—
My boat, you shall find none fairer afloat,
In river or port.
Long I looked out for the lad she bore,
On the open desolate sea,
And I think he sailed to the heavenly shore,
For he came not back to me—

Ah me!
Jean Ingelow.

THE VILLAGE BLACKSMITH

UNDER a spreading chestnut tree
  The village smithy stands;
The smith, a mighty man is he,
  With large and sinewy hands:
And the muscles of his brawny arms
  Are strong as iron bands.

His hair is crisp, and black, and long,
  His face is like the tan:
His brow is wet with honest sweat,
  He earns whate'er he can,
And looks the whole world in the face,
  For he owes not any man.

Week in, week out, from morn till night,
  You can hear his bellows blow;
You can hear him swing his heavy sledge,
  With measured beat and slow.
Like a sexton ringing the village bell,
  When the evening sun is low.

And children coming home from school
  Look in at the open door:
They love to see the flaming forge,
  And hear the bellows roar.
And catch the burning sparks that fly
  Like chaff from a threshing floor.

He goes on Sunday to the church,
  And sits among his boys:
He hears the parson pray and preach;
  He hears his daughter's voice
Singing in the village choir,
  And it makes his heart rejoice.

It sounds to him like her mother's voice,
  Singing in Paradise !
He needs must think of her once more
  How in the grave she lies;
And with his hard, rough hand he wipes
  A tear out of his eyes.

Toiling,—rejoicing,—sorrowing,
  Onward through life he goes ;
Each morning sees some task begun,
  Each evening sees its close ;
Something attempted, something done,
  Has earned a night's repose.

Thanks, thanks to thee, my worthy friend,
  For the lesson thou hast taught !
Thus at the flaming forge of life
  Our fortunes must be wrought;
Thus on its sounding anvil shaped
  Each burning deed and thought.

Longfellow.

THE GREATNESS AND GLORY OF GOD.

I.

Thou art, O Lord, the life and light
  Of all this wondrous world we see;
Its glow by day, its smile by night,
  Are but reflections caught from Thee :
Where'er we turn thy glories shine,
And all things fair and bright are Thine.

II.

When day, with parting beam, delays
  Among the op'ning clouds of ev'n ;

And we can almost think we gaze
   Through golden vistas into heav'n;
Those hues that mark the sun's decline,
So soft, so radiant, Lord! are thine.

III.

When night, with wings of starry gloom,
   O'ershadows all the earth and skies,
Like some dark, beauteous bird, whose plume
   Is sparkling with unnumber'd dyes;—
That sacred gloom, those fires divine,
So grand, so countless, Lord! are Thine.

IV.

When youthful Spring around us breathes,
   Thy Spirit warms her fragrant sigh;
And every flow'r the Summer wreathes
   Is born beneath that kindling eye:
Where'er we turn thy glories shine,
And all things fair and bright are Thine.

T. Moore.

THE SONG OF MIRIAM.

Sound the loud timbrel o'er Egypt's dark sea!
Jehovah has triumph'd—his people are free.
Sing—for the pride of the tyrant is broken,
His chariots and horsemen, all splendid and brave;
How vain was their boasting! The Lord hath but
   spoken,
And chariots and horsemen are sunk in the wave;
Sound the loud timbrel o'er Egypt's dark sea,
Jehovah has triumphed—his people are free!

ıe to the Conqueror, praise to the Lord,
ɼord was our arrow, his breath was our sword!—
 shall return to tell Egypt the story
ıose she sent forth in the hour of her pride?
:he Lord hath look'd out from his pillar of glory,
 all her brave thousands are dash'd in the tide;
.d the loud timbrel o'er Egypt's dark sea!
vah has triumph'd—his people are free!

T. Moore.

HE NEVER SMILED AGAIN.[1]

ıɛ bark that held a prince went down,
The sweeping waves rolled on;
ıd what was England's glorious crown
To him that wept a son?
: lived—for life may long be borne,
Ere sorrow break its chain;—
hy comes not death to those who mourn?
He never smiled again!

ıere stood proud forms before his throne,
The stately and the brave;
ıt which could fill the place of one,
That one beneath the wave?
fore him passed the young and fair,
ın pleasure's reckless train;
t seas dashed o'er his son's bright hair—
He never smiled again!

is recorded of Henry the First, that, after the death
son Prince William, who perished by shipwreck off the
ɔf *Normandy,* he was never seen to smile.

He sat where festal bowls went round;
　He heard the minstrel sing ;
He saw the tourney's victor crowned
　Amidst the knightly ring :
A murmur of the restless deep
　Was blent with every strain,
A voice of winds that would not sleep—
　He never smiled again !

Hearts, in that time, closed o'er the trace
　Of vows once fondly poured,
And strangers took the kinsman's place
　At many a joyous board ;
Graves, which true love had bathed with tea:
　Were left to heaven's bright rain,
Fresh hopes were born for other years—
　He never smiled again !

　　　　　　　　　　Mrs. He

THE MARINER'S SONG.

A wet sheet and a flowing sea,
A wind that follows fast,
And fills the white and rustling sail,
And bends the gallant mast ;
And bends the gallant mast, my boys,
While, like the eagle free,
Away the good ship flies, and leaves
　　Old England on the lee.

" Oh for a soft and gentle wind ! "
I heard a fair one cry ;
But give to me the snoring breeze,
And white waves heaving high ;

And white waves heaving high, my boys,
The good ship tight and free—
The world of waters is our home,
    And merry men are we.

There's tempest in yon horned moon,
And lightning in yon cloud;
And hark the music, mariners,
The wind is piping loud;
The wind is piping loud, my boys,
The lightning flashing free—
While the hollow oak our palace is,
    Our heritage the sea.

Allan Cunningham.

THE STORMY PETREL.

A THOUSAND miles from land are we,
Tossing about on the roaring sea;
From billow to bounding billow cast,
Like fleecy snow on the stormy blast;
The sails are scattered about like weeds,
The strong masts shake like quivering reeds;
The mighty cables and iron chains,
The hull which all earthly strength disdains,
They strain and they crack; and hearts of stone
Their natural hard proud strength disown.

Up and down! up and down!
From the base of the wave to the billow's crown,
Amidst the flashing and feathery foam
The *stormy* petrel finds a home;

A home—if such a place can be
For her who lives on the wide wide sea,
On the craggy ice, in the frozen air,
And only seeketh her rocky lair
To warm her young, and teach them to spring
At once o'er the waves on their stormy wing!

Procte

WAR.

THE hunting tribes of air and earth,
Respect the brethren of their birth;
Nature, who loves the claim of kind,
Less cruel chase to each assigned:
The falcon, poised on soaring wing,
Watches the wild duck at the spring;
The slow-hound wakes the fox's lair,
The greyhound presses on the hare,
The eagle pounces on the lamb,
The wolf devours the fleecy dam:
E'en tiger fell and sullen bear
Their likeness and their lineage spare
Man only mars kind nature's plan,
And turns the fierce pursuit on man,
Plying war's desultory trade,
Incursion, flight, and ambuscade;
Since Nimrod, Cush's mighty son,
At first the bloody game begun.

Walter S

THE BIRD AND THE SHIP.

From the German of Müller.

The rivers rush into the sea,
    By castle and by town they go;
The winds behind them merrily
    Their noisy trumpets blow.

The clouds are passing far and high,
    We little birds in them play;
And everything that can sing and fly
    Goes with us, and far away.

" I greet thee, bonny boat! Whither or whence,
    With thy fluttering golden band ? "—
" I greet thee, little bird! To the wide sea
    I haste from the narrow land.

" Full and swollen is every sail;
    I see no longer a hill,
I have trusted all to the sounding gale,
    And it will not let me stand still.

" And wilt thou, little bird, go with us?
    Thou mayest stand on the mainmast tall,
For full to sinking is my house
    With merry companions all."

" I need not and seek not company,
    Bonny boat, I can sing all alone;
For the mainmast tall too heavy am I,
    Bonny boat, I have wings of my own.

" High over the sails, high over the mast,
    Who shall gainsay these joys?

When thy merry companions are still, at last
Thou shalt hear the sound of my voice.

" Who neither may rest, nor listen may,
God bless them every one!
I dart away, in the bright blue day,
And the golden fields of the sun.

" Thus do I sing my weary song,
Wherever the four winds blow;
And this same song, my whole life long,
Neither poet nor printer may know."

Longfellou

THE HEBREW MOTHER.

THE rose was in rich bloom on Sharon's plain,
When a young mother, with her first-born, thenc
Went up to Zion; for the boy was vowed
Unto the Temple service.[1]   By the hand
She led him, and her silent soul, the while,
Oft as the dewy laughter of his eye
Met her sweet serious glance, rejoiced to think
That aught so pure, so beautiful, was hers,
To bring before her God.

So passed they on,
O'er Judah's hills; and wheresoe'er the leaves
Of the broad sycamore made sounds at noon,
Like lulling rain-drops, or the olive-boughs,
With their cool dimness, crossed the sultry blue
Of Syria's heaven, she paused that he might rest;

[1] See 1 Sam. i. 24.—The presentation of Samuel is
posed to have taken place when he was about three years

Yet from her own meek eyelids chased the sleep
That weighed their dark fringe down, to sit and
    watch
The crimson deepening o'er his cheek's repose,
As at a red flower's heart; and where a fount
Lay, like a twilight star, midst palmy shades,
Making its banks green gems along the wild,—
There too she lingered, from the diamond wave,
Drawing clear water for his rosy lips,
And softly parting clusters of jet curls,
To bathe his brow.

      At last the fane was reached—
The earth's one sanctuary; and rapture hushed
Her bosom, as before her, through the day,
It rose, a mountain of white marble, steeped
In light like floating gold. But when that hour
Waned to the farewell moment,—when the boy
Lifted, through rainbow-gleaming tears, his eye
Beseechingly to hers—and, half in fear,
Turned from the white-robed priest, and round her
    arm
Clung even as ivy clings; the deep spring-tide
Of nature then swelled high; and o'er her child
Bending, her soul brake forth, in mingled sounds
Of weeping and sad song.—"Alas" she cried,

"Alas, my boy! thy gentle grasp is on me;
The bright tears quiver in thy pleading eyes;
    And now fond thoughts arise,
And silver cords again to earth have won me;
And like a vine thou claspest my full heart;—
    How shall I hence depart?

" How the lone paths retrace where thou wert
    playing
So late among the mountains at my side; .
    And I, in joyous pride,
By every place of flowers my course delaying,
Wove, even as pearls, the lilies round thy hair,
    Beholding thee so fair?

" Under the palm-trees, thou no more shalt meet
    me,
When from the fount at evening I return,
    With the full water urn !
Nor will thy sleep's low dove-like murmurs greet
    me
As midst the silence of the stars I wake,
    And watch for thy dear sake.

" And thou, will slumber's dewy cloud fall round
    thee,
Without thy mother's hand to smooth thy bed?
    Wilt thou not vainly spread
Thine arms, when darkness as a veil hath wound
    thee,
To fold my neck; and lift up, in thy fear,
    A cry which none shall hear?

" What have I said, my child? Will HE not hear
    thee.
Who the young ravens heareth from their nest?
    Will HE not guard thy rest,
And, in the hush of holy midnight near thee,
Breathe o'er thy soul, and fill its dreams with
    joy ?—
    Thou shalt sleep soft, my boy !

" I give thee to thy God !—the God that gave thee,
A well-spring of deep gladness to my heart !
   And, precious as thou art,
And pure as dew of Hermon, HE shall have thee,
My own, my beautiful, my undefiled !
   And thou shalt be HIS child.

" Therefore, farewell !—I go ; my soul may fail me
As the stag panteth for the water-brooks,
   Yearning for thy sweet looks ;
But thou, my first-born, droop not, nor bewail me ;
Thou in the shadow of the Rock shalt dwell,
   The Rock of strength—Farewell."

Mrs. Hemans.

THE CHILD IN THE WILDERNESS.

ENCINCTURED with a twine of leaves,
   That leafy twine his only dress—
A lovely boy was plucking fruits,
   In a moonlight wilderness.
The moon was bright, the air was free,
   And fruits and flowers together grew,
And many a shrub and many a tree ;
   And all put on a gentle hue,
Hanging in the shadowy air
Like a picture rich and rare !
It was a climate where, they say,
The night is more beloved than day.
   But who that beauteous boy beguiled,
That beauteous boy, to linger here,
   Alone by night, a little child,
   In place so silent and so wild?—
Has he no friend, no loving mother near?

Coleridge.

SEEDS AND FRUITS.

WE scatter seeds with careless hand,
And dream we ne'er shall see them mo:
　　But for a thousand years
　　　Their fruit appears
　In seeds that mar the land
　　Or healthful store.

The deeds we do—the words we say
Into still air they seem to fleet;
　　We count them ever past,—
　　　But they shall last—
　In the dread judgment, they
　　And we shall meet! *Lyra Inn*

———◆◇◆———

THE FIFTIETH BIRTHDAY OF AGAS

MAY 28, 1857.

IT was fifty years ago,
　In the pleasant month of May,
In the beautiful Pays de Vaud
　A child in the cradle lay.

And Nature, the old nurse, took
　The child upon her knee,
Saying, "Here is a story-book
　Thy Father has written for thee."

[1] *Agassiz*—the distinguished Swiss naturalist,
been for many years a Professor in Harvard Coll
bridge, Massachusetts. It was he who once wr
study Nature in the house, and when you go out
you cannot find her.'

" Come wander with me," she said,
  " Into regions yet untrod;
And read what is still unread
  In the manuscripts of God."

And he wandered away and away
  With Nature, the dear old nurse,
Who sang to him night and day
  The rhymes of the universe.

And whenever the way seemed long,
  Or his heart began to fail,
She would sing a more wonderful song,
  Or tell a more marvellous tale.

So she keeps him still a child,
  And will not let him go,
Though at times his heart beats wild
  For the beautiful Pays de Vaud;

Though at times he hears in his dreams
  The Ranz des Vaches of old, '
And the rush of mountain streams
  From glaciers clear and cold;

And the mother at home says, " Hark !
  For his voice I listen and yearn;
It is growing late and dark,
  And my boy does not return ! "
Longfellow.

THE WRECK OF THE HESPERUS.

IT was the schooner Hesperus,
  That sailed the wintry sea;
F F 2

And the skipper [1] had taken his little daughter
   To bear him company.

Blue were her eyes, as the fairy-flax,
   Her cheeks like the dawn of day,
And her bosom white as the hawthorn buds,
   That ope in the month of May.

The skipper he stood beside the helm,
   With his pipe in his mouth ;
And watched how the veering flaw [2] did blow
   The smoke now west, now south.

Then up and spake an old sailor,
   Had sailed the Spanish Main :
" I pray thee, put into yonder port,
   For I fear a hurricane.

" Last night, the moon had a golden ring,
   And to-night no moon we see ! "
The skipper, he blew a whiff from his pipe,
   And a scornful laugh laughed he.

Colder and colder blew the wind,
   A gale from the north-east ;
The snow fell hissing in the brine,
   And the billows frothed like yeast.

Down came the storm and smote amain
   The vessel in its strength ;
She shuddered and paused, like a frighted steed
   Then leaped her cable's length.

---

[1] *Skipper*—man of the ship, captain.
[2] *Flaw*—a sudden burst or gust of wind.

" Come hither! come hither ! my little daughter,
  And do not tremble so ;
For I can weather the roughest gale,
  That ever wind did blow."

He wrapped her warm in his seaman's coat,
  Against the stinging blast ;
He cut a rope from a broken spar,
  And bound her to the mast.

" O father! I hear the church-bells ring,
  O say, what may it be ? "
" Tis a fog-bell on a rock-bound coast ! "—
And he steered for the open sea.

" O father! I hear the sound of guns,
  O say, what may it be ? "
" Some ship in distress, that cannot live
  In such an angry sea ! "

" O father! I see a gleaming light,
  O say, what may it be ? "
But the father answered never a word,—
  A frozen corpse was he.

Lashed to the helm, all stiff and stark,
  With his face to the skies;
The lantern gleamed through the gleaming snow
  On his fixed and glassy eyes.

Then the maiden clasped her hands, and prayed
  That saved she might be ;
And she thought of Christ, who stilled the waves
  On the Lake of Galilee.

And fast through the midnight dark and drear,
  Through the whistling sleet and snow,

Like a sheeted ghost, the vessel swept
  Towards the reef of Norman's Woe.

And ever the fitful gusts between
  A sound came from the land;
It was the sound of the trampling surf,
  On the rocks and the hard sea-sand.

The breakers were right beneath her bows,
  She drifted a dreary wreck,
And a whooping billow swept the crew
  Like icicles from her deck.

She struck where the white and fleecy waves
  Looked soft as carded wool,
But the cruel rocks, they gored her side,
  Like the horns of an angry bull.

Her rattling shrouds, all sheathed in ice,
  With the masts, went by the board; [1]
Like a vessel of glass, she stove [2] and sank,
  Ho! ho! the breakers roared!

At daybreak on the black sea-beach,
  A fisherman stood aghast,
To see the form of a maiden fair,
  Lashed close to a drifting mast.

The salt sea was frozen on her breast,
  The salt tears in her eyes;
And he saw her hair, like the brown sea-weed
  On the billows fall and rise.

[1] *Went by the board*—went over the side of the v
were destroyed and lost.
[2] *Stove*—was staved in, or broken into.

Such was the wreck of the Hesperus,
   In the midnight and the snow !
Christ, save us all from a death like this,
   On the reef of Norman's Woe !

                        Longfellow.

WILLIAM TELL.[1]

Come, list to me, and you shall hear
   A tale of what befel
A famous man of Switzerland ;
   His name was William Tell.

Near Reuss's bank, from day to day,
   His little flock he led,
By prudent thrift, and hardy toil,
   Content to earn his bread.

[1] In the centre of the little town of Altorf, near the Lake of Lucerne, there stands a stone fountain, surmounted with the figures of William Tell and his son. It is said to cover the spot on which the father stood when he took aim at the apple on his child's head. It is right, however, to say that it is now seriously doubted whether such a person as William Tell ever existed. The story stands on much the same footing as those about Robin Hood and William of Cloudesly. In the latter, indeed, there is a similar incident. William of Cloudesly saves his life by cleaving with his arrow an apple placed on the head of his son at "six score paces." The ballad tells us that—

   " There even before the king
   In the earth he drove a stake,
   And bound thereto his eldest son,
   And bade him stand still thereat ;
   And turned the childes face him fro,
   Because he should not start ;
   An apple upon his head he set,
   And then his bow he bent, &c., &c."

Nor was the hunter's craft unknown;
   In Uri none was seen
To track the rock-frequenting herd
   With eye so true and keen.

A little son was in his home,
   A laughing, fair-haired boy;
So strong of limb, so blithe of heart,
   He made it ring with joy.

His father's sheep were all his friends,
   The lambs he called by name;
And when they frolicked in the fields,
   The child would share the game.

So peacefully their hours were spent
   That life had scarce a sorrow;
They took the good of every day,
   And hoped for more to-morrow.

But oft some shining April morn
   Is darkened in an hour;
And blackest griefs o'er joyous homes
   Alas! unseen may lower.

Not yet on Switzerland had dawned
   Her day of liberty;
The stranger's yoke was on her sons,
   And pressed right heavily.

So one was sent in luckless hour,
   To rule in Austria's name;
A haughty man of savage mood,—
   In pomp and pride he came.

One day in wantonness of power,
   He set his cap on high;—

" Bow down, ye slaves," the order ran ;
  " Who disobeys shall die ! "

It chanced that WILLIAM TELL, that morn,
  Had left his cottage home,
And with his little son in hand,
  To Altorf town had come.

TELL saw the crowd, the lifted cap,
  The tyrant's angry frown—
And heralds shouted in his ear,
  " Bow down, ye slaves, bow down ! "

Stern Gesler marked the peasant's mien,
  And watched to see him fall ;
But never palm tree straighter stood
  Than TELL before them all.

" My knee shall bend," he calmly said,
  " To God, and God alone ;
My life is in the Austrian's hand,
  My conscience is my own."

" Seize him, ye guards," the ruler cried,
  While passion choked his breath ;
" He mocks my power, he braves my lord,
  He dies the traitor's death.

" Yet wait.   The Swiss are marksmen true,
  So all the world doth say ;
That fair-haired stripling hither bring ;
  We'll try their skill to-day."

Hard by a spreading lime-tree stood,
  To this the youth was bound ;
They placed an apple on his head ;—
  He looked in wonder round.

" The fault is mine, if fault there be,"
 Cried TELL in accents wild ;
" On manhood let your vengeance fall,
 But spare, oh spare my child ! "

" *I* will not harm the pretty boy,"
 Said Gesler tauntingly ;
" If blood of his shall stain the ground,
 Yours will the murder be.

" Draw tight your bow, my cunning man,
 Your straightest arrow take ;
For, know, yon apple is your mark,
 Your liberty the stake."

A mingled noise of wrath and grief
 Was heard among the crowd ;
The men, they muttered curses deep,
 The women wept aloud.

Full fifty paces from his child,
 His cross-bow in his hand,
With lip compressed, and flashing eye,
 TELL firmly took his stand.

Sure, full enough of pain and woe
 This crowded earth has been ;
But never, since the curse began,
 So sad a sight was seen.

The noble boy stood bravely up,
 His cheek unblanched with fear ;
" Shoot straight," he cried, " thine aim is su
 It will not fail thee here."

" Heaven bless thee now," the parent said,
  " Thy courage shames me quite ; "
Then to his ear the shaft he drew,
  And watched its whizzing flight.

" 'Tis done, 'tis done, the child is safe ! "
  Shouted the multitude :
" Man tramples on his brother men,
  But GOD is ever good."

For, sure enough, the arrow went,
  As by an angel guided ;
In pieces two, beneath the tree,
  The apple fell divided.

" 'Twas bravely done," the ruler said,
  " My plighted word I keep ;
'Twas bravely done by sire and son—
  Go home, and feed your sheep."

·" No thanks I give thee for thy boon,"
  The peasant coldly said ;
" To God alone my praise is due,
  And duly shall be paid.

" Yet know, proud man, thy fate was near,
  Had I but missed my aim ;
Not unavenged my child had died,
  Thy parting hour the same.

" For see ! a *second* shaft was here,
  If harm my boy befel ;
Now go and bless the heavenly powers,
  My first has sped so well."

G G

GOD helped the right, GOD spared the sin,
    HE brings the proud to shame,
HE guards the weak against the strong,—
    Praise to His Holy name !

Rev. J. H. Gurn

———◦◦◦———

SIR PATRICK SPENS.[1]

THE king sits in Dunfermline town
    Drinking the blude-red wine :
" O where will I get a skeely skipper[2]
    To sail this new ship of mine ? "

O up and spake an eldern knight
    Sat at the king's right knee :
" Sir Patrick Spens is the best sailor
    That ever sailed the sea."

Our king has written a braid letter,
    And sealed it wi' his hand,
And sent it to Sir Patrick Spens—
    Was walking on the strand.

To Noroway, to Noroway,
    To Noroway o'er the faem ;[3]
The king's daughter to Noroway,
    'Tis thou maun bring her hame.[4] "

The first word that Sir Patrick read,
    Sae loud laughed he ;

---

[1] This old ballad probably refers to the escorting to N
way of King Alexander the Third's daughter, the Princ
Margaret, to marry Eric, King of Norway, in 1282.

[2] *Skeely skipper*—skilful captain.

[3] *Faem*, foam ; *hame*, home ; *maun*, must ; *bring*, take.

[4] *Bring her hame*—take her to her new home in Norw

The neist [1] word that Sir Patrick read,
    The tear blinded his ee.[2]

" O wha is this has done this deed,
    And tauld the king o' me,
To send us out at this time of the year,
    To sail upon the sea ?

" Be it wind, be it weet, be it hail, be it sleet,
    Our ship must sail the faem ;
The king's daughter to Noroway,
    'Tis we must bring her hame."

They hoisted their sails on Monenday morn,
    Wi' a' the speed they may ;
They hae landed safe in Noroway,
    Upon a Wodensday.

They hadna been a week, a week,
    In Noroway but twae,
When that the lords of Noroway
    Began aloud to say :—

" Ye Scottishmen spend a' our king's goud,
    And a' our queenis fee." [3]
" Ye lie, ye lie, ye liars loud,
    Fu' loud I hear ye lie ;

" For I brought as mickle white monie
    As gane [4] my men and me ;
And I brought a half-fow o' gude red goud
    Out o'er the sea wi' me.

---

[1] *Neist*—next.   [2] *Ee*—eye.
[3] *Queenis fee*—queen's property or possessions.
[4] *Gane*—suffice for.

"Mak ready, mak ready, my merry men a',[1]
    Our gude ship sails the morn "
" Now ever alak! my master dear,
    I fear a deadly storm.

" I saw the new moon late yestreen,[2]
    Wi' the auld moon in her arm ;
And if we gang to sea, master,
    I fear we'll come to harm ! "

They hadna sailed a league, a league,
    A league but barely three,
When the lift [3] grew dark, and the wind blew
    And gurly [4] grew the sea.

The ankers brak, and the topmast lap,[5]
    It was sic a deadly storm ;
And the waves cam o'er the broken ship,
    Till a' her sides were torn.

" O where will I get a good sailor
    To tak my helm in hand ;
Till I gae up to the tall topmast
    To see if I can spy land ? "

" O here am I, a sailor gude,
    To tak the helm in hand,
Till you go up to the tall topmast ;—
    But I fear you'll ne'er spy land."

He hadna gane a step, a step,
    A step but barely ane,

[1] *A'*—all.   [2] *Yestreen*—yestereven, last nig
[3] *Lift*—air.   [4] Gurly—stormy.
[5] *Lap*—gave a spring, fell overboard.

When a bolt [1] flew out of our goodly ship,
    And the salt sea it came in.

" Gae fetch a web o' the silken claith,
    Anither o' the twine,
And wap [2] them into our ship's side,
    And let na the sea come in."

They fetched a web o' the silken claith,
    Anither o' the twine,
And they wapped them round that gude ship's side,
    But still the sea came in.

O laith,[3] laith were our good Scots lords
    To weet [4] their milk-white hands;
But lang ere a' the play was ower
    They wat their gouden bands.

O laith, laith were our good Scots lords
    To weet their cork-heeled shoon;
But lang ere a' the play was played
    They wat their hats aboon.[5]

And mony was the feather-bed,
    That floated on the faem;
And mony was the gude lord's son
    That never mair cam hame.

The ladies wrang their fingers white,
    The maidens tore their hair;
A' for the sake of their true loves,—
    For them they'll see nae mair.

[1] *Bolt*—bar, or fastening of the planks.
[2] *Wap*—wrap, drive into a hole.   [3] *Laith*—loth.
[4] *Weet*—wet.
[5] *Wat their hats aboon*—got wet above their heads.

O lang, lang may the ladies sit
　Wi' their fans into their hand,
Before they see Sir Patrick Spens
　Come sailing to the strand !

And lang, lang may the maidens sit
　Wi' their goud kaims [1] in their hair,
Awaiting for their ain [2] dear loves, —
　For them they'll see nae mair !

Half ower, half ower to Aberdour
　It's fifty fathoms deep ;
And there lies gude Sir Patrick Spens,
　Wi' the Scots lords at his feet.

---

[1] *Kaims*—combs.　　　　　　[2] *Ain*—own.

LONDON : PRINTED BY
SPOTTISWOODE AND CO., NEW-STREET SQUARE
AND PARLIAMENT STREET

Sixth Edition, revised and enlarged, Crown 8vo. 480 pp. in
new and elegant cloth binding, price 5s.

STUDIES

IN

ENGLISH POETRY

WITH

SHORT BIOGRAPHICAL SKETCHES, AND NOTES EXPLANATORY AND CRITICAL.

Intended as a Text-Book for the Higher Classes in
Schools, and as an Introduction to the
Study of English Literature.

Extracts from Critical Notices.

'This is one of the best publications of the kind we are
acquainted with. It has our unqualified approbation as
admirably adapted to the higher orders of schools. It
follows out the laudable object of its beautiful predecessor,
"Select Poetry for Children," in an effective manner, by an
ample supply of materials for the cultivation of the youthful
taste.'—*Christian Witness.*

'The selection is both extensive and varied, including
many of the choicest specimens of English poetry, and
eminently adapted to purify the taste and to invigorate some
of the best affections of the heart.'—*Eclectic Review.*

'A volume of well-selected short pieces, and extracts from
larger poems, all of which are already stamped with approbation by the popular taste, and adapted to the young.'
                                        Tait's Magazine.

'Mr. Payne is entitled to the highest praise for the care
bestowed on the antiquated orthography of the earlier
authors, and the ability and judgment displayed in the
annexed notes throughout the volume.'—*The Student.*

London: LOCKWOOD & Co., 7 Stationers'-Hall Court

Crown 8vo. 480 pp. in new and elegant cloth binding, price 5s.

STUDIES

IN

ENGLISH PROSE:

CONSISTING OF

Specimens of the Language in its Earliest, Succeeding, and Latest Stages, with Notes, Explanatory and Critical; together with a Sketch of the History of the English Language, and a Concise Anglo-Saxon Grammar.

INTENDED AS A TEXT-BOOK FOR SCHOOLS AND COLLEGES.

' Besides furnishing a chronological view of the history of the English language, it has been the Editor's aim to illustrate, by means of the extracts themselves, the various powers of our mother tongue. These have been carefully chosen, not less for the sake of the material than of the workmanship; not less for the worthiness of the thoughts than for the style in which they are presented ; and they furnish, it is believed, a matchless exhibition of strength, beauty, grace, energy, and freedom of language.'—Extract from the *Preface.*

' "Studies in English Prose" admirably accomplishes the object aimed at by its Editor, which is to furnish, in the form of specimens, a continuous and systematic view of the development of the English language. It is a rare collection of literary gems, and it is difficult to imagine a more useful manual.—*Scotsman*, March 8, 1872.

'An unique attempt, so far as we are aware, to give specimens of the English language from the period previous to the Norman Conquest down to quite modern times. The design, which we think a good one, has been well executed. The selected passages are worthy to represent the style and opinions of their respective authors, and deserve to be carefully studied. The contents of this volume are worthy of its pretty exterior.'—*John Bull*, March 9, 1872.

London: LOCKWOOD & Co., 7 Stationers'-Hall Court.

A LIST

OF

School and Juvenile Books

PUBLISHED BY

LOCKWOOD & CO.

7 STATIONERS'-HALL COURT, LUDGATE HILL, E.C.

WORKS BY JOSEPH PAYNE,

Vice-President of the Council of the College of Preceptors, &c.

PAYNE'S SELECT POETRY for CHILDREN, with brief Explanatory Notes, arranged for the use of Schools and Families. *Sixteenth Edition*, with fine Steel Frontispiece. 18mo. cloth, 2s. 6d.

PAYNE'S STUDIES in ENGLISH POETRY; with short Biographical Sketches, and Notes Explanatory and Critical, intended as a Text-Book for the Higher Classes of Schools. *Sixth Edition*, revised. Post 8vo. in new and elegant cloth binding, 5s.

'The selection is both extensive and varied, including many of the choicest specimens of English poetry, and eminently adapted to purify the taste and to invigorate some of the best affections of the heart.'— *Eclectic Review.*

PAYNE'S STUDIES in ENGLISH PROSE. Specimens of the Language in its various stages; with Notes Explanatory and Critical. By JOSEPH PAYNE, Vice-President of the Council of the College of Preceptors, Author of 'Select Poetry for Children' &c. Post 8vo. in new and elegant cloth binding, 5s.

'"Studies in English Prose" admirably accomplishes the object aimed at by its Editor, which is to furnish, in the form of specimens, a continuous and systematic view of the development of the English language. It is a rare collection of literary gems, and it is difficult to imagine a more useful manual.'—*Scotsman.*

'An unique attempt, so far as we are aware, to give specimens of the English language from the period previous to the Norman Conquest down to quite modern times. The design, which we think a good one, has been well executed. The selected passages are worthy to represent the style and opinions of their respective authors, and deserve to be carefully studied. The contents of this volume are worthy of pretty exterior.'—*John Bull.*

M'HENRY'S SPANISH COURSE.

M'HENRY'S NEW and IMPROVED SPANISH GRAMMAR. Containing the Elements of the Language and the Rules of Etymology and Syntax Exemplified; with Notes and Appendix, consisting of Dialogues, Select Poetry, Commercial Correspondence, Vocabulary, &c. Designed for every class of Learners, especially for such as are their own Instructors. *New Edition*, revised and corrected by ALFRED ELWES. 12mo. bound, 6s.

'Justice compels us to say that this is the most complete Spanish Grammar for the use of Englishmen extant. It fully performs the promises in the title-page.'—*British Neptune.*

M'HENRY'S EXERCISES on the ETYMOLOGY, SYNTAX, IDIOMS, &c. of the SPANISH LANGUAGE. *New Edition*, revised by ALFRED ELWES. 12mo. bound, 3s. *** KEY to the EXERCISES, revised and corrected by ALFRED ELWES. Price 4s. bound.

'Unquestionably the best book of Spanish Exercises which has hitherto been published.'—*Gentleman's Magazine.*

M'HENRY'S SYNONYMS of the SPANISH LANGUAGE EXPLAINED. 12mo. bound, 4s.

'Anxious to render the work as interesting as possible, the Author has expended considerable time and labour in making a selection of characteristic extracts from the most approved writers, which, while they serve to exemplify or elucidate the particular synonyms under consideration, may at the same time recommend themselves to the learner by their intrinsic value.'—*Extract from the Preface.*

RAGONOT'S VOCABULAIRE SYMBOLIQUE.

A SYMBOLIC FRENCH and ENGLISH VOCABULARY, for Students of every age in all classes; in which the most Useful and Common Words are taught by Illustrations. By L. C. RAGONOT, Professor of the French Language. *Ninth Edition*, with upwards of 850 Woodcuts and 9 full-page Copper-plates. 4to. cloth, 5s.

Ragonot's Symbolisches Englisch-Deutsches Wörterbuch.

THE SYMBOLIC ANGLO-GERMAN VOCABULARY, adapted from RAGONOT'S 'Vocabulaire Symbolique Anglo-Français.' Edited by FALCK LEBAHN, Dr. With 850 Woodcuts and 8 full-page Lithographic Demy 8vo. cloth, 6s.

CIVIL SERVICE EDUCATIONAL HANDBOOKS.

THE CIVIL SERVICE GEOGRAPHY. Arranged especially for Examination Candidates and the Higher Forms of Schools. By the late LANCELOT DALRYMPLE SPENCE, of H. M. Civil Service; revised throughout by THOMAS GRAY, of the Board of Trade. *Third Edition*, revised and enlarged. With Woodcuts and Six Maps. Fcp. cloth, price 2s. 6d.

'A thoroughly reliable as well as a most ingenious compendium of geography.'—*Civil Service Gazette.*

THE CIVIL SERVICE BOOK-KEEPING—Book-keeping No Mystery : Its Principles Popularly Explained, and the Theory of Double Entry Analysed ; for the use of Young Men commencing Business, Examination Candidates, and Students generally. By an EXPERIENCED BOOK-KEEPER, late of H.M. Civil Service. *Second Edition*, fcp. cloth, 2s.

'We have never seen a work which expressed with greater force and plainness the mode of keeping accounts.'—*Civil Service Gazette.*

THE CIVIL SERVICE ORTHOGRAPHY : a Handy Book of English Spelling. With ample Rules and carefully arranged Exercises. Adapted for the use of Schools, and of Candidates for the Civil and other Services. By E. S. H. B. Fcp. cloth, price 2s. 6d.

'This is a very handy, carefully written, and complete little book.'— *Pall Mall Gazette.*

THE CIVIL SERVICE HISTORY of ENGLAND : being a Fact-Book of English History. By F. A. WHITE, B.A. Edited and completed by H. A. DOBSON, of the Board of Trade. Maps, &c., *Second Edition*, 2s. 6d.

'Four maps, genealogical tables, and an index, supply all that is necessary to render the work superior to most others, as a help to Candidates for Examination. We do not remember having seen anything of the kind at once so compendious, complete, accurate, and convenient for use.'—*Athenæum.*

THE CIVIL SERVICE CHRONOLOGY of HISTORY, ART, LITERATURE, and PROGRESS, from the Creation of the World to the Conclusion of the Franco-German War. The Continuation by W. D. HAMILTON, F.S.A., of H.M. Public Record Office. Fcp. 8vo. cloth boards, 3s. 6d.

'An admirable little work, and one that will be welcomed by the young men who are seeking admission into the Civil Service.—*City* Accurate, wide, and thorough.'—*English Churchman.*

FOR NURSERY OR MATERNAL TUITION.

ENGLISH.

CHICKSEED WITHOUT CHICKWEED : being very Easy and Entertaining Lessons for Little Children. New Edition, with Frontispiece. 12mo. cloth, 1s.

*** *A book for every mother.*

COBWEBS to CATCH FLIES ; or, Dialogues in short sentences, adapted for Children from the age of three to eight years. Part I. Easy Lessons ; Part II. Short Stories. Cloth, 2s. complete. *** The Parts separately, 1s. each.

THE FIRST or MOTHER'S DICTIONARY. By Mrs. JAMESON. *Tenth Edition.* 18mo. cloth, 2s. 6d.

*** *Words unsuited for children are omitted, and the definitions given adapted to the infant capacity.*

SCHOOL-ROOM LYRICS. A selection of 143 poems for youthful Readers, compiled and edited by ANNE KNIGHT. New Edition. 18mo. cloth, 1s.

FRENCH.

LA BAGATELLE ; intended to introduce Children of five or six years old to some knowledge of the French Language. Revised by Madame N. L. New and improved Edition, with entirely new cuts. 18mo. bound, 2s. 6d.

BARBAULD, LEÇONS pour des ENFANTS de l'Âge de Deux Ans jusqu'à cinq. Traduites de l'Anglais de Mme. BARBAULD par M. PASQUIER. Suivies des HYMNES en PROSE pour les ENFANTS, traduites de l'Anglais de Mme. BARBAULD par M. CLÉMENCE. Nouvelle Edition, le tout revu par CLOTILDE NORRIS. Avec un Vocabulaire complet Français-Anglais. 18mo. cloth, 2s.

BARBAULD, HYMNES EN PROSE, pour les Enfants, traduites de l'Anglaise par M. Clémence. 18mo. limp, 1s.

GERMAN.

THE LITTLE SCHOLAR'S FIRST STEP in the GERMAN LANGUAGE. By Mrs. FALCK LEBAHN. 18mo. cloth, 1s.

THE LITTLE SCHOLAR'S FIRST STEP in GERMAN READING. Containing Fifty Short Moral Tales from CHRISTOPH VON SCHMID, with Notes and Vocabulary. By Mrs. FALCK LEBAHN. 18mo. cloth, 1

EVENTS to be REMEMBERED in the HISTORY of ENGLAND. A Series of Interesting Narratives of the most Remarkable Occurrences in each Reign. By CHARLES SELBY. *Twenty-sixth Edition*, 12mo. fine paper, with 9 beautiful Illustrations by Anelay, 3*s*. 6*d*. cloth elegant, gilt edges.

A SCHOOL EDITION, without the Illustrations, cloth, 2*s*. 6*d*.

** Great care has been taken to render this book unobjectionable to the most fastidious, by excluding everything that could not be read aloud in schools and families, and by abstinence from all party spirit, alike in politics as in religion.

THE HISTORICAL FINGER-POST : a Handy Book of Terms, Phrases, Epithets, Cognomens, Allusions, &c. in connection with Universal History. By EDWARD SHELTON, Assistant Editor of 'The Dictionary of Daily Wants,' &c. *Cheaper Edition*, 1 vol. crown 8vo. cloth, 2*s*. 6*d*.

TOMKINS' POETRY.—POETRY for SCHOOLS and FAMILIES ; or, the Beauties of English Poetry. Selected for the Use of Youth. By E. TOMKINS. *Twenty-second Edition*, with considerable Additions and fine Steel Frontispiece. Fcp. 8vo. cloth, 2*s*. 6*d*. ; gilt edges, 3*s*.

THE ART of EXTEMPORE SPEAKING : Hints for the Pulpit, the Senate, and the Bar. By M. BAUTAIN, Vicar-General and Professor at the Sorbonne, &c. Translated from the French. *Fourth Edition*, fcp. cloth, 3*s*. 6*d*.

WHEN to DOUBLE YOUR CONSONÂNTS. See the WRITER'S ENCHIRIDION, a List of all the Verbs that Double their Consonants on taking ED, EST, ING, &c. By J. S. SCARLETT. 18mo. cloth limp, 1*s*.

MIND YOUR H's and TAKE CARE of YOUR R's. Exercises for Acquiring the Use and Correcting the Abuse of the Letter H ; with Additional Exercises on the Letter R. By CHAS. WM. SMITH, Author of ' Clerical Elocution,' &c. Fcp. cloth limp, 1*s*.

THE YOUNG REPORTER : a Practical Guide to the Art and the Profession of Shorthand Writing, with Dictionary of Latin Quotations. &c. Fcp. cloth, 1*s*.

THINGS NOT GENERALLY KNOWN FAMILIARLY EXPLAINED. By JOHN TIMBS. *New Edition*, in 3 double volumes (VOL. I. General Information; VOL. II. Curiosities of Science; VOL. III. Curiosities of History, and Popular Errors Explained), either cloth elegant or strongly half-bound, gilt backs, 15s.

'A remarkably pleasant and instructive book ; a book to take a bite of now and then, and always with a relish ; as full of information as a pomegranate is full of seed.'—*Punch.*

*** *The above are sold separately, price 5s. each, and in Single Volumes as follows :*—

GENERAL INFORMATION. 2 vols. 2s. 6d. each, cloth.

CURIOSITIES of SCIENCE. 2 vols. 2s. 6d. each, cloth.

CURIOSITIES of HISTORY ; POPULAR ERRORS EXPLAINED. 2 vols. 2s. 6d. each, cloth.

TRUTHS ILLUSTRATED BY GREAT AUTHORS; A Dictionary of nearly Four Thousand Aids to Reflection, Quotations of Maxims, Metaphors, Counsels, Cautions, Proverbs, Aphorisms, &c. &c. In Prose and Verse. Compiled from the Great Writers of all Ages and Countries. Fourteenth Edition, fcp. 8vo. cloth, gilt edges, pp. 568, 5s.

'The quotations are perfect gems ; their selection evinces sound judgment and an excellent taste.'—*Dispatch.*
'We accept the treasure with profound gratitude—it should find its way to every home.'—*Era.*

THE FABLES of BABRIUS : Translated into English Verse, from the Text of Sir G. CORNEWALL LEWIS, by the Rev. JAMES DAVIES, Lincoln College, Oxford. Fcp. cloth antique, 6s.

'"Who was Babrius?" The reply may not improbably startle the reader. Babrius was the real original Æsop.'—*Daily News.*

THE POCKET ENGLISH CLASSICS. 32mo. neatly printed, bound in cloth, lettered, price 6d. each :—

The Vicar of Wakefield	Scott's Lady of the Lake
Goldsmith's Poetical Works	Scott's Lay of the Last Minstrel
Falconer's Shipwreck	Walton's Angler, 2 Parts, 1s.
Rasselas	Elizabeth ; or, the Exiles
Sterne's Sentimental Journey	Cowper's Task
Locke on the Understanding	Pope's Essay and Blair's Grave
Thomson's Seasons	Gray and Collins
Inchbald's Nature and Art	Gay's Fables
Bloomfield's Farmer's Boy	Paul and Virginia

E LAWGIVER OF THE PLAYGROUND.

3OY'S OWN BOOK : a Complete Encyclopædia
>orts and Pastimes, Athletic, Scientific, and Re-
A New and greatly enlarged Edition, including the
Games and Amusements ; with more than 600
>ns (many of them quite new), 10 Vignette Titles
1 Gold, and over 700 pages. Handsomely bound
8s. 6d. ; or in French morocco, gilt edges, 12s.

PRINCIPAL CONTENTS.

;PORTS : Games with —with Tops—with Balls Ball Game—Sports of and Speed—Miscella-utdoor Sports—Indoor Sports with Toys.

G-ROOM GAMES : ames—Shadow Panto-Bouts Rimés—Defini-orfeits — Acting Cha-cting Proverbs—Ta-ivants, &c.

C SPORTS : Cricket Football — Croquet — Iockey—Rackets and ennis and Pallone—Bowls, Skittles, &c.—ly— Fencing — Broad-Single-stick—Archery — Driving — Gymnas-ing and Wrestling, &c.

SPORTS : Angling, ng—Swimming—Row-oeing — Sailing—Skat-ing—Curling, &c.

THE NATURALIST : Singing Birds—Talking Birds—Poultry-Yard — Pigeons — Rabbits — Guinea-pigs — Dogs — Cats — Squirrels—White Mice — Silk-worms—Bees—Aquarium, &c.

SCIENTIFIC RECREATIONS Arithmetical Amusements — Magnetism — Electricity — Gal-vanism and Electro-Magnetism — Chemistry — Fireworks — Aërostatic Amusements—Acous-tics and Pneumatics—Optics—The Microscope — The Tele-scope—Photography, &c.

GAMES OF SKILL : Chess—Draughts — Backgammon—Do-minoes—Solitaire — Bagatelle—Billiards—Minor Games, &c.

LEGERDEMAIN, &c. : Simple Deceptions and Easy Tricks—Tricks with Money—with Cards —Feats requiring Special Appa-ratus or Confederacy — Para-doxes and Puzzles, &c.

DIX : *The Young Velocipedist—The American Na-l Game, Base Ball—La Crosse, the Canadian Game.*

: amongst its rivals—not half-a-dozen of them rolled into one h our old favourite. . . . It is still peerless ! . . . More truly he lawgiver of the playground.'—*Sun.*

Boy's Own Book" has had many imitators, but they have uny counterfeits, and the new edition just issued may bid them all. Brought up to the present day, it is "itself alone." or boys.'—*Bailey's Magazine of Sports.*

oy's Own Book" is still *the* book which English lads take in, and read with the greatest interest. It stands alone, ar stand alone for many generations to come, as the you sury of pleasant, instructive, and entertaining knowledg Gazette.

'MANY HAPPY RETURNS of the DAY !' A Birth
day Book for Boys and Girls. By CHARLES an
MARY COWDEN CLARKE, Authors of the 'Concordance
Shakspeare,' &c. *Second Edition.* Profusely illustrated b
the Brothers DALZIEL and others. Post 8vo. with illum
nated cloth binding, gilt edges, 6*s.*

'Mr. and Mrs. Clarke have here invited all our "big little people
to a grand conversazione. Who will not desire to partake of the enjo
ment offered by such hosts?'—*Athenæum.*

'A very charming little book. . . . . The volume does not contain
chapter from which something may not be learnt, and as we had eve
right to expect, from the names upon its title-page, it evinces a v
amount of elegant and discursive reading. We can strongly and c
scientiously recommend it to those parents and friends who, in makin
present, consult not only the gratification, but also the benefit of
recipients, who will, we feel assured, at any season, on receiving
mentally wish themselves "Many Happy Returns of the Day !"'
Literary Gazette.

'An unobjectionable child's book is the rarest of all books. "Ma
Happy Returns of the Day !" is not only this, but may rely, with
shrinking, upon its positive excellencies for a long and deserved po
larity.'—*Westminster Review.*

MERRY TALES for LITTLE FOLK. Edited
Madame DE CHATELAIN. Illustrated with more th
Two Hundred Pictures. Cloth gilt, price 3*s.* 6*d.* ; gilt edg
4*s.* Containing—

The House that Jack Built—Little Bo-Peep—The Old Woman
her Eggs—Old Mother Goose—Cock Robin—Old Mother Hubbar
Henny Penny—The Three Bears—The Ugly Little Duck—The Wh
Cat—The Charmed Fawn—The Eleven Wild Swans—The Blue Bir
Little Maia—Jack the Giant Killer—Jack and the Bean Stalk—Sir C
of Warwick—Tom Hickathrift—Bold Robin Hood—Tom Thumb—P
in Boots—Little Red Riding-Hood—Little Dame Crump—Little Goo
Two Shoes—The Sleeping Beauty in the Wood—The Fairy One w
Golden Locks—Beauty and the Beast—Cinderella—Princess Rosett
The Elves of the Fairy Forest—The Elfin Plough—The Nine Mo
tains—Johnny and Lisbeth—The Little Fisher Boy—Hans in Luc
The Giant and the Brave Little Tailor—Peter the Goatherd—F
Jacket ; or, The Nose Tree—The Three Golden Hairs—The Jew in
Bramble Bush.

'A charming collection of favourite stories.'—*Athenæum.*

'A comfortable, pretty and charmingly illustrated volume, wh
ought to be placed in every nursery by Act of Parliament.'—*A
Judy's Magazine.*

'All good uncles and aunts—all dear grandfathers and grandmot
—as you wish to contribute to the happiness of the little darling
love you, take with you, on your next visit, these "Merry T
le Folk."'—*Lady's Own Paper.*

THE BOY'S HOME BOOK of SPORTS, GAMES,. EXERCISES and PURSUITS. By Writers of 'THE BOY'S OWN MAGAZINE.' Beautifully printed on toned paper, with Two Hundred Engravings, and Coloured Frontispiece and Title. Cloth elegant, gilt edges, 2s. 6d.

CONTENTS : In-door Games—The Playground—Football—Hockey—Golf—Croquet—Cricket—Skittles—Quoits—Bowles—Running and Walking—Gymnastics—Fencing—Archery—Angling—Swimming—Rowing—Skating—Riding—Driving—Chess—Draughts—Dominoes—Singing and Talking Birds—The Poultry Yard—Rabbits—Dogs—Bees.—Silkworms—Gold and Silver Fish, &c. &c.

'It is a charming little volume, especially suited for holiday times, and full of information healthful to mind and body.'—*Civil Service Gazette.*

THE WAY to WIN : a Story of Adventure, Afloat and Ashore. By CHARLES A. BEACH, Author of 'Lost Lenore,' 'Ran Away from Home,' &c. With full-page Engravings, cloth elegant, 3s. 6d.

'A delightful work to read, with a good moral.'—*Rock.*
'We have seldom read a book which has pleased us more than this. The subject matter is extremely interesting, the moral running through it is excellent, the style in which it is written is at once manly and simple, and the work, as a whole, is eminently instructive.'—*Civil Service Gazette.*

CAST AWAY on the AUCKLAND ISLES ; a Narrative of the Wreck of the 'Grafton,' and of the Escape of the Crew, after Twenty Months' Suffering. From the Private Journals of Captain THOMAS MUSGRAVE. Edited by JOHN J. SHILLINGLAW, F.R.G.S. Post 8vo. with Portrait and Sketch Map, 3s. 6d.

The *Times'* Correspondent says that Captain Musgrave's Diary almost as interesting as Daniel Defoe, besides being, as the children say, "all true."'
'A more interesting book of travels and privation has not appeared since "Robinson Crusoe ;" and it has this advantage over the work of fiction, that it is a fact.'—*Observer.*
'Captain Musgrave has added another name to the muster-roll of those who prosper by self-help. He fully deserves a place in Mr. Smiles's volume.'—*Saturday Review.*

A MANUAL of SWIMMING ; including Bathing, Plunging, Diving, Floating, Scientific Swimming, and Training ; with a Chapter on Drowning, Rescuing, &c. By CHARLES STEEDMAN, several years Champion Swimmer of Victoria. With Thirty-one Illustrations. Fcp. cloth, 5s.

'The most complete work of the kind we have seen, and we have eve confidence in recommending it.'—*Educational Times.*

SCHOOL-DAYS of EMINENT MEN. Containing School and College Lives of the most celebrated British Authors, Poets, and Philosophers; Inventors and Discoverers; Divines, Heroes, Statesmen, &c. By JOHN TIMBS. *Second Edition.* Frontispiece by John Gilbert. 13 views of public schools, and 20 Portraits by Harvey. Fcp. price 3*s.* 6*d.* cloth.

'A book to interest all boys, but more especially those of Westminster, Eton, Harrow, Rugby, and Winchester; for of these, as of many other schools of high repute, the accounts are full and interesting.'—*Notes and Queries.*

'A most amusing volume, and will be a most acceptable present to any schoolboy ambitious of figuring in a future edition as one of England's "Eminent Men."'—*Gentleman's Magazine.*

STORIES of INVENTORS and DISCOVERERS in SCIENCE and the USEFUL ARTS. By JOHN TIMBS. *Second Edition.* Many illustrations, price 3*s.* 6*d.* cloth.

'Another interesting and well-collected book, ranging from Archimedes and Roger Bacon to the Stephensons.'—*Athenæum.*

'These stories by Mr. Timbs are as marvellous as the "Arabian Nights' Entertainments," and are wrought into a volume of great interest and worth.'—*Atlas.*

BEST EDITION OF LAMB'S TALES FROM SHAKESPEARE.

TALES from SHAKESPEARE. Designed for the Use of Young Persons. By CHARLES and MARY LAMB. 15th Edition, with Steel Portrait and Twenty beautiful full-page engravings, by HARVEY. Fcp. 8vo. extra cloth gilt, price 3*s.* 6*d.* ; gilt edges, 4*s.*

COMPANION VOLUME TO LAMB'S TALES.

TALES from CHAUCER, in PROSE. With a Memorial of the Poet. Designed chiefly for the Use of Young Persons. By CHARLES COWDEN CLARKE, Author of 'The Riches of Chaucer,' 'Shakespeare Characters,' &c. New and revised Edition, with Twelve full-page engravings Fcp. 8vo. extra cloth gilt, price 5*s.*

'For intelligent young folk a pleasanter, and at the same time more profitable gift, it would be hard to desire, than the Prose "Tales from Chaucer."'—*Daily Telegraph.*

'Mr. Clarke has done that for Chaucer which Charles and Mary Lamb did for Shakespeare. The quaint old Stories, with their digressions and entanglements and disfigurements, have been taken in hand by him, and are here presented thoroughly purged from their impurities, and newdressed.'—*City Press.*

RIDDLES in RHYME : a Book of Enigmas, Charades, Conundrums, &c., with Answers. Edited by EDMUND SYER FULCHER. In cloth extra, gilt edges, 2*s.* 6*d.*

DOUBLE ACROSTICS. By various Authors. Edited by K. L. *Second Edition,* revised and enlarged. In cloth extra, gilt edges, price 2*s.* 6*d.*

DO YOU GIVE IT UP? A Collection of the most amusing Conundrums, Riddles, &c. of the Day, with Answers. *Second Edition.* In cloth limp, lettered, price 1*s.*

BEETON'S BOOK of ANECDOTE, WIT, and HUMOUR : being a Collection of Wise and Witty Things in Prose and Verse : together with a Selection of Curious Epitaphs. *Fourth Edition,* in coloured wrapper, price 1*s.*

BEETON'S BOOK of JOKES and JESTS ; or, Good Things Said and Sung. *Second Edition,* in coloured wrapper, price 1*s.*

GOOD THINGS for RAILWAY READERS. One Thousand Anecdotes, original and selected. By the Editor of 'The Railway Anecdote Book.' Large type, crown 8vo. with Frontispiece, price 2*s.* 6*d.*

'A capital collection, and will certainly become a favourite with all railway readers.'—*Reader.*
'Fresh, racy, and original.'—*John Bull.*

THE LAWS and BYE-LAWS of GOOD SOCIETY : a Code of Modern Etiquette. 32mo. neatly bound, price 6*d.*

THE ART of DRESSING WELL : a Book of Hints on the Choice of Colours to suit the Complexion and the Hair ; with the Theory and Practice of the Art of Dress, &c. 32mo. neatly bound, price 6*d.*

'Two pretty little volumes for those who have the privilege of entering into society, but are unacquainted with its forms.'—*Sunday Times.*
'These little books are superior to those usually published on similar subjects ; they are gems in their way.'—*Civil Service Gazette.*

A TRAP to CATCH a SUNBEAM. Thirty-eighth Edition, price 9*d.* cloth ; or in coloured wrapper, 6*d.*

'*Aide toi, et le ciel t'aidera*, is the moral of this pleasant and interesting story, to which we assign in this Gazette a place immediately after Charles Dickens, as its due, for many passages not unworthy of him, and for a general scheme quite in unison with his best feelings towards the lowly and depressed.'—*Literary Gazette.*

Also, by the same Author, each cloth lettered, price 9d. ; or in Coloured Wrapper, 6d. :—

MARRIED and SETTLED.
'COMING HOME ;' a New Tale for all Readers.
OLD JOLLIFFE ; not a Goblin Story.
The SEQUEL to OLD JOLLIFFE.
The HOUSE on the ROCK.
'ONLY ;' a Tale for Young and Old.
The CLOUD with the SILVER LINING.
The STAR in the DESERT.
AMY'S KITCHEN, a VILLAGE ROMANCE.
'A MERRY HRISTMAS.'

SUNBEAM STORIES. A selection of the Tales by the Author of 'A Trap to Catch a Sunbeam,' &c. Illustrated by Absolon and Anelay. FIRST SERIES. Contents :—A Trap to Catch a Sunbeam—Old Jolliffe—The Sequel to Old Jolliffe — The Star in the Desert—'Only'— 'A Merry Christmas.' Fcp. cloth elegant, 3*s.* 6*d.*

Uniform with the above:—

SUNBEAM STORIES. SECOND SERIES. Illustrated by Absolon and Anelay. Contents :—The Cloud with the Silver Lining—Coming Home—Amy's Kitchen—The House on the Rock. Fcp. cloth elegant, 3*s.* 6*d.*

SUNBEAM STORIES. THIRD SERIES. Illustrated by James Godwin, &c. Contents :—The Dream Chintz—Sibert's Wold ; or, Cross Purposes. Fcp. cloth elegant, 3*s.* 6*d.*

SUNBEAM STORIES. FOURTH SERIES. Contents :—'Minnie's Love,' and the New Tale, Married and Settled. Illustrated with four full-page Engravings. Fcp. cloth elegant, 3*s.* 6*d.*

THE BIBLE OPENED for CHILDREN. In Two Series. Comprising numerous Stories from the Old and New Testament. By MARY BRADFORD. Illustrated with Twelve full-page Engravings by DALZIEL Brothers. Small crown 8vo. cloth, price 2s. 6d.

'The stories of the lives and adventures of Scriptural characters are herein simply told, and all those parents who feel the impossibility of giving children of tender years the Bible to read, may overcome the difficulty they have in conveying to their minds the facts of the sacred narrative by consulting this neat little volume, which is adequately illustrated by the famous Dalziels.'—*Weekly Dispatch.*

'The writer of this book has made a successful attempt to relate several of the principle narratives embodied in the Old and New Testaments, in simple language, and in an easy style, suited to the comprehension of young children, who are thereby led to gain a more intimate acquaintance with the principal events in Bible history than they would if they had read them for the first time in the Bible itself.'—*Bookseller.*

LITTLE SUNSHINE : a Tale to be Read to very Young Children. By the Author of 'A Trap to Catch a Sunbeam.' In square 16mo. coloured borders, engraved Frontispiece and Vignette, fancy boards, price 2s.

'Just the thing to rivet the attention of children.'—*Stamford Mercury.*

'Printed in the sumptuous manner that children like best.'—*Bradford Observer.*

'As pleasing a child's book as we recollect seeing.'—*Plymouth Herald.*

SIDNEY GREY : a Tale of School Life. By the Author of 'Mia and Charlie.' *Second Edition*, with 6 beautiful Illustrations. Fcp. cloth, 3s. 6d.

SIBERT'S WOLD ; or, Cross Purposes. A Tale. By the Author of 'A Trap to Catch a Sunbeam,' &c. &c. *Third Edition*, cloth limp, 2s.

THE DREAM CHINTZ. By the Author of 'A Trap to Catch a Sunbeam,' &c. With Illustrations by JAMES GODWIN. *Second Edition*, in appropriate fancy cover, cloth, 2s. 6d.

'We take leave of this little book with unfeigned regret. Its whole spirit and tendency is to purify, strengthen, console : to make us contented with our lot ; to lead us never to doubt Almighty mercy, not to relax in our own proper exertions ; to be kind and charitable to our fellow-creatures, and to despise none, since none are created in vain ; to hope, believe, love here, as we desire hereafter to meet again the loved ones who have gone before into "the beautiful country."'—*Literary Gazette.*

BOHN'S MINIATURE LIBRARY.

A Series of elegantly-printed Pocket Volumes, each containing a Steel Frontispiece or Portrait, and bound in best red cloth, gilt and sides.

BARBAULD and AIKIN'S EVENINGS at HOM 2s. 6d.

BOURRIENNE'S MEMOIRS of NAPOLEON. 3s.

BYRON'S POETICAL WORKS, with Life H. LYTTON BULWER. 3s. 6d.

BUNYAN'S PILGRIM'S PROGRESS, with a Life a Notes. Frontispiece, and 25 full-size Woodcuts. 3s.

CHEEVER'S LECTURES on BUNYAN'S PILGRIM PROGRESS, and the Life and Times of Bunyan. 2s.

COLERIDGE'S SELECT POETICAL WORKS.

COWPER'S POETICAL WORKS, with all the Cop right Poems, and a Short Life by SOUTHEY. 3s. 6d.

DRYDEN'S POETICAL WORKS. 3s. 6d.

ENCYCLOPÆDIA of MANNERS and ETIQUETT comprising Chesterfield's Advice, &c. 2s.

HEBER'S (Bp.), HEMANS' (Mrs.), and RADCLIFFE (Ann) POETICAL WORKS. 3 Vols. in 1. 2s. 6d

HERRICK'S POETICAL WORKS. 2s. 6d.

MILTON'S POETICAL WORKS, Complete. Wi Life by Dr. STEBBING. 3s. 6d.

OSSIAN'S POEMS. Translated by MACPHERSON. 2s. 6

POPE'S HOMER'S ILIAD, with Notes and Index.

SCOTT'S POETICAL WORKS. 3s. 6d.

STURM'S REFLECTIONS on the WORKS of GOD. 3

THOMSON'S SEASONS, with his CASTLE of IND LENCE. With 4 fine Woodcuts by HARVEY. 2s.

VATHEK and the AMBER WITCH. 2s. 6d.

Stddiswode & Co. Printers, New-street Square, Lon

Milton Keynes UK
Ingram Content Group UK Ltd.
UKHW011528230124
436534UK00004B/263

9 783368 848545